THE
LAST DRAGON
CHARMER
BOOK 2

QUEST MAKER

THE
LAST DRAGON
CHARMER
BOOK 2

QUEST MAKER

LAURIE McKAY

HARPER
An Imprint of HarperCollins*Publishers*

Library of Congress Control Number: 2015943569

ISBN 978-0-06-230846-7 (trade bdg.)

Typography by Robert Steimle

16 17 18 19 20   CG/RRDH   10 9 8 7 6 5 4 3 2 1

First Edition

To my mom

Contents

THE RED LIGHTNING

There was magic on the night wind, and it wasn't the good kind. Caden knew from the acrid smell, from the way his skin itched. He stood on the mountainside, peering down, and listened to the tree branches creak and the leaves rustle.

In the valley, the city gleamed with scattered yellow streetlights. The rectangular buildings looked asleep. Above, the three-quarters moon was half-hidden by clouds.

Suddenly, the sour scent grew stronger. Caden felt goose bumps pucker down his arm. There was a thunderous crack and the sky shattered. Red tendrils streaked across it. Everything—the trees with their spring leaves, the buildings below, the sky above—was bathed in a sickly red glow. Magic born of hate and anger often burned red like those passions. He was witness to a spell, and it was one backed by brutal emotions.

Caden felt the wind ruffle his short brown hair. He pulled his coat tighter. The wool was enchanted with warmth and protection. The royal Winterbird, the symbol of his people and family, was embroidered in silver and gold threads on the back. It reminded him of his family. It reminded him he was trapped in Asheville, North Carolina, and he needed to find his way home to the Greater Realm.

Then the red light disappeared. The smell diminished. The static in the air returned to an itch. Brynne, the young sorceress, stepped up beside him. Her silvery eyes reflected the moonlight, and her dark hair blew across her face. "That almost looked like lightning," she said.

Caden disagreed. "It was red."

"And it felt like sorcery," she said. "Angry sorcery at that."

On that, Caden agreed. Sorcery was one of the three magics. When cast with rage it tingled and scorched. Unlike ritual magic, which was attached to a place, and enchantment, which was attached to an item, sorcery was always attached to a person. The light show tonight was connected to someone, somehow.

"That red lightning—" Brynne said. It wasn't lightning, but Caden held his tongue. "It's like nothing I've seen in this land." She talked quickly. "That magic felt like home. And spells can send things from the Greater Realm to here. A spell sent us, after all."

Maybe so, but it was the reverse they needed. Caden pointed this out. "But we need magic that will send us there."

They'd been stranded in Asheville from February to June. Caden hadn't seen his father, King Axel, or his older brothers: first-born Valon, second-born Maden, third-born Lucian, fourth-born Martin, fifth-born Landon, or seventh-born Jasan, in four months. It had been longer since he'd seen sixth-born Chadwin—but Chadwin he wouldn't see again. He'd been killed by a rigging dagger to his back ten months prior. Caden and his brothers were devastated. King Axel was devastated.

No doubt Caden's father and brothers now thought Caden dead as well. He mustn't continue to cause them pain. He must return home. A future Elite Paladin turned heartache into action.

Although Brynne wasn't a royal like he was, certainly her parents also missed her.

That was why this night, like many recent nights, they had snuck out of their foster home to search for a way back. Until now, the most interesting thing they'd seen in their searches was a low-flying helicopter. But tonight there was red-tinted and powerful magic. Such a spell was rare enough in the Greater Realm. It was not a sight either of them expected to see in the Ashevillian sky. What did the spell mean? Why were they seeing it now?

Caden felt his skin tingle. Brynne pulled her cell phone

from her pocket and aimed it up. The sour scent flared again, and a moment later, the red tendrils branched over the city once more. This time they were brighter. More intense. Brynne clicked a picture.

Once the red faded out, the night felt more normal. The air smelled of cedar and earth. Brynne turned to him with a dazzling smile and held up her dimly glowing phone. "Look, prince," she said. "The red lightning seems to have touched ground."

In the picture, the tendrils joined and furrowed down like fire channeling to the earth. The point of impact was just beyond downtown. In his free time, Caden had memorized the city layout. It was important for a future Elite Paladin to understand terrains. He guessed the spell made ground at Biltmore Village, near the large house there that the locals mistook for a castle.

"What type of spell was it?" he said.

Brynne wasn't listening, though. "If we can get to the point of impact, maybe we can use the residual magic to return."

There were others from the Greater Realm trapped in Asheville. They were not, however, stranded like he and Brynne. They were villains, the vilest and most evil of people. They were those the Greater Realm Council had sentenced to banishment and certain death in the Land of Shadow. The spellcasters who executed the punishment were powerful, practiced. Certainly, they could break open a sky a realm away.

Of course, Caden and Brynne had learned the Land of Shadow was a lot nicer than described. It was not a realm of eternal torment. Matter of point, it was Asheville, North Carolina. The locals called it the Land of Sky and had recently deemed it the happiest city in the region.

Somewhere along the line, the Greater Realm Council had gotten very confused.

Caden suspected that the red lightning meant another infamous villain had just been banished to the happy city. What other type of spell would connect the realms and be attached to someone? He turned to Brynne. She was the sorcery expert. "Brynne," he said, "was it a banishment spell?"

She caught his gaze. "I think so. If it opened a portal here, maybe we can sneak through before it's completely closed."

As far as Caden understood, the paths between worlds opened but one way—from the Greater Realm to Asheville. They didn't open the other way. That was their problem. That was why they were trapped, why the villains were trapped.

"You can latch on to a banishment spell?"

"Maybe." Brynne was often offended when her knowledge of magic was questioned. Her eyes narrowed. "If we do it right, we could get back to the Greater Realm this very night. Do you not want to try? We must hurry. Before the magic completely burns out." She secured her phone and pulled back her hair. "Where'd your horse go?" she said. "We must hurry."

Caden's horse, Sir Horace, had fallen across realms with Caden. Caden whistled for him now. "He was uninterested in the spell."

"You mean he was spooked," she said.

Sir Horace was a Galvanian snow stallion, the eighth-finest horse in the Greater Realm. He was housed by the local horse rescue, but at night, the winds called to him and the small mountains beckoned. He romanced mares around Asheville. Neither wooden stable nor meager fence could keep him captive.

"Sir Horace doesn't need to explain his noble self," Caden said.

A moment later, Sir Horace stuck his majestic head around a cedar. His white-and-gray coat shimmered in the moonlight. Caden patted Sir Horace's mane and swung up to his back. If there was a chance they could return, Brynne was right—they must try. It was their duty to their families and their peoples.

Caden held his hand out to Brynne. A prince always was chivalrous even to difficult spellcasters like her. She glanced at Caden's hand, ignored it, and pulled herself up without his aid. Sir Horace turned back to look at them. Obviously, he wasn't happy with his second rider.

"Brynne is our ally," Caden reminded him.

After a brief moment, long enough for Sir Horace to convey his displeasure, he returned his gaze to the front. Then they galloped down the mountain, a streak of white on the dark slope.

The night air rushed against Caden's face. He listened to the pounding of Sir Horace's hooves. Caden's heart beat faster and faster as they hurried down to the road and onto a bike path beside it. Could they really get home to Razzon this night? He dared to hope.

He turned back and spoke into the wind. "If someone was sent here," Caden yelled, "he or she is dangerous and may still be at the point of impact."

"The banishment spell is painful magic meant to punish." Even over the wind's roar, she sounded quite happy about that. "For a time, anyone sent here will be in too much agony to do anything!"

Caden wasn't so sure. People of normal talent and constitution were rarely banished. Only those evil and exceptional were fated to the not-so-horrible Land of Shadow.

Soon they stood at the undersized gate of the Biltmore house. In Razzon, Caden's homeland, the walls of the Winter Castle touched the clouds. These were tiny by comparison.

Brynne reached over Caden's shoulder and pointed. "That way," she said, and he could tell she was concentrating, trying to locate the exact place where the magic had come to ground. "Past the gate and down the road."

Caden directed Sir Horace to jump over the gate. They soared above it and sped down the curving path. As they approached the not-castle, all was quiet.

"To the left, down the hill." Brynne jabbed Caden's back. "Hurry! The magic is fading!"

Caden directed Sir Horace to gallop at top speed. They flew through a bed of lilies, bright white with moonlight, and toward the manicured gardens and ornamental trees beside the Biltmore house. At first, there was nothing unusual. Caden slowed Sir Horace to a trot. Uphill, the house looked down as if it held contempt for their plight.

Brynne pinched his arm. This time, she whispered. "Beyond that hedge," she said. "The ground there looks scorched."

"Better to continue on foot," Caden said.

He swung down from Sir Horace's back and reached up to help Brynne. She rolled her eyes. In a smooth, swift hop, she jumped down beside him.

Near the charred dirt, he felt a slight static in the air. There was a lingering sour smell, too. It was hard to discern over the scents of jasmine and roses. There wasn't time to worry about who might have been banished, no time to fear who could be hiding behind a hedge. The magic was fading.

Brynne darted to the point of impact, a broken stone bench. She placed her hand between the crumbling sides of the seat and onto burned dirt, then closed her eyes. Caden saw no one else, but that didn't mean there wasn't a villain nearby.

He patrolled the perimeter of the charred dirt, and Sir Horace followed. On the edge were red roses, fragrant and newly bloomed. There were large hedges with purple rhododendron blossoms. Every few strides, manicured and flowering trees had been planted.

He reached out to touch the smooth bark of a small magnolia. Its white flowers reminded him of snow, of his home in Razzon in the Winterlands of the Greater Realm. Maybe, soon, the heavy snows would again fall around him.

A cardinal landed on a nearby branch. It was a bright red bird that looked a bit like the burn birds of the Greater Realm Autumnlands. Unlike the burn birds, however, cardinals were small, not poisonous, and didn't like to eat children.

Still, the cardinal was a bad sign. Animals tended to stay away from magic. There wasn't much time left. He glanced back at Brynne. Her brow was wet with sweat, her eyes squeezed shut. She mumbled to herself.

Caden stepped toward her and his boot hit a mound of dirt near the base of the magnolia tree. Some of the dirt was burned, some was not—like it had been packed after the spell.

Just because he and Brynne hadn't found a banished villain screaming in pain, that didn't mean there wasn't someone dangerous near. Best Caden not forget that. He scanned the area. Three strides away, where the ground was spring soft and not scorched, he saw a boot print. Farther away, he saw another. The marks were angled oddly, like their maker had staggered, but placed far enough apart to show that he or she had been running. He looked back at the mound. Before the villain had run away, had he or she buried something at the base of the magnolia tree?

He knelt down and dug into the dirt. The earth was cool and damp.

Someone touched his shoulder.

Caden spun around. He looked up to find Brynne standing above him. He was about to chastise her for sneaking up on him, but he saw her shaking. She was pale. Caden grabbed her hand. When she used too much magic, she became weak.

"The magic is gone," she said softly. She jerked away and wiped at her eyes. Sometimes, Caden forgot she was as homesick as he. "I almost latched on to it. Almost."

She was one girl trying to ride the spell that seemed to be the work of the Greater Realm Council spellcasters. "Almost" was impressive. "We will find our way home, sorceress," he said, and he tried to sound more confident than he felt. Then he motioned to the prints and the dirt mound. "Look at this."

She took a shaky breath but looked. "Someone was here," she said. "Someone banished?"

"It seems likely," Caden said. "And that person hid something." He returned to digging. His fingers touched something hard, something of jagged metal. It felt heavy. Careful, so not to cut himself, he pulled it from the ground.

"What is it?" Brynne said.

He shook dirt from the object. For a moment, he froze. He held a rigging dagger. Its hilt was wrapped in blue-and-gold leathers. It had a beveled blade. The blade was stained brown—the rust-colored shade of dried blood. The tip was broken just so. It looked like the weapon that had killed his sixth-born brother, Chadwin.

He felt cold dread deep in his being. He wanted to let it go, but he couldn't seem to do so.

"Caden?" Brynne said.

No, it didn't look like that dagger. It was that dagger. The one Caden dreamed about at night before he awoke in a cold sweat. It was supposed to be in the Greater Realm, not in Asheville.

"Caden?" Brynne said again. This time she sounded alarmed. He felt her hand touch his shoulder. She was still shaking. "What's wrong? What is that?"

"I'm taking this with me," he said. "This dagger . . ."

Caden was quick to talk and answer questions. Like all princes and princesses born in Razzon, he'd been gifted as an infant, given an ability that would aid him through his royal life. His gift was speech. Any language he heard, he could speak, and he often knew what to say to get his way.

For a fleeting moment, however, his words failed him. His jeans felt damp where his knees pressed against the ground. He reminded himself to breathe. "This dagger killed my brother."

"Maybe you should leave it," Brynne said.

Caden wouldn't leave it. It was connected to Chadwin. He wrapped the dagger in magnolia leaves and set it in his inside coat pocket. "I'm taking it."

The spring breeze rustled the branches. The sky was turning blue with dawn. Caden called for Sir Horace, climbed atop, and offered Brynne his hand. This time, she accepted. The dagger's hilt bumped his side as they galloped past surprised morning cyclists.

Why was the dagger here?

Who had buried it?

THE ENCHANTED CHAIN

They needed to get inside their foster home before Rosa caught them.

She was a local metal artist and knew nothing of magic or of the Greater Realm. Truth be told, when Caden shared information with her about his noble birthright and his homeland, she seemed to doubt his royal sanity.

If she caught them, she wouldn't tie them to the ground or dunk them in the French Broad River. But she would take their cell phones away. Caden had grown fond of his phone, and Rosa had made sure his new one was legally acquired, unlike his first one, which Brynne had taken in stealth from the local market known as a "mall."

The house was three stories high and surrounded by her metal-and-found-object sculptures. Among the emerging green grasses were twisted and sharp-petaled copper flowers. One of her newer projects, a pewter-and-steel waterfall, leaned two stories tall against the house. When the metal caught the morning sunlight, it mimicked cascading water.

Caden and Brynne dismounted near the twinkling metal, and Caden ordered Sir Horace to return to the horse rescue. Then he and Brynne snuck back to their respective rooms—hers on the second floor, his in the repurposed attic. Unimpressively, Brynne crept in the back door, which she'd left unlocked. Caden, however, took the more appropriate reentry. He scaled up the escape rope he'd used to get out.

The attic's planked floor was covered in mismatched rugs, but it still creaked when Caden climbed through the window and stepped onto it. The walls were slanted and a length of black tape divided the room. One side—the neat side—was Caden's. His bed was made, his pink-and-orange quilt pulled taut. His clothes were folded. The other side—the cluttered, book-and-clothes-strewn side—belonged to his foster brother, Tito.

Tito was about Caden's build and height, although Tito claimed he was taller. His hair was long and midnight black, his dark eyes striking, and his face sharp featured. When he frowned, the left side of his mouth was always higher than the right.

Tito was awake and sitting up in bed. His hair was pulled back. Around his neck, he wore a necklace of braided wire with an obsidian stone—a gift from their foster sister and Brynne's current roommate, the half elf enchantress, Jane Chan.

Tito had stacked books on his bed to make a table, and his booklet of hard-to-spell words was open atop it. He studied for some odd Ashevillian spelling contest to be held midweek. He didn't look up. "You snuck out," Tito said.

"I let you sleep."

"You gotta sleep, too, and if Rosa catches you, you'll get grounded again."

Tito was a local, but he knew of Caden and Brynne's plight. He had proven himself a worthy and loyal ally. Matter of point, Caden had deemed Tito worthy of training in the ways of the Elite Paladin. If Tito would dust his books and fold his clothes, Caden wouldn't even mind sharing the room with him. "Brynne and I sought a way home," Caden said. "We won't give up."

Tito looked up at that. "Did you find one?"

As Caden was standing in their bedroom and not in Razzon, he felt the answer was obvious. "No," he said. "But we found evidence that a new villain arrived in the city." And he'd found the dagger, but he couldn't show that to Tito. Truth be told, he wished Brynne hadn't seen it. It felt too private for anyone else to see but him.

"Huh," Tito said, and sounded nowhere near as concerned as he should have been.

Caden reached across the taped line, grabbed a clean-looking shoe, and tossed it at him. "No doubt it's someone dangerous. Put on your sparring clothes, Sir Tito. There is a new villain in our midst, and neither you nor Jane has mastered sword form five or seven."

"Maybe that's because we've been practicing with a mop."

"Practice is practice."

Caden sought out his after-training, after-shower clothes. Rosa had bought him several short-sleeved shirts and, for school, he picked the midnight blue one with the picture of a magnificent smoke-colored horse. He found comfort in the colors of Razzon and the image of the horse.

It seemed Tito's opinion of the shirt differed. "Please tell me you didn't pick that yourself."

Of course Caden had picked it. "It matches my coat."

"It's got a huge-butted horse on the front."

The magnificent steed reminded Caden of Sir Horace riding on the wind. After spending the presunrise hour galloping up the mountains, Sir Horace deserved such a tribute. "Indeed, it honors Sir Horace."

"Dude, don't blame your horse for that shirt."

As Tito only wore dull colorless clothes, Caden had long ago deemed his opinion on fashion meritless. Also, since Tito looked as if he wasn't going to move from his bed, Caden threw a second shoe at him. "Daily training is essential for a future Elite Paladin."

"You know, you're lucky I put up with you," Tito said, but he set his booklet aside.

While Tito disappeared into the bathroom, Caden pulled his secret box of Ashevillian treasures from under his bed. It was filled with items he thought would be beneficial to bring back to Razzon and the Greater Realm, things his father would be able to use: a light bulb, Lysol, cleaning wipes, toothpaste, and mouthwash. He grabbed the dagger from his inside coat pocket and stuffed it inside the box. With shaky fingers, he pushed the box back under the bed.

That dagger had killed Chadwin. Now it was in Asheville. The Greater Realm Council often banished people with tokens of their crimes. Did that mean Chadwin's killer was here? Caden felt his heart race. His chest hurt. He needed to know, and he knew exactly who to ask.

The villains sent to happy Asheville weren't completely free. They were kept under control—and sometimes eaten—by Ms. Primrose, the local middle school vice principal. Fussy and proper, she was not the prim old lady the locals believed her to be. She was a fickle and powerful Elderdragon, one of four, and one of the eight legendary Elderkind that had founded the Greater Realm.

The nondragon Elderkind were said to have formed the lands of the Greater Realm. The first was the majestic Winterbird, protector of the Winterlands. The second was the Walking Oak, the great tree that had rooted to form the Springlands and defended the elves, gnomes, and spellcasters. Third was the great Sunsnake. Its movements were said to turn the sands of the Summerlands deserts. Last was the Bloodwolf. Its red and brown fur could still be seen in the Autumnlands' great prairies and red-leaved forests.

The powerful Elderdragons, on the other hand, were fickle. Two of them—the Gold Elderdragon and the Silver Elderdragon—were charmed by man's intellect and curiosity. They taught strategy, medicine, and helpful magic to people. The Blue Elderdragon and the Red Elderdragon, however, were angered by man's greed and disrespect. They punished the lands with disease, war, and dark magic. Magic of hate, jealousy, and anger glowed in sickly reds and cool blues like their scales. And it was these dark magics that spawned the normal dragons that Caden quested to slay.

Caden knew Ms. Primrose was either the vicious Blue Elderdragon or the less vicious Silver, but he didn't know which. Still, he was certain of one thing: if the villain who buried the dagger was here, she would know who it was. Caden just needed to go to school, ask her, and not get gobbled up in the process.

As he dragged the sparring mop from the kitchen closet, he considered what he should say. Maybe he'd start with something flattering about her button collection? It was important to be truthful and respectful when talking to beings of great power and old people. Ms. Primrose was both.

Brynne wasn't waiting on the porch for practice when he walked outside, but Jane was. She wore pink shorts and a cream-colored top. Her dark, shoulder-length hair was braided. Part elf, part enchantress, she was a girl belonging to both Asheville and the Greater Realm, and, always, she was disarmingly calm.

Her calm hid a deeper storm, though. And she took training seriously. Her strikes with the training mop had deadly intent. Her concentration was complete. Perhaps it was because she'd so recently suffered at the hands of the local villains.

When Caden and Brynne were first stranded, Jane had been missing. While searching for her, they'd discovered mysteriously labeled vials that the lunch witches and Rath Dunn—Caden's great enemy and math teacher—sought to fill with ingredients for dark magic. Three were empty: the first, "Essence of Dragon," referred to Ms. Primrose's per-fume; the second, "Magical Locks," Caden suspected was connected to Brynne somehow; and the third, "Blood of Son," referred to the seventh-born son of a king.

The fourth vial, however, "Tear of Elf," was full. Caden now knew it was Jane's tears that had filled it, and he hated to think how they'd been caused. Whatever horrors Rath Dunn and the lunch witches had inflicted on her, it was clear she had rage in her that wanted to get out.

Caden pointed the mop to the green and white speckled

hillside. "First we sprint the mountain. Then drills."

They ran. They practiced staff formation two and sword formation seven. Caden found it hard to concentrate and Tito knocked the mop twice from his hand with a large twig they were using for the second sword. After a while, however, Tito's schoolbooks called to him.

"I really need to study before school," he said.

Getting Tito to do what Caden wanted required a two-part strategy. One, persistence was essential. Two, it was important to agree to his strange study habits. "So be it," Caden said.

"Oh, it be, bro," Tito said.

After Tito left, Caden and Jane ran the mountain once more, then took a break on a log midslope. A tree beside them bore an orange ribbon, a symbol that indicated the city limits. Caden suspected it also indicated the border of Ms. Primrose's territory. He really needed to talk to her.

"I want to tell you something," Jane said. Her gaze drifted toward the misty morning path. "And I don't want you to tell Tito." She reached in her pocket as if she grasped on to something, and turned back to him. "I want you to promise."

A promise was binding; a promise must be kept. Jane seemed honorable enough, but Tito was Caden's close friend. The idea of keeping information from him felt wrong. He hesitated.

"I'll consider that a yes," she said.

"It's not."

She nodded as if he'd said the opposite and pulled out a chain of silvery paper clips. Caden had limited knowledge of paper clips. In the Greater Realm, tomes, deeds, and documents were bound in sun griffin hair and inspected by the spellcasters' librarian. For unimpressive and uninteresting Ashevillian paper clips, however, these seemed especially fine.

Jane held them out. "I enchanted them," she said.

Caden took them. As he held them, their magical nature became more obvious. He felt a soft hum of power in the metal. The chain glittered in the light.

There were only one hundred and twenty-eight known magic items in the Greater Realm. Caden's coat was number one hundred and twelve. His brothers envied him for owning it. Enchanted items were rare and valuable even among princes.

In Asheville, Jane had created two more. Item one hundred and twenty-nine, the Half Elf's Necklace of Protection, which hung always around Tito's neck, and now, item one hundred and thirty, the Magical Chain of Paper Clips that dangled from Caden's fingers.

The ability to put magic into an inanimate object, Jane's enchantment magic, was different from the other magics. To permanently power an item, she had to put part of her life force into it. It shortened her lifespan. It took a burst of emotion and a droplet of blood. Enchanters died young for a reason.

He frowned and handed them back to her. "You will die

if you keep enchanting things. You must control yourself."

"I'll die eventually anyway. We all will."

"You'll die much sooner if you don't stop."

She shrugged. "Maybe."

But there was no maybe about it.

Jane rebraided her hair and seemed at ease.

This, to Caden, was the most puzzling thing about Jane. Historically, enchanters—although rare—had reputations for being emotional. It supposedly took great feeling to put a piece of one's soul in an item, yet Jane was the calmest person Caden had ever met. When she'd been rescued, she'd kept her wits. When she'd found out the surviving lunch witch, Ms. Jackson, had killed her mother, she'd become quiet. Caden again wondered what would happen when that calm broke.

"I worry for you," he said.

"It's only a small enchantment," she said with another shrug. The chain of paper clips hung from her fingers like a talisman. She held it out again with a small smile. "It's for you. You saved me from the lunch witches."

"Tito and Brynne did more than me," Caden said. "They slew the ice dragons." Even as he said it, he felt annoyed. It should've been him.

Jane smiled. "I already gave Tito my necklace."

True—Tito's necklace was a far finer gift than a chain of paper clips. If Caden took it, he'd have two magic items: his coat—the very symbol of his father and his people—and the paper clips. None of his brothers had two.

Still, what use did he have for paper clips? "What do they do?" he said.

"They hold things together."

Suddenly, he wasn't sure he wanted a second magic item. No doubt his brothers would find amusement in magic paper clips. They always found their amusement at his expense. "Perhaps you should give them to someone else," he said.

"I made them for you," Jane said. "I want you to take them."

With a furrowed brow, he took them. It seemed rude not to do so. "Thank you," he said. He took a deep breath. "But you must stop enchanting. The boy who enchanted my coat died at seventeen turns."

"I know more about enchanting than you."

"Then you know you should stop."

"Brynne and I are working on something. Don't worry, we have a plan," she said, and smiled, but she didn't elaborate and she didn't look like she was going to stop.

He said the only thing that he thought might make her reconsider. "If Tito and Rosa lose you again, they'll not recover. At the very least, tell Tito what you're doing."

Her expression clouded. Her smile flattened. She looked down at her lap. In a quiet, firm voice she said, "I'm going to enchant a stapler next."

THE HALF-MOON'S PROMISE

Caden needed to discuss a villain with a dragon. And he had to take a reading quiz. Neither of these were trials he ever expected to face. He must be brave and keep his wits.

He stood on the school's lawn. The breeze felt soft, and the air smelled of dirt, grass, and, oddly, rotting plants. In the blue sky, the moon was a white slip. The waning moon was yet another of his problems.

Four months ago, Brynne had cursed him with compliance. For three days each cycle—when the moon was half-full—he was forced to do as he was told. This Sunday, it would recur. He turned and scowled at her.

She wore an ivory-colored, high-collared blouse and faded jeans. Her clothes appeared pressed and her hair fell neatly past her shoulders. No doubt she'd magicked her appearance. It was beyond a foolish thing to do. She was already worn out from the magic she'd used in the Biltmore gardens. His annoyance grew. Any magic she used now should be used to find a way to uncurse him.

Like Brynne could read his thoughts, she said, "You know it was an accident."

"It was partly an accident. You said you'd fix it, sorceress."

Jane placed her hand on his arm. "She's working on it. Every night."

Brynne arched her brow. "Well," she said, "when I feel like it."

That deserved no reply. Caden walked toward the school's entrance.

The school was built right into the side of the mountain; the stone walls were carved into the granite and surrounded by green trees and vines. Around the perimeter of the building, however, the azalea bushes looked withered and dead. Workers in green jackets ripped them from the soil and replaced them with yellow rosebushes. Only three weeks ago, the same workers had pulled out dried box hedges and planted the now-dead azaleas in their place.

They piled the dead bushes beside the walkway. The blackened stems looked liked they oozed death thistle sap. Caden wasn't yet an expert on Ashevillian gardening, but wasn't this the spring? Weren't plants supposed to be growing? It seemed strange that they kept dying. He stopped and frowned.

Jane stopped beside him. She said nothing, but Caden suspected the dead plants bothered her as well. Elves were known to be close to nature.

"C'mon," Tito said, and yanked Caden toward the heavy double doors. "I don't want to be late." Inside, the tiles were gritty with dirt and the occasional grass blade tracked in by careless Ashevillian students. The walls echoed with laughter and the clanging of lockers. The warning bell rang.

Caden's gift of speech allowed him to speak any language, but it didn't translate to the written word. While Brynne, Tito, and Jane had English, Caden had his literacy class. He split from the others, but paused when he reached the classroom door.

All he could think about was the rigging dagger—the dagger that had killed his sixth-born brother, Chadwin.

If Caden hurried down the long hall, he could speak to Ms. Primrose before the final bell rang. Any tardiness after that could be excused. Caden could use his gift of speech to persuade her. And she'd once told him to practice his charms if he wanted to get better. He darted to the long hall that led deeper into the mountain and toward Ms. Primrose's office.

By the busy classrooms, light filled the school. There were sounds of teachers lecturing, students asking questions, and books slamming closed. The long hall, though, was dim, lit only by the buzz of fluorescent light. It was lined with lockers, but never had Caden seen a student at one of these. No one came this way unless they were summoned to the vice principal's office.

At the hall's end, Ms. Primrose's assistant, Mr. Creedly, sat behind a mahogany desk. His palms were flat on the desktop, his elbows upturned. He'd slicked back his dark hair. He was spindly and odd, and not for the first time, Caden felt like Mr. Creedly's true, villainous form was bent and crammed inside his human flesh.

"You're here already?" Mr. Creedly cocked his head. "You were just summoned."

Now Caden was confused. "She wanted to see me?"

Mr. Creedly untangled his long limbs and pointed to the large oak door behind him. "Yesss, go in, young one," he said with a sneer. "They await you."

Caden knew Ms. Primrose was inside. He hadn't known she had called for him, nor did he know why, and he didn't know who else was with her. That might make it difficult to ask about the dagger.

He stood for a moment, unsure, and brushed off his jeans. In the face of the unknown a prince was cautious, a prince was neat. That was what his father and brothers had taught him.

"She's the principal today," Mr. Creedly said.

Caden raised a brow. He'd never heard her go by that title before, and he didn't know what it meant that she was doing so today. He took a deep breath and walked through the heavy door.

Ms. Primrose's office was spotless. Her treasured,

cheap-looking beads looked polished, and she had them displayed on shelves. She'd added some square buttons to her button bowl. Her bowl of rocks had been rearranged in an order Caden was certain only she understood. A window overlooked the mountainside, and the room glittered in the light.

Ms. Primrose sat sword straight behind her carved desk. She wore a pink pansy-patterned suit. Her distinct, rose-scented perfume filled the office, and her gray hair was in a tightly centered bun. She was speaking in the royal tongue of Razzon, the tongue of Caden's family, and his ears ached at the familiar flow of words.

But it was the second person in the room who took Caden's breath away. Even from behind, Caden recognized the tall figure. His hair was mussed and golden blond. He wore the padded gray practice uniform of the Elite Paladin, though the fabric had turned the rusty color of blood and grime. The royal Winterbird—always embroidered in gleaming gold and silver threads—was a mere dark shadow on his uniform's shoulder.

Caden felt his mouth hang wide. His heart pounded in his chest. His seventh-born brother, Jasan, gifted in speed and favorite son of Razzon, stood before the unseen and gaping hunger of the now principal.

How had Jasan gotten to Asheville? Had he come to rescue Caden? "Jasan?" Caden tried to say, but his voice was weak and died on his tongue.

It took great will not to run to Jasan and latch his arms

around his older brother.

Caden couldn't yet match any of his brothers in hand-to-hand and Jasan was the fastest. If Caden surprised him, he'd throw Caden across the room before their identities were established. Caden would crash into Ms. Primrose's cheap treasures. She'd eat him. Jasan would attack her, then she'd eat Jasan as well. Such was why composure in adversity was a necessary skill.

Caden brought his mouth back to its non-wide-open, normal state and aligned his posture. His thoughts whirled but he spoke louder and clearer. "Jasan."

Jasan spun so fast that he was facing Caden before Caden had finished the first syllable of his name. Then Caden better saw his brother's unkempt state. Jasan's clothes were tattered, burned in places. His eyes looked tired. His mouth was fixed in a tight line. He was often in a sour mood, though, so the unhappy expression was familiar.

Jasan seemed equally stunned, and his surly expression faltered. "Caden?"

Caden had been stranded long enough for the Ashevillian seasons to shift from winter to spring. Jasan looked shocked. He reached to Caden and gently touched his arm as if surprised Caden was real and alive. Unlike Jasan's frown, this tenderness did worry Caden. Jasan didn't do such things. He was honorable and brave, but he wasn't friendly.

The gentleness didn't last. Jasan was gifted in speed

and quick in all ways—quick in movement, quick in mind, and quick to anger. He seemed to coil up. He squeezed Caden's arm tighter. It was with his voice that he lashed out. "Where have you been?" he yelled.

Caden had been in the hallway.

Before he could explain that and all it meant, Caden felt creeping cold. Jasan spun back to face the front of the room. Ms. Primrose's arms shimmered with blue scales. Caden felt as if the sharpest teeth were near Jasan's throat.

"Indoor voices, please," Ms. Primrose said. Then she looked at Jasan and licked her lips.

As she seemed versed in the royal tongue, Caden spoke in it, and not the long drawl of the local English. "Please don't eat my brother."

Ms. Primrose turned to Caden. To him, she spoke English. "I'm hungry, dear." She'd said things like that to him before, but she seemed more intense than usual. Her stomach rumbled, and her beads and baubles clanked on their shelves. "He's so tempting."

It was obvious Jasan didn't understand English. It was possible, however, that he understood Ms. Primrose's growling stomach. He looked to Caden to translate.

Caden, of course, understood both English and Royal Razzon. As well as Spanish, Japanese, Gnomish, and all other languages of note. He returned to English. Ms. Primrose liked him to answer in whatever language she spoke to him. "He's a skilled Elite Paladin," he said as calmly as he could muster. "He's Razzon's champion."

"Dear, you're always thinking everyone's a threat." She didn't seem to understand. She continued. "First Mr. Rathis, and now this pretty and tasty-looking one."

Jasan wouldn't have been pleased with that particular description, and her mention of Mr. Rathis—Rath Dunn to those who knew his true history—frustrated Caden. Rath Dunn wasn't to be trusted or underestimated. Why didn't Ms. Primrose see that? "Rath Dunn is a threat. He moves against you. He wants your perfume for a spell. If you're hungry, eat him. He—"

Jasan interrupted. "Speak so I can understand." He sounded as if he expected Caden to obey.

Caden's worry intensified. As he spoke Rath Dunn's name, he realized Jasan was doubly in danger. Ms. Primrose might eat him. But Rath Dunn, the villainous math teacher, wanted the blood of a seventh son and Jasan was Caden's seventh-born brother. No doubt that ingredient, like all those Rath Dunn was collecting, was for the darkest of ritual magic. Rath Dunn was the worst of villains, the scourge of the Greater Realm. He was the tyrant of the math room. Perhaps he had brought Jasan here to make him bleed.

Until this moment, Caden had believed Jasan a realm away and safe from Rath Dunn's reach. Now Jasan stood just down the hall from the villain who wanted his blood, and in front of an ancient and hungry dragon. Maybe it was Caden who needed to save Jasan.

And there was still the rigging dagger.

Someone had buried it under the magnolia tree blossoms that had reminded Caden of Razzonian snow. His stomach churned. Why was Jasan here?

Ms. Primrose, of course, was unperturbed. She kept to her English and spoke unhurriedly, as if she relished her words. "I'm not eating my best teacher. Not unless he breaks his contract, and he's far too clever for that. And, pish, I'm not giving him my perfume. It's too precious." She sat back in her chair. "But you, dear," she said and pointed at Caden, "amuse me at times, and you've been working hard on your reading. That pleases me, and you know I reward those who please me."

Once, she'd rewarded him by giving him a copy of an employee contract that he couldn't read. Maybe this time the reward would be worth more. If it was about Jasan, it would be.

Caden tried to ignore Jasan's scorched uniform and intense glare, and held Ms. Primrose's gaze. His heart raced. "You're rewarding me?" he forced out.

"That's why I called you." She leaned forward. "If you can give me one good reason I shouldn't eat your brother," she said with a little tut, "I won't. Not right away, anyway." Her cheek twitched like it was a decision that was difficult for her. "It's in my nature to give my meals a chance to live before I eat. I always do. I always follow my rules."

She was acting strangely. Caden wondered when—and

who—her last meal had been. It was like her control had cracks, like it could shatter at any moment. He didn't doubt she'd eat Jasan if Caden was unable to provide a reason. With the way she was looking at Jasan, she might eat him regardless.

When Caden had first arrived, Ms. Primrose had mentioned losing her physical education teacher. Well, if he were to be precise, she'd mentioned devouring her physical education teacher. To Caden's knowledge that position remained unfilled. "You need a physical education teacher," he said. "Jasan's talents in athleticism are unmatched."

She seemed to consider. "As principal, I get final say in who is hired and who sates my appetite." The room was as cold as the Winterland Ice Falls. Ms. Primrose looked at Jasan, then Caden, and licked her lips again. Was she thinking of eating Caden, too?

"If you're hungry, eat one of your villains," Caden said. Better a villain than Jasan and Caden. "They plot against you, Ms. Primrose."

"It's in their natures, dear." There was sincere-sounding fondness in her next words. "Bless their conniving little hearts."

Ms. Primrose's affection for villain keeping was foolish, but there was no convincing her of that. She believed herself beyond their schemes. There was one thing, however, that she seemed to value even more than her evil teachers.

"I thought the school was your true treasure," Caden said.

Ms. Primrose narrowed her ice-blue eyes, and Caden saw Jasan's fingers twitch at his side. "Do you have a point, dear?"

Caden did have a point. In his mind, he conjured images of Razzon, of the deep snows and the majestic beauty of the Winter Castle. He felt honor for his homeland. Searching, he found a small spark of the same for Asheville. "I have pride in my home and in your school."

The room warmed a bit. "Is that so?"

The secret to charming Ms. Primrose was sincerity. He nurtured the spark. "It is," he said, "and it's a quality too many of your villains lack."

A glint of amusement returned to her hungry eyes. "Perhaps you think I should collect heroes instead?"

She shouldn't collect people at all. He doubted she'd ever be convinced of that. But Caden couldn't lose Jasan like he'd lost his sixth-born brother, Chadwin. The rigging dagger flashed in his mind. He pushed thoughts of it aside. Right now, he needed to save Jasan. And better Jasan be kept than be dead. "Let Jasan teach," Caden said.

"I'll consider," she said. It didn't sound like she was happy about the idea.

Jasan's quick gaze darted back and forth between them. His right hand was tight around Caden's arm, his left hand hung loosely at his side, his concentration appeared intent. Caden moved closer to him. He needed to keep Jasan from attacking, and he needed to convince Ms. Primrose that

Jasan was teacher material.

"Jasan is better than any villain you could collect," he said. "He could be your first hero."

Ms. Primrose glanced at Jasan like he was a tasty bit of meat. "Heroes aren't sent here, dear."

Never had an Elderdragon uttered a more ridiculous statement. Truth be told, Caden hadn't met any other Elderdragons, but he was still certain. Caden was a future Elite Paladin and Jasan already a hero many times over. Ms. Primrose was obviously wrong. But neither the Elderdragon nor the old lady in her seemed to appreciate it when he told her of her failings. Few creatures did.

Ms. Primrose peered at him, then flapped her hand at the door. "You've said your piece. You can return to class." When he didn't move, she added, "I'm going to eat you both if you don't run along." Then she arched a brow, perhaps amused, definitely hungry, and rubbed her stomach. When Caden still didn't leave, she shook her head and pushed the button under her desk. "Mr. Creedly," she said, and Caden knew he was done pleasing her at that point. "Escort Caden out."

A moment later, Mr. Creedly slunk into the office. He wrapped his long, cold fingers around Caden's right wrist. "Come with me, young one."

Caden's skin felt like it was being pricked by a hundred tiny teeth. He tried to catch Jasan's gaze. He needed to warn him to be respectful and unappetizing, but Jasan was now watching Mr. Creedly like he knew exactly what he was and was calculating the easiest way to dispatch him while removing Caden from his grasp. It seemed Caden was moments from being tugged between the two of them.

Foolish they all were, however, to forget the dragon in the room. Suddenly, Caden felt dwarfed by the small old woman behind the desk. Caden, Jasan, and Mr. Creedly looked at her. The pansies on her dress seemed stark, like flowers on rock; the skin on her arms shimmered blue as if made of scales.

There was no time to explain to Jasan the danger of Ms. Primrose and her fickle nature, or that the math teacher down the hall was Rath Dunn, the great enemy of their people. If Caden stayed in the room, Ms. Primrose would lose her fragile temper.

The best way to appeal to Jasan was with emotion. Caden feared for him. If Caden showed Jasan that fear, Jasan might believe the situation was dire. He pulled away from both Mr. Creedly and Jasan and spoke in the royal tongue. "I'll survive my classes."

Jasan reached for Caden like he wanted to keep him close. There was no time for that now. Caden couldn't stand to lose another brother.

"Agree to teach the Ashevillian physical education class. Sign her contract." Caden lowered his voice. "Do whatever it takes. Please. Just don't get eaten."

THE LOST PRINCE

As Caden trudged back down the hall to class, a noise louder than a herd of stampeding thunder cattle roared down the hall. He almost jumped out of his boots. The booming came from the front of the building. Then there was a second loud boom. The hall tiles fractured and a crack traveled from floor to wall, then up between two sets of lockers.

The school's alarm bells began to wail, and the pale pink-gray doors vibrated. The emergency lights turned on and off, on and off. Green gas began to seep up from the crack. Caden smelled something foul, like the fruits of a Razzonian fartenbush.

In the Greater Realm, inhaling green gases was often deadly, and the green gasses that didn't melt people turned them into giant frogs. Neither was a good fate.

He turned back toward Ms. Primrose's office, but that end of the hall had become shadowed in blue. Over the alarms, he heard a low, hungry growl. Every instinct Caden possessed screamed that that direction was not the escape he needed.

Then he realized Jasan was still there.

Caden felt a rush of air at his back as the green, choking gas surrounded him. There was no time. He needed to be free of the gas, and he couldn't help Jasan if he was dead or froggy.

He used his coat sleeve to cover his mouth and nose, turned, and dashed toward the main exit. The enchanted wool would protect him from the gas. At least, he was mostly certain it would. It was best he run fast, though, and keep his head above the densest parts of it.

Near the front entrance, the gas was thin and diffused. He heard sirens blaring outside. The heavy double doors were open, the day bright beyond them. A short man in a firefighter's uniform saw Caden running, grabbed his arm, and dragged him outside.

As Caden felt spring grass slick under his boots, he turned back. The school looked like a gray castle. The mountain behind it was brown and green, the sky a piercing blue. With green gas billowing from the broken science-classroom window, it seemed no mere middle school. It truly did look like a prison where monstrous villains were kept.

Was Jasan still inside? Was he all right?

"What did you do?" Brynne said.

Always, she snuck up on him. One day, he'd surprise her. She looked him up and down with a concerned frown. Her long hair blew in the breeze. Her ivory blouse was the slightest bit wrinkled. She shifted her gaze from him to the green gas flowing from the science-classroom window. "No signs you're turning into a frog, prince," she said.

"Good. You were unbearable as a frog that last time." Then she scrunched up her face and sniffed. She leaned closer, did it again, and flinched. "But you smelled better."

Caden smelled nothing but prince-like and pleasant. He scanned the crowd for signs of Jasan or Ms. Primrose. "That's the gas," he said.

She scrunched up her nose. "It's you who walked through it." She stepped back. "Don't get that smell on me."

The firefighter looked between them and frowned. "Are you two all right?"

"I'm fine," Brynne said, and smiled. "He's as he always is, difficult and troublesome."

Caden was neither difficult nor troublesome. He was charming and easy. He told the firefighter so but the firefighter looked skeptical.

No matter. Caden didn't have time to convince peasants of his likable nature. He needed to find Jasan. Where was he? Caden took in a deep breath.

Something did smell bad. Brynne sent him a pointed look. He was about to reiterate that it was the gas, not him, and they needed to find Jasan, but before he could, a familiar voice said, "Caden, Brynne, are you all right?"

Officer Levine, the police officer who had imprisoned them in foster care, walked toward them. He was short and stout with bushy brows. Like Rosa, he didn't see the truth of the middle school, its villainous teachers, and its Elderdragon administration. To him, it was just a middle school.

"You look pale, son." Officer Levine said. "And you smell like a sewer."

"It's gas," Caden said.

"Yeah, that happens to me sometimes, too."

Caden didn't respond. He leaned around Officer Levine. Likely, Jasan was outside. Jasan was smart enough and fast enough to avoid noxious, green, frog-causing hazes. Maybe he was near the building's corner? There was a firefighter there, but no one else.

Officer Levine leaned down and blocked Caden's view. "Son, we should get you checked out. Did you inhale any of the gas?"

With a sigh, Caden motioned to himself. "I'm obviously not a frog," he said. That didn't seem to alleviate Officer Levine's worry. Caden demonstrated his sleeve-to-mouth strategy for defeating the haze. Putting his hand back down, he said, "My magical coat protected me."

"Uh-huh."

Officer Levine pointed to a group of sequestered students and paramedics. "Go sit over there with the other kids who were exposed to the gas and wait for a paramedic. Rosa's coming. We're closing the school until the gas is purged."

Reluctantly, Caden joined the group of other smelly kids. Brynne sat atop a small, nearby brick wall and watched while a paramedic poked Caden's royal person and checked his vital signs. While the paramedic took his pulse, Caden scanned the area.

Tito and Jane stood in a huddle of students. Mrs. Belle, the science teacher, was hunched over near another student group. Her clothes were more wrinkled than usual. She tapped her bloodred fingernails against her hip. She was ashen. As she should be—it was from her science-classroom window that the green gas billowed. And there was the matter of Ms. Primrose seeming hungrier and less in control than usual.

Mr. Bellows, the tall, skeletal-looking English teacher, stood near the lawn's edge. He had the distinctive look of a necromancer—one that animated and controlled the dead. Ms. Jackson, the beautiful young-looking lunch witch and dark magic master, stood on his right. She cackled. The grass by their feet looked dead. More dead plants.

Near them stood Rath Dunn. He was dressed in a rich crimson-colored shirt and tie, and burgundy pants. His bald head shone in the sun. His left eye was dark and crinkled with laugh lines; the right was pale blue and split by the deep scar that reached from that eye to his mouth. When he saw Caden, Rath Dunn grinned like a wolf and waved at him. Caden caught the glint of red metal under his sleeve.

It was magical item number forty-three, the blood dagger. It was the evil token with which Rath Dunn had been banished. Any wound by the dagger would reopen in its presence and would never be fully healed. It was supposed to be useless in the Land of Shadow.

That uselessness was yet another thing the Greater Realm Council had wrong. Rath Dunn had slashed Caden's upper arm with the dagger. Although it was a small wound, Caden could attest that the blood dagger still worked. He spontaneously began to bleed whenever he was too near it.

But it was not Caden's blood that Rath Dunn needed. Although with Chadwin dead, Caden was the seventh son, Jasan was still and always would be the seventh born. It was Jasan's blood that Rath Dunn was after. No matter how Jasan had wound up in Asheville, he was here, and he was in danger. Ms. Primrose wanted to eat him. Rath Dunn wanted his blood.

Caden turned to the students around him, fellow victims of the gas, told them of his noble brother, and asked if they'd seen him. None had. Truthfully, many seemed too distraught to answer.

When the paramedic turned, Caden eased away from the group. He went to Brynne. She would understand.

"Go back to the smelly group," she said.

There were matters more pressing than tile-cracking green gases and stink. "Jasan is here. I saw him."

Brynne blinked at him for a moment. "What?" Her gaze darted around, and she straightened her blouse.

"Prince Jasan is here?"

"I have to find him before Rath Dunn does. And before Ms. Primrose devours him."

Brynne remained stunned for a moment. Then she hopped from the wall. "I'll help."

The crowd parted for Caden. It seemed his classmates were finally acknowledging his status. Then Olivia, a girl with freckles and glasses from his math class, shooed him away. "I'm sorry, but you smell so bad," she said. "Please go somewhere else."

In the school's drive, parents picked up students. Rosa drove up in her extended cab pickup, parked, and stepped out. She was dressed like an Ashevillian sunrise in a bright orange shirt and deep pink pants. Her gray-brown hair was pulled back and frizzed around her face. She scanned the crowed and waved Tito and Jane to the truck. No doubt she'd also want Caden to return home.

He couldn't do that. Not before he found his brother.

He grabbed Brynne's hand and pulled her toward the side of the building. Once they were hidden by the stone wall and a Dumpster, she pulled her hand from his. "The Dumpster smells better than you, prince."

Brynne liked to insult Caden, but she also often helped him, and she was a sorceress. She knew how to find lost things. "Would a location spell find Jasan?" From what he knew of mind magic, location spells weren't simple. But Brynne was strong. "Could you do that?"

She bit her lower lip. "Maybe," she said. "I don't really

know him that well. And it won't work at all if he's too far away, or asleep, or unconscious." Her voice trailed off. "Or eaten" hung unspoken in the air between them.

Caden's cell phone buzzed in his left pocket. He pulled it out and checked. It was Rosa. He didn't answer.

A moment later, Brynne's phone started playing harp music—her ringtone for Rosa. Brynne had separate ringtones for everyone. To Brynne's credit, she looked momentarily guilty. "We'll get in trouble for ignoring her," she said.

He held her gaze. "Just find Jasan, sorceress."

Any signs of guilt vanished, and she grinned, seemingly lost in the thrill of magic and mayhem. "I'll need something of his. Something related."

Caden catalogued his possessions. He had his Summerlands compass in his right pocket. It was engraved with the kindly Sunsnake. The compass could, usefully, locate freshwater, test for edible plants, and navigate direction. It had been given to him new, though. Never had Jasan owned it. He had his coat, but it was a gift from his father. The only other things he owned were his Ashevillian clothes, his cell phone, and his magic paper clips. None of these things were related to Jasan.*

Brynne reached out and grabbed Caden's hair. She yanked him closer. He felt his face flush. With an arched brow and a sly smile, she jerked out several of his short hairs.

"Ow," he said, and rubbed his head.

"There," she said. "You're related to him. Your smelly hair should do."

His face was still hot. "You don't amuse me."

Her delighted expression implied Brynne amused herself plenty, however. Then she closed her eyes. Her brows furrowed together, and beads of sweat formed on her forehead.

Caden felt his phone buzz with another call. Likely, it was Rosa again. She didn't believe Caden about many things, but she treated him well. It was unkind not to answer. On the stone wall, there was a small fissure, and he traced it with his finger.

After a moment, Brynne opened her eyes. Now her face looked strained, her eyes tired. "He's close," she said. "The woods—downslope from the cafeteria."

Caden was a flash of speed on soft, green grass. He bolted down the hill. Brynne called after him, but he didn't stop until he was past the mixed fir trees and oaks that guarded the perimeter of the forest.

A few strides past the edge, the woods became strange. Something was wrong even by Ashevillian standards. At his feet, the ground seemed dead. Little sunlight entered and no spring saplings sprouted from the dark leaf litter. The trees were devoid of green leaves. The oak bark was brittle and the evergreen cedars were a mud-brown color. He saw neither living plant nor animal nor Jasan.

Brynne caught up with him. She rested her hand against a dead oak and caught her breath.

Caden peeked behind the trunk of a large black-barked tree. "Where is he?"

"Here?" she said.

Here there were only dead trees and rotten earth. "He's not here," Caden said.

He felt his phone buzz again and pulled it out, untangling it from the enchanted chain of paper clips. Another call. This time it was Tito.

Caden answered. "Hello," he said as he searched the trees and ground.

Tito spoke in a hush. There was an echoing quality to his voice, like he was in a small space. Caden imagined him hunched in the backseat of the pickup. "Bro, where are you? Rosa's looking for you and Brynne."

Caden kicked at the dead leaves and dirt around his feet. "We'll be back when we can."

"And when's that?" Tito said. "Look, come back, now. Don't annoy Rosa." Tito was protective of Rosa. Truth be told, Tito was protective of many people. If Tito understood, he'd help.

"My brother is—" Caden started.

Over the connection, Caden heard Jane. "Rosa's coming back."

Tito hung up.

Brynne's phone started playing harp music again. "Maybe I should answer?"

Among the dead leaves, something glittered in silver and gold. Caden reached down and grabbed it. In his hand, he held a ripped and soiled emblem of the Winterbird. He held it up to show Brynne.

His heart jumped. Behind Brynne, behind the dead oak where she rested her hand, a dark figure loomed. It wasn't Jasan. Nor was it Rosa.

"Brynne!" Caden tried to warn her, but it was too late. The figure grabbed her elbow.

It was Rath Dunn.

His red clothes stood out in the dark woods. The wound on Caden's arm started to ache. Rath Dunn had his blood dagger. That meant that unlike Caden, Rath Dunn was armed.

"You two disappeared. We've been looking for you," Rath Dunn said. Brynne grimaced, and Caden knew he was holding her arm too tightly. Rath Dunn turned. In a booming voice, he called uphill. "I've found them."

Caden stuffed the emblem in his pocket.

Rath Dunn turned back. "I just followed the smell," he said. "And did I hear a harp? It's good you two keep some culture." Then he looked between Caden and Brynne. "What are you doing out here? Looking for someone?" He laughed, and Caden felt he knew exactly who it was they sought. "Too bad. Students aren't allowed out here."

Brynne wriggled in his grip. "Then we'll return," she said. "Rosa is waiting for us."

"And I'm taking you back to her," Rath Dunn said. "In a minute." He waved for Caden to come closer. Caden stayed put. "Now, boy, do you want the young sorceress to be the only one punished for running into the woods?"

Rath Dunn began to drag Brynne out of the woods.

Caden followed and the ache in his arm deepened. "Where's my brother?" he said in a low, dangerous voice.

"Which one?" Rath Dunn said. "The one who bled out on the night no snow fell? Worm food in the crypt." How did Rath Dunn know there'd been no snow that day? Caden hadn't told him that detail. The math tyrant continued. "Or maybe you mean the soon-to-be-dead ones?" He paused to turn and grin at Caden. "Or maybe you mean the traitor?"

As soon as they stepped from the woods, the sun was bright. Brynne jerked herself loose. Rath Dunn took a moment to glower at her. "You'll regret it if you run." He pointed uphill to the gathered crowd. Rosa, with her bright clothes, was waiting at the edge with her hands on her hips.

Caden caught Rath Dunn's gaze. "I mean Jasan," he said. "Where is he?"

"Hmm. I'm looking for him myself." He directed them up the hill. "I do hope Ms. Primrose hasn't eaten him already."

Caden felt himself go pale.

Brynne moved farther from Rath Dunn. "That would be bad for you," she said, "as you want his blood."

That was right. Rath Dunn still needed Jasan's blood. Whatever Rath Dunn's plot was, it required Jasan's blood specifically. It wasn't in Rath Dunn's interests that Jasan be eaten.

Rath Dunn guffawed. "What makes you think it's not bloody when she eats?"

osa drove them in angry silence. Once home, she ordered Caden to go take a shower. After he was pleasant smelling and freshly dressed, she made him sit next to Brynne on her interrogation seat—the living room's green couch.

Rosa stood in front of Caden and Brynne, her bright shirt catching sun rays from the window, and crossed her arms. Officer Levine stood beside her. Apparently, he'd come as soon as he could. Whenever Rosa needed support, Officer Levine always came immediately. Jane and Tito weren't in the room, but Caden suspected they listened from the vent in the attic.

"An emergency situation isn't the time to run off," Rosa said.

Caden leaned forward. He looked her in the eyes. "I am

truly sorry to have worried you, but we had to go to the woods."

Her cheek twitched. "Why?"

Beside Caden, Brynne was quiet. She'd closed her eyes. No matter, Caden would explain without her help. "I feared Ms. Primrose would eat my seventh-born brother, Jasan." Rosa wasn't fond of Caden's tales of the Greater Realm, but she wanted her questions answered. "I still do. And Rath Dunn wants his blood."

"So you ran into the woods?" Officer Levine said. There was a concerned wrinkle to his brow. "Because of that?"

"I suspected Jasan was there."

Some of the anger had drained from Rosa's face. For a moment, she didn't say anything. Finally, she said, "Go to your room, Caden."

"Jasan is in danger."

Rosa's expression became like iron. "Go to your room, now. You, too, Brynne."

Brynne opened one eye. "Yes, Rosa."

"And young lady," Rosa said in a weary voice. "Stop encouraging him."

As they trudged to the steps, Brynne whispered, "If Jasan were dead, my spell wouldn't have located anything. He still lives."

Caden wasn't so confident. "But your spell didn't find him," he said. He thought about his curse by the half-moon; he thought about the Winterbird emblem. "And your magic doesn't always work the way it should."

He intended to sneak out again, but Officer Levine and Rosa stayed up late, and Caden fell asleep atop his pink-and-orange quilt. It was Tuesday morning way too soon.

At school, the science classroom was sealed up, but the rest of the school was open and normal smelling. Caden wore his blue T-shirt with snowflakes on it and his coat. Today, his garments honored his homeland in the Winterlands.

The hallway was a sea of black, brown, red, and blond hair, but his tall and noble brother wasn't there. He tapped Brynne on the shoulder. "Let's search the grounds," Caden said.

"You know," Brynne said, "you'd think he'd be looking for you."

"What do you mean by that?"

"He knows where you are, right? Let him find you. What do you think I mean, prince?"

Caden thought she meant to start an argument. Jane touched his arm and smiled. "Give her a break, Caden. She's still worn out from the spell." Then Jane grabbed Tito's hand—which made Tito grin like a Razzonian snickle puppet—and pulled him down toward the side hall. "We'll check the cafeteria for you."

Truth be told, Caden suspected Brynne was worn out, and Caden could search on his own. He zigged and zagged, dodged a group of studious-looking sixth-grade girls, and ran to the gymnasium.

It was large, with a wooden floor and exposed metal beams. There were skylights, and rays of sun shone down. Caden's classmate Derek and Derek's friends Tyrone and Jacob played basketball inside. It was a game with hoops and nets, but no baskets. Like many things in the odd land, the name made no sense.

Derek, Tyrone, and Jacob weren't Caden's favorite people, but he needed information. "I need to ask you something," he said.

Derek threw Tyrone the basketball and turned. "Hey, Fartenbush, we're busy here." It seemed Caden shouldn't have explained the terrible smell to his classmates. Besides, it wasn't the fartenbush that smelled bad, it was its fruits. And Caden cared not about insults from peasants.

"Listen," Caden said. "I seek my brother. He may be the new gym teacher. He's tall, royal, and doesn't speak English. Have you seen him?"

They stared at him. "Nah," Derek said. "Sorry, Fartenbush, we haven't seen him."

Caden was tempted to interrogate them further, but the first warning bell rang. Ms. Primrose ate students who missed class. Well, she had rules about eating locals. Derek, Tyrone, and Jacob would only get detention for being late. Caden, however, wasn't local. He'd be brunch.

Tyrone dropped the basketball. As he and the others walked out, Tyrone said, "Good luck, Nutcase."

Nutcase? Truly, Derek's name-calling skills were far superior. Caden wasn't pleased to be called Fartenbush, but he would be proud to be compared to a nutcase. Cases for nuts were tough and protective and useful. Had Caden not been worried about his brother, he might have explained that.

Caden hurried to his locker: unlucky number twelve-four. He would use each break to search a different part of the school. It seemed the best strategy. As he grabbed his reading book, a paper fell out.

Every morning for the past five school days, someone had been putting papers with Ashevillian handwriting in his book. They cluttered his locker, and he couldn't read them. He bent down to pick up the note. The writing was local and large, and the paper pink, so it wasn't from Jasan.

He folded this note and set it back in his locker with the others, then turned toward his reading class. When he got a chance, he should ask Tito what the notes said. Not knowing was foolish. They could be threats.

Speaking of threats, Mr. Creedly waited near Caden's classroom door like a malevolent shadow. "She's sent me to summon you," he said. "She wants to see you."

"Ms. Primrose?"

"Yes."

Yesterday, Jasan had been there. Maybe he was there now, too.

Caden followed Mr. Creedly. His lanky shadow

stretched abnormally across the tiles and the lockers, making it appear as if he had too many arms and legs. At the end of the long hall, Mr. Creedly slunk into his desk. There was hate in his eyes, in the long flat line of his mouth, but he pointed to the heavy office door. It shut with a thud behind Caden.

Ms. Primrose sat behind her marble desk. Her suit was patterned with blue irises and she was on the phone. "Certainly," she was saying. "The smell is completely gone. No, it wasn't toxic. We did tests. No one was hurt. It seems likely it was an overzealous student and a science experiment gone awry."

On the mountainside outside the office window, small white flowers peeked up from cracks in the rock, reaching for sun. The incoming light, however, did nothing to warm the room. Icicles hung from the office shelves. Frost covered the button bowl. If not for his magical coat, Caden would be shivering. She was angry. Oh, but he could feel it in the chill, see it in the wild glint in her eyes. He felt his heart rate jump. Was that why she'd called for Caden? Because she was furious? Jasan wasn't here. Had she eaten him in a fit of rage?

Ms. Primrose set down the phone. It didn't seem like she'd squeezed it with much effort, but the receiver cracked in her gnarled hand. She looked at Caden with no signs of amusement or fondness. Her pupils were too small and her skin scaly and blue.

It seemed today she was more Elderdragon than usual,

and more ferocious Blue Elderdragon than somewhat benevolent Silver. Her bad mood aside, Caden was here. She'd called him. And he saw no reason not to speak first. He did, however, speak as respectfully as he could muster.

First, he needed to know Jasan wasn't in her stomach. His voice wavered on the words. "Where is my brother?"

"I sent him shopping with Manglor." Manglor was the school janitor and father to Caden's friend Ward. Ms. Primrose continued. "My teachers are expected to look the part."

Caden felt tension he didn't know he'd carried loosen. He would do what he could to protect his brother, to help him in this backward land. Certainly, a compliment was also smart now. "You are wise beyond measure to have hired him," he said. "He's a great talent."

"I haven't decided to keep him yet. He's a probationary hire. Bless his heart, he wears such a sour expression." She seemed to think on that. "It's been awhile since I've eaten something sour." She peered at Caden. "Is he so important to you?" The words sounded kind, but her tone less so. If Caden had to characterize it, he'd call it cold curiosity.

"He is," Caden said, and squared his shoulders. She kept licking her lips. The slightest bit of drool had collected on the side of her mouth. He wasn't sure what she wanted, but she seemed hungry. Although it was likely unwise, he felt she must understand the consequences of ever eating his brother. "If you kill Jasan," he said, "we will be enemies."

For a moment she stared at him with her too-small pupils and pale-blue eyes. Then her icy expression broke. The sides of her mouth tipped up. She noticed the drool, pulled a flowery handkerchief from her pocket, and dabbed at it. "Oh my," she said, and the entire room seemed to warm up. "How terrifying, dear."

His threat was by no means trivial. Truly, Caden was insulted. He pointed at her. "I still have a dragon to slay. I'd prefer it not be you." Likely he was saying things he shouldn't, but he felt no need to stay quiet. He was too wound up from the events of the last two days. Besides, his words seemed to only better her mood. "So don't eat my brother or my friends, else I reconsider."

"I quake in my scales, dear." Then she laughed and wiped her eyes. The icicles hanging from the shelves started to melt. "This is why I'm glad I haven't eaten you. In my foulest moods, you cheer me."

If this was why he was here, he'd rather be in reading class. "Is that why you summoned me?" he said. "To amuse you?"

"Oh pish. Don't get huffy." She leaned back and flapped her handkerchief at him. "You said you had pride in my school. You meant that."

With Ms. Primrose, Caden was always sincere. "I did."

She puffed up. "It's my jewel. My greatest treasure." She'd appreciated his pride in the school more than he'd realized. "Yet someone dares tarnish it. Not everyone shares our love. Yesterday's incident—" On the word "incident" her voice became sharp again. The cold returned. "The police deemed it an accident."

It seemed Ms. Primrose didn't share the opinion that it was an accident. "You disagree with the police," he said.

"It's not my job to agree or disagree with them. It's my job to follow my rules." She was getting irritated again. It seemed he'd charmed her for but a moment. He would get better as he continued to practice. "I've gotten calls from parents." The temperature in the room plummeted. "Derek's mother has called five times."

Ms. Primrose disliked Derek's mother. Derek's mother was a lawyer and a local, though, and it seemed the combination made her less appetizing.

"Oh, they'll stop soon, but my school is getting bad press. All the magical work to make them forget is making me irritable. I haven't the time to polish my buttons or rearrange my treasures." Then she leaned forward. "Now, if I was brought proof someone caused that accident . . ." She blinked—a slow unnatural movement. "Then I'd have someone to eat." She paused. "Oh my, pardon me, someone to blame. That's what I meant. Yes. Blame." She nodded as if to agree with herself. "Then eat."

Caden wasn't to blame for the smelly green gas, and she didn't seem overly inclined to eat him just yet. So it seemed she was asking him for help. "What is it you want from me?"

"You're a prince, aren't you?" She leaned forward and clasped her gnarled hands together like she was about to deliver the most exciting of news. "Well, dear, I've got a quest for you," she said.

Caden perked up. A quest? Elite Paladins were often sent on quests. Technically, he wasn't fully an Elite Paladin, and he was already on a quest to slay a dragon, but he was confident he could handle another quest. "What type of quest?"

"One to unmask a saboteur. Find out who released the gas. If you succeed, I'll grant your brother's life, regardless of that temper of his. Don't get me wrong, he'll still have to work at the school. He'll serve me, but I'll overlook his disrespectful attitude."

When she next spoke, her words had a guttural sound. The room seemed to vibrate. Each syllable felt like a physical blow, like something hard and unyielding striking his temple. When Caden heard a new language, sometimes, fleetingly, the words had a strange cadence. Then his gift of speech would fix the foreign words into something familiar.

She spoke another language now. It wasn't a regular language, though. It was a forgotten tongue, a language of power. It took a moment for the meaning to register.

Her sentences started to unscramble in his mind.

"Find the one responsible. Bring me Ashevillian evidence of their misdeeds. Give me something I can act upon.

Do these three things and Prince Jasan will be spared."

Unlike other languages, Caden didn't retain the forgotten ones. When he concentrated, he could understand and reply to her. But afterward the powerful words vanished like stabbing pains. He couldn't retrieve the language at will. She'd spoken a forgotten tongue to him two other times. Like those other times, Caden now felt like his head might break open. He brought his palm to his temple. It was important that he answer in the same harsh language. When she spoke to him, she expected that. He dreaded forming the words, though. They made his tongue feel split at the seams, and his mouth taste of blood.

He forced out the next words.

"Jasan will be spared, and you agree not to eat Brynne."

He thought about Ms. Primrose's recent behavior, about how she seemed short on control. He also thought about how she'd told him she rarely ate locals. Not never. He added:

"And you agree not to eat any of the students or parents."

His vision was blurring, but he thought she smiled, and her skin and eyes and hair all shone silver. "Are you negotiating in a tongue of power?" she said in the Ashevillian tongue. He heard something that might have been a laugh. "That is a dangerous thing to do, but I must say I am impressed. Very well." She returned to speaking the ear-splitting forgotten tongue.

"If you succeed, I'll spare him. I'll spare your friends and the others.

"Though, really," she added in normal Ashevillian, her tone huffy. "You needn't worry. I don't eat locals that often."

Caden's head felt like it was being crushed. He took a deep breath. Through the pain, something occurred to him, something he should have said earlier. He forced his hand back to his side.

He forced out the painful forgotten language again. "And if I fail?"

Ms. Primrose spoke it with ease. "Then I eat him. And you."

"Why me, too?" His tongue hurt more with each word.

"As you've added to the reward the safety of your friends and classmates, I must add punishment. That is negotiation in a tongue of power. I'm being quite generous only adding you to my dinner plans. Would you rather I add your friends instead?"

Caden hunched over.

"No."

"I thought not. It wouldn't be in your nature."

He grew dizzy from the pounding in his head and the pain in his tongue. Ms. Primrose seemed unaffected. She spoke to him as if she spoke in English or Spanish.

"Do you accept?"

Even with his aching head, he felt pride bubble deep within him. This was an honorable quest. He would be bringing a villain to justice and protecting his brother. And, truth be told, he didn't think he had a choice. Refusing the quest seemed the same as failing it.

He tried to focus on her and forced the guttural language out once more.

"I accept."

As soon as he'd uttered the words, the air suffocated him. He felt as if his soul was being branded. He couldn't breathe and fell to his knees. A moment later, he felt his cheek hit the cold tile floor.

The pressure soon let up. He blinked at the sideways room and realized he was lying on the floor. With a silent curse, he pushed up to his knees.

Ms. Primrose was now standing. When she spoke, she mercifully did so in English. "Get off the floor, dear."

Caden tottered to his feet. "What was that?"

She looked nostalgic. "Contracts made in a tongue of power are unbreakable. They're powerful. Once an agreement is made, nothing can breach it. Not even I can stop how it concludes."

"I see," Caden said.

She let out a soft sigh. "There are so few capable of the words, so few. None I know of in the last millennia but you." She frowned at him. "The fainting was a bit dramatic, though."

"It wasn't intentional," he said.

She waggled her finger at him. "Well, don't do it next time."

It seemed the exchange had mostly returned her old

lady persona. Then her phone rang. Any amusement Caden had brought her seemed to fly away. With a gnarled hand that shimmered with blue scales, she reached for the phone. Before she picked it up her gaze skittered back to him. "Now, chop, chop, back to class. Don't neglect your studies." She put the phone to her ear. "That will be tantamount to failure, dear."

Times such as these were times for confidence. "I'll master reading and unmask the saboteur."

"For your sake and your brother's, I hope so."

Caden bowed to her. With time and effort, he would find the ones responsible. He would save Jasan and his friends would be protected. "I take this quest with honor and good intent."

"Find out who's embarrassing my school." She picked up the phone and the room was again bathed in blue light. She kept her hand over the receiver. "You have seven days."

Wait. What? Caden's confidence faded. "You said nothing about a time limit."

"Don't take that tone with me. What did you expect? Such quests have rules." She shook her head. "Princes these days," she said. "Seven days is standard. Those are the rules."

They stared at each other. The silence of the room was broken by a low, hungry growl. Her pupils narrowed until they seemed to disappear in the icy blue of her eyes. Caden felt cold, damp breath on his neck; he felt like he was near jagged, tearing teeth. He dared not move; he dared not look away.

"Fail and I'll gobble you up."

At that moment, she sounded like she wanted to eat him. Caden uttered a respectful farewell. Then he bolted out the door.

THE NIGHT RIDE

Seven days. That's all. Next Tuesday, Caden and Jasan would either be saved or be dead.

Caden composed his royal self as he walked. When he stepped from the blue-tinted long hall into the main corridor, it was like emerging from the Winter Castle catacombs to the bustle of the grand floor. There was sun and color. There was life. Once he was standing outside his literacy classroom, he inhaled deeply. He needed to investigate. At lunch, he'd sneak to the science room.

Mr. McDonald, his teacher, opened the door. His hair was thick and white. His shoulders had a constant downtrodden slump. "You have a note?" Mr. McDonald said.

In his dash to get away from the hungry Elderdragon, Caden hadn't asked for a note. He crossed his arms. "No, but she wanted to see me."

"You still need a note."

"I still have none."

Mr. McDonald shook his head. "Then you'll have to stay with me after school today." He fiddled with some papers on a nearby desk and pulled out a pink detention slip. "That's her policy."

The class consisted of two other students. The first was Tonya. She was pale and pudgy, with pretty blond hair and glasses. "B-but," she said, "Caden was excused." She was also a good, respectable ally.

Beside her sat Ward. He was small with brown skin and brown eyes. He nodded. Ward, too, was a good ally, though a quieter one. As Caden was in seventh grade, they were also his eyes and ears in the sixth grade.

Mr. McDonald started to fill in the form. "You don't have a note, though." He kept glancing at Caden like he expected a debate.

Well, it would be wrong to deny him one. "I see," Caden said, and smiled. "Then I'll return to Ms. Primrose during the break and tell her you demanded a note."

He turned a ghostly white. "That's not necessary—"

"Of course it is," Caden said. "You don't trust that she summoned me. I'll tell her you require proof. She'll understand." With a smile, he added, "Probably."

Mr. McDonald stared for a moment. Then he crumpled up the slip. "Forget it," he said. "But if you're late again, it's detention."

"Agreed."

With a huff, Mr. McDonald trudged to his chair on the other side of the room. Caden took his computer seat between Tonya and Ward. In a lower voice, he said, "The gas incident was no accident."

Neither Tonya nor Ward seemed surprised.

Tonya and Ward were excused at the normal time for first lunch. Normally, Caden would go to science. Sadly, the science room was locked and class was cancelled. Today, he had to spend an extra session in the literacy class. Caden's attention wandered back to Mr. McDonald. Caden raised his hand and asked him who caused the gas explosion.

Mr. McDonald's eyes went wide. "I don't know anything about anything," he said. Caden couldn't argue with that. "Why don't you ask the science teacher?"

Caden intended to ask everyone. "I will." And he needed to look inside the science classroom. His and Jasan's lives depended on it. "Anyone else I should ask?"

Mr. McDonald stomped to the other side of the classroom. "I wouldn't know," he said as he plopped into his chair. "Don't meddle," he warned.

"I'm not meddling," Caden said, and turned to his computer. "I'm on a quest."

When the bell finally tolled, Caden hurried to unlucky locker twelve-four. He returned his reading book. Tito walked up to him and leaned against less unlucky locker twelve-three. "Found Speedy yet?"

"No, Jasan is shopping with Ward's father."

Tito looked confused. "Shopping?"

"It means he's alive." Caden closed the locker door, wiped it down, and threw away the cleaning cloth. "We need to get inside the science classroom. Let's go."

Tito didn't go. "Bro, it's lunchtime. Best time of the day. For an evil guy I hate, Mr. Rathis makes really good food."

Rath Dunn helped in the cafeteria only so that he had permission to leave the city limits for farm-fresh food, to go beyond Ms. Primrose's territory even if only for a moment. Tito knew this. Was he trying to aggravate Caden? Yes. Probably so. "There's no time for discussion. Come with me, now."

"You know, you shouldn't order people around so much," Tito said, but he fell in step beside Caden. He dropped his voice so no one else could hear. "On Sunday, you'll be following orders, and payback is a—"

Caden cut him off. "What will happen on Sunday isn't funny."

"It's a little funny."

Caden had seven days to complete his quest. But for three of them, he'd be cursed with compliance. And he still hadn't asked Jasan about that dagger. Suddenly, he felt sick. He stopped walking and brought his arm to his middle. A group of eighth-grade girls passed them and bumped him. It was possible he might throw up.

"Hey." Tito pulled him from the middle of the hall.

"Um . . . Brynne will fix that. And until she figures out how, Jane and I will help you when it happens."

"Now you sound worried," Caden said. "As you should."

"Well, you turned green."

Caden looked at his hands. They were the usual fleshy color.

"It's a figure of speech, your bossiness." The hall was starting to empty. Tito nodded in the direction of the science room. "Check it out." Mr. Creedly stood guard in front of it like a Summerlands prison attendant.

Behind Mr. Creedly, there were several splintered cracks in the door's oak frame. The small window in it must have shattered, for it had been replaced with a rough wooden plank.

Mr. Bellows, the skeletal English instructor, walked past from the other side of the hall. He had a key in his hand. He slowed as he approached Mr. Creedly.

"This is not your room," Mr. Creedly said.

Mr. Bellows looked ready to argue, but stepped back. "I just need to enter for a moment."

Mr. Creedly raised his spindly arms. The shadows stretched across the door and wall behind him. "She is angry. You've angered her."

Mr. Creedly was right about that. Ms. Primrose was angry. And hungry. Both. They seemed to be interwoven. The angrier she got, the hungrier she was.

Mr. Bellows snickered. "I don't know what you're

talking about," he said, but he looked at Mr. Creedly's outstretched arms and stepped back. "I'll come back after lunch." As Mr. Bellows passed Caden and Tito, he turned to Tito. "Win the spelling bee Thursday, and you'll definitely get the English award next week."

"Awesome," Tito said. "A-W-E-S-O-M-E."

"Nicely done, Tito. Smart," Mr. Bellows said. "S-M-A-R-T."

Caden was feeling sick once more.

Then Mr. Bellows shifted his attention to Caden. "And you." Mr. Bellows and Caden had never before spoken. "You, young Razzonian prince, enjoy my spelling contest as well."

What was there to enjoy about that? "Doubtful," Caden said.

After Mr. Bellows left, Tito turned to Caden. "Everyone really does seem to know about you."

"My family is famous in the Greater Realm. All know of us." He nodded to Mr. Bellows's retreating figure. "He's evil, you understand that?"

"I still need him to give me an A." Tito grinned, the left side of his mouth higher than the right. "It's better to lull them into a false sense of friendliness. Keeps them off guard."

"Perhaps," Caden said. Mr. Creedly remained stationed at the classroom door. Now he watched Caden and Tito like he wanted to sink poisonous fangs into them. "He doesn't look lulled," Caden said.

"Yeah, I don't think he's going to let us in that room

either." Tito leaned back against the wall. "That room blew up, and if your brother is out shopping, he's not inside it. Why do you need to get in there?"

Caden needed to get inside because his and Jasan's lives depended on him finding out what had happened. Seven days would be up in the flap of a fairy wing. "Because there is something new I must tell you," Caden said. He also needed to tell the sorceress and enchantress. "Brynne and Jane must know, too."

"Okay. Then tell us over delicious, evil-people-prepared food."

The cafeteria was noisier than usual. Caden waited at the middle table for Brynne, Tito, and Jane. Near the front, Derek and his group laughed and pointed at him. No matter. Caden was certain he could flatten them if he wanted.

Toward the back, the teachers who ate with second lunch were gathered. Mr. Bellows was there. He and Mrs. Belle were arguing. That was interesting, considering the scene by her destroyed classroom, but not that unusual. The villainous teachers often argued. They hated one another as much as everyone else.

As he turned back, a group of sixth-grade girls and boys waved at him. As Caden was gracious and royal, he smiled and waved back. They broke into giggles.

Tito clanked his plate down on the table. It was full of apple-and-cheese something—apple gratin, Tito called it—and vegetarian pizza. "Don't you already have a beautiful sorceress?" he said, and motioned to the pack of students. "Stop flirting with sixth graders. She'll curse you again."

Caden was offended. And confused. How was this flirting, and why was he being accused of it? "I was being gracious," he said.

"You tell Brynne that and see how that works for you."

Brynne and Jane sat down across from them. Jane had a plate of food, and Brynne had a spoon. "Tell me what?" Brynne said.

Though Caden's graciousness was none of her concern, it was more important to share what had happened. He explained his agreement with Ms. Primrose, then added, "It's a great honor to be given a quest."

He glanced at the cafeteria line. Rath Dunn was there, handing out sweet potato and walnut rolls. Had he been involved in the accident? Caden had seen him standing with Mr. Bellows and Ms. Jackson on the lawn, and Mr. Bellows had wanted to get into the destroyed classroom.

"If Rath Dunn was involved in that not-accident," Caden said, "Ms. Primrose will eat him. Jasan will then be safe from her and him."

Tito paused with the pizza a finger's length from his mouth. "Bro, you always think Rath Dunn's involved. You thought he poisoned that bunch of hedges."

Jane glared toward the serving line.

"It's more likely Ms. Jackson's doing," Jane said. "She's the ritual magic master."

Ms. Jackson was Jane's greatest enemy. Like every other day, Jane had gone through the lunch line, had her plate filled, but wasn't eating. Once lunch ended, Jane made a show of throwing it away.

Caden appreciated that type of commitment. He considered. "I agree—she's likely involved, too."

Brynne stole a spoonful of apple gratin from Tito's plate. Jane never allowed her to steal bites from her plate. "So, prince, we must find a saboteur to save your banished brother." She set the spoon down. "And if we fail, he and you die?"

"That's right."

"And we have only seven days."

"Yes."

Brynne scrunched up her pretty face. "Ms. Primrose likes you. I didn't think she'd eat you unless you did something stupid." She peered at him as if she sensed he hadn't told her every detail. "It seems strange to me."

There was no reason to tell her that his negotiations for her and others' safety had led to the danger for his life. That information would change nothing. "She is hungry. Perhaps it clouds her judgment?"

Tito chewed on his pizza. Jane nodded in agreement.

Brynne looked unconvinced. "You still shouldn't have agreed to it," she said.

"I didn't really have any choice," Caden said.

* * *

That night, Caden couldn't sleep. He hadn't warned Jasan about Rath Dunn. Despite searching the halls between classes, he'd found no clues as to who had caused the gas not-accident. Worst of all, the rigging dagger remained tucked in his treasure box. How could he sleep with that item under his bed? Chadwin's blood was on it.

On the other side of the taped line, Tito was sprawled across his purple quilt. His hair was loose and falling over his face, and he was drooling. Quietly, so as not to wake Tito, Caden got out of bed and got dressed. He lowered his escape rope from the window. If he couldn't sleep, he could find somewhere to bury the rigging dagger.

He landed quietly on the soft grass. The night was dark, the moon completely covered in clouds. Caden was grateful. Not seeing the moonlight kept the curse further from his mind, and there were more important matters tonight.

"Caden?" said a hushed voice near the metal waterfall.

Caden squinted. "Jane?" He walked to her. As he got closer, he saw she wore her sweatshirt and sweatpants. In her hand, she held a bunch of flowering weeds. "Why are you collecting weeds in the dark?"

Jane looked to the hills and shrugged. "My mom liked wildflowers. She liked the spring and the night," she said. "Sometimes I just like to collect them."

"To honor her?" Caden said.

"To remember her," Jane said. She was quiet for a moment. "Why are you out here?"

The rigging dagger felt heavy in his coat pocket. He looked down at the flowers in her hands. It seemed they were outside for similar reasons. "To remember my brother Chadwin." He fidgeted. "I have to bury something for him." He blurted out the next part. "The dagger that killed him."

He hadn't intended to say that. Jane looked shocked. Caden felt shocked. He looked away.

After a moment, Jane said, "Where are you going to bury it?"

He looked back at her. "I'll call for Sir Horace. He and I will find a place."

In Caden's royal opinion, this was one of the more awkward conversations he'd had. He kicked at the grass. The rigging dagger knocked against his side.

"I'll come with you," Jane said.

Jane didn't know Chadwin. And while she and Caden were friends, she wasn't close to him like she was to Tito and Brynne. Caden blinked at her. "Why?"

"Because that's what my mom would have done."

Sir Horace showed up soon after Caden whistled for him. His snow-white mane was tousled, and his white-gray coat had a few strands of brown horsehair mixed with it. Caden suspected young foals would be born in Asheville that were part Galvanian stallion and part common brown horse.

"You must stop romancing mares, Sir Horace," Caden

said, but Sir Horace seemed unashamed. Jane reached out and Sir Horace nosed her fingers.

Soon after, he, Jane, and Sir Horace trotted up the dark mountainside.

He remembered the first time he'd ridden at night. He'd been ten. That night the stars had shone like white pixie flames. The air was so cold his hands ached in his leather gloves. His enchanted coat was snug and warm around his body; his sword was belted to his back. He couldn't see beyond his arm's reach. As they'd cantered up the long trail, Caden had felt Sir Horace twitch, tense with nerves.

Up ahead and out of sight, Caden's five oldest brothers led the way. The *clip-clop* of their mounts echoed in the night. Occasionally, his eldest brother, Valon, would shout an order, or second-born Maden would loose a laugh. He could hear the whisper-soft voices of third-born Lucian and fourth-born Martin, but he couldn't make out their words. Every few minutes, he'd hear fifth-born Landon sigh.

His other two brothers, Chadwin and Jasan—the sixth and seventh born—rode in the rear. They, too, were beyond his vision, but they were closer and their quiet words carried on the cold winds.

"We should ride with Caden." That was Chadwin.

"I ride enough with Caden," Jasan answered. "He's safe between us and the others."

"It's a dark night." Chadwin's voice dropped lower.

"And he's new to the Galvanian saddle."

At that, Caden bristled. While he was new to the Galvanian saddle, he wasn't new to riding. And he and Sir Horace had practiced without stop for days on end. He was a competent rider.

"We trained all last week. He's good enough," Jasan said. Caden sat a little straighter. It was rare that Jasan complimented Caden's abilities. Jasan continued. "And he and that horse are of one mind. He talked Father into knighting him."

Chadwin laughed. "I should ask Father to knight my Starlight," he said, and Caden had the impression of him scratching his mare's silvery mane. "She's a true lady."

"You find our half brother amusing," Jasan said. Caden knew Jasan was irritated. That was when he brought up that Caden only shared one parent, that only their father was the same.

"He is amusing," Chadwin said. "And he tries, Jasan. You know what he's like."

"Yes, I do. I'm the one ordered to train with him day and night." There was a pause. Jasan made little attempt to keep his words whispered. "He's like his mother."

Caden froze and Sir Horace jerked beneath him, seeming to read Caden's surprise. No one ever mentioned his mother—not his father or brothers, not the elite guard, not the cooks or the maids or the butlers. Caden slowed Sir Horace so he could better hear.

Jasan, though, said nothing more. After a moment, Chadwin spoke. "Don't say that in front of Father." They rode in silence after that.

Now, this Ashevillian night was quiet, too. Near the peak of the mountain, there was a granite and mica outcropping. Even in the cloudy night, the rocks shimmered. By the base of the outcropping, there was a small fir tree.

"My mom would've liked it here," Jane said.

"As would've Chadwin."

Caden buried the dagger near the tree beneath loose rocks. Then he took the torn Winterbird emblem he'd found in the dead woods and placed it on top. Sir Horace nuzzled Caden's neck.

Jane placed her mother's flowers beside the emblem. She stepped back and looked at Caden. Her voice was soft, but her eyes flashed. "We can't let the villains keep hurting people."

Caden squared his shoulders. "As future Elite Paladins, we won't."

"No, we won't." Then she peered at him. "And make sure you don't lose your paper clips. I feel like you need to have them."

Truth be told, Caden didn't need the paper clips. That wasn't the point, however. He pulled them from his pocket and showed her. "They are with me always, enchantress."

Jane smiled.

Around them, the night was giving way to morning. Caden helped Jane atop Sir Horace, climbed up behind her, and they galloped back to Rosa's as fast as the spring winds would carry them.

THE SEVENTH BORN

The next morning, there were two notes in Caden's locker. He put the pink one in the neat stack of other pink ones. The other was written on thin paper that looked like a store receipt. The words were written in Royal Razzon; the letters were small, closely spaced, and looked rushed—Jasan's writing. Maybe Jasan hadn't found Caden, but he'd found his locker. Caden's rush of euphoria turned to confusion when he read Jasan's words:

> *Stay away from me. Find your way home at once. Take the sorceress with you.*

He'd not signed the note with his title or the seal of Razzon. Not that it mattered, as Caden couldn't comply with Jasan's wishes anyway. One, Caden had to warn him of Rath Dunn. Two, they'd yet to find a path back to Razzon, and Brynne said it would take four years before the sun, moon, and magic aligned in a way that might allow normal magical transport back. Three, Caden had a quest to complete. In six more days, their fates would be decided.

He folded the paper and put it in his coat pocket with his magic paper clips. He would find Jasan and explain that he couldn't simply go home. Caden took the side hall toward the gymnasium. It had been the classroom of the previous, eaten physical education teacher. Jasan could very well be there now.

By the doors, a group of seven students peeked inside. They looked perplexed, and their faces were various shades of red. Derek was among them and looked annoyed with the others' reactions. From within the gymnasium, Caden heard a thunk. Then silence followed by another thunk.

Caden tapped one of the students—a girl with dark braids and golden skin—on the shoulder. She was an eighth grader. Her name was Kali.

"Who's inside?" Caden said.

Kali turned. "Oh, hi, Caden." She looked at her feet, and her cheeks grew redder. "We were just checking out the new gym teacher."

The tanned blond girl in front of them—Caden didn't know her name—giggled. Caden peeked over her to see who was inside. His knees went weak. "He's my brother," he said.

"Oh," Kali said.

The blond girl squinted up at him. "Really?"

Derek scoffed. "Sure, Fartenbush."

"His name is Jasan," Caden said. "And he'll expect your respect." He pushed past them and into the gym. Sun from the skylights left bright stripes on the wooden-planked floor. A back door was open to a supply room. Jasan stood near the far wall beside a pile of basketballs. He wore a dark blue sweatshirt and slate-colored slacks.

It was strange to see Jasan without the royal Winterbird embroidered somewhere on his clothes, to see him in Asheville surrounded by Ashevillian things. To see him holding the confusingly named basketball and not his sword.

But it was good to see him. Caden felt his eyes itch as emotion threatened to overcome him. Jasan picked up a basketball. As it slammed into the far wall, it flattened with the force of his throw, then slumped to the floor. Balls were no match for any Razzonian prince.

Caden felt seven pairs of eyes on his back. He glanced back at the other students. Kali, Derek, and the others needn't watch them. He shut the door, then turned to Jasan. "I need to talk to you," he said in the elegant tongue of Royal Razzon.

Jasan didn't turn around. "I told you to leave," he said. "Evil is here. That office assistant, the witch in the cafeteria . . ." He stopped and clenched his jaw.

At least Jasan knew of the villains around them. He'd not mentioned Rath Dunn, though, and it was Rath Dunn Jasan needed to know about most. Caden considered how to tell him. Best he choose his words with care.

Jasan turned. With measured control, he said, "Go away. This is no place for children."

Caden disagreed. One, as of the blustery Ashevillian month of March, Caden was thirteen turns. He was no child. And two—"It's a school," Caden said.

"It's a prison."

The second morning bell—the bell that meant Caden was once again late for his class—rang. Although technically he was with a teacher. He simply needed a note. "There are things you don't know."

Jasan grabbed another basketball. "I know you need to go home. And I know I can't help you with that." When Jasan was the maddest, when he could barely contain his temper, he kept his voice low. This was how he spoke now. "Our people think you dead. As Brynne's people think her dead." His voice was a growl. "You need to show them it isn't so. Make that sorceress cast a spell and go back. Then go straight to Father. Trust no one. Only him." Jasan's eyes narrowed. "He needs to know not all is as he believes. You're proof of that. Understand?"

No, Caden didn't understand. Also, what Jasan wanted wasn't possible. He and Brynne couldn't return. They'd yet to find a way back that didn't involve waiting several years. They continued to search, but Caden was beginning to doubt their efforts. He held his chin high. "We can't get back. We're stranded."

Jasan dropped the basketball and stalked toward him. "Explain."

Finally, something Caden could do. He told Jasan of the magic that had trapped him and Brynne, and of Ms. Primrose.

"So neither of you can return home?"

"You should be more concerned with the Elderdragon in the office."

"Elderdragons are myths."

He was wrong. They weren't myths. They were old ladies. "Why do you think the evil teachers behave? We're all subject to her whims."

"So I'm a trinket collected by an Elderdragon." He looked unconvinced. "This is what you think?"

This was what Caden knew, but Jasan didn't seem ready for certainty. "I believe so."

Jasan grimaced and gazed up at the sun-filled skylights. "I admit, this isn't the torture I was expecting." Although from his tone, he still found it torture. "I expected something more than a sentence of babysitting."

Caden was very late for literacy class now. The rigging dagger remained fresh in his mind. Was it a coincidence that Caden had found the weapon that had killed one brother just after another was stranded in the Land of Shadow?

This isn't the torture I was expecting.

Heroes aren't sent here, dear.

Caden looked sharply at his brother.

"How did you get here?"

Jasan's face flushed red. "Don't ask when you know the answer."

Did Caden know the answer? Jasan was in Asheville, the land of the banished, stripped of sword and royal emblem. He'd arrived around the time Caden and Brynne had witnessed the banishment spell. Like the villains, it seemed he now belonged to Ms. Primrose. And the rigging dagger had been buried. Under the magnolia that reminded Caden of snow. Perhaps with reverence? Maybe how Jasan got to Asheville wasn't the question that had been bothering Caden. Maybe the how wasn't what had kept him from sleep and turned his stomach sour. He shifted on his feet and asked what he really wanted to know.

"Why were you banished?"

With a voice that wounded like a blade, Jasan said, "For killing Chadwin."

In the expanse of the gym, the silence sat between them like a barbed wall. Jasan watched. His whole body looked loose, like he was waiting for a punch, like he was waiting to be condemned.

Caden's first instinct was to ask if it was true, but that question would surely upset Jasan. Truthfully, asking it would upset Caden. He needed to concentrate. If he were to learn how to use the deeper aspect of his gift of speech, the part that allowed him to charm, he had to think about the words he said, and why he said them. He had to focus.

Emotion was the key to talking with Jasan, but which emotion? Not anger, certainly. Jasan had enough of that. Compassion? "You'd never hurt Chadwin."

Jasan picked up another basketball. "Father disagrees with you. And Chadwin's not the only one he thinks I'd hurt." He turned and slammed the basketball into the wall. *Thunk.* It slumped to the floor in a hissing, deflated heap. "You've been missing for months."

Did their father think Jasan had done something to Caden? That made no sense. Caden frowned and felt his brows draw close. "Father sent me away. He knows that. Why would he think—"

"You didn't come back." Jasan clenched and unclenched his fists as if wanting to hit a memory. "And there was proof," he said, his voice low. "Bloody clothes and ashes. Your favorite sword was broken. They found it in my room."

"No," Caden said. "My sword is here, in Asheville. The police have it. It fell to this land with Brynne and me."

"Then a copy," Jasan said, and for a moment, he seemed to look sad, "and a good one."

Proof or not, how could their father believe Jasan would hurt Chadwin? Hurt Caden? Jasan was an Elite Paladin. He was noble and brave. "Why would they think that you'd hurt me?"

"They all know I don't like you." His words echoed against the bleachers. Anyone in fifty strides or a nearby classroom would have heard.

Caden felt the color drain from his face.

It wasn't the first time Jasan had said something like that. When they were younger, when Jasan was about Caden's age, he'd even said it in front of the castle staff. Caden's own anger began to build, but he fought it down. People usually grew to like Caden, and Jasan did like him, even if he didn't realize it.

Besides, it annoyed Jasan more when Caden didn't get upset. He squared his shoulders. "I know you didn't kill Chadwin or me." He glanced down at himself. "Especially me. I'm obviously not dead."

"But Chadwin is dead," Jasan said.

It was said like a challenge. It was said in anger. Caden wasn't sure why Jasan would say something like that, but Caden needed to reply thoughtfully.

That was when three things happened all at once.

One, Caden felt his phone buzz with a new call.

Two, the emergency lights started flashing.

Three, a loud scream echoed from the front of the school.

8

THE HAIR CHAIR

Banished or not, Jasan was a trained Elite Paladin. He ran toward the scream so fast he was a blur. Caden chased after him. After all, Caden was a future Elite Paladin.

More screams echoed down the hall, followed by cursing in the common tongue. And cursing in Spanish and English. Caden dodged students exiting to the lawn (no doubt they were worried about more smelly gas) and ran to the classroom where Brynne, Tito, and Jane had their honors English while he was in his literacy class. The hall alarm outside it had been pulled.

From inside, he heard Jane say, "Get away from her!" Jane didn't normally shout. Caden burst into the room.

Brynne was hunched by a desk, her neck at an awkward angle, her long dark hair glued to the back of the chair where Caden assumed she'd been sitting. Jane was beside her, a small figure of fury with her cell phone out. It seemed it was Jane who had called him. Tito was near the door. Likely, it was he who had pulled the alarm. Caden had to admit he was proud that his friends knew how to take action in an emergency.

The English teacher, Mr. Bellows, stood near the front with gleaming silver scissors raised like a weapon. His gray skin looked dull under the yellow light. His pointed features were pulled into a sneer. Jasan stood between Mr. Bellows and the girls.

"Move," Mr. Bellows said. "My student's hair is stuck to the chair." The scissors glinted in the light. "I must cut it free."

That was a very unwise thing to say. Brynne's eyes narrowed. She struggled like a frost lynx caught in a bowman's pit. "No one's cutting my hair," she growled.

Caden hurried to his brother's side. The blood-dagger wound on his arm started to ache and he heard someone else enter the room. Caden knew who it was without turning. Rath Dunn. And Caden hadn't yet warned Jasan of the danger awaiting him.

When Jasan turned and saw Rath Dunn, his face lost all expression, and his chest moved with slow breaths. Never had Caden seen his brother react like this. Caden was certain Jasan would attack. However, Caden wasn't certain Jasan would win. Even if Jasan prevailed, Ms. Primrose would devour him for it. Killing was against the rules in her contract. She would have to be extremely distracted not to notice an attack.

Caden locked his arm around his brother's and turned sideways so that he could see everyone in the room. Rath Dunn was dressed in a bloodred vest, dark shirt, and brown slacks. As fast as Jasan was, it would be difficult for him to fight with Caden latched on to him. "Not here, brother," Caden said in Royal Razzon.

Rath Dunn spoke in the same language. "Listen to the boy," he said, and grinned. The scar splitting his face tugged at his mouth. "You don't want to get hurt."

Caden felt the bandage he kept wrapped around his wound dampen, and blood dripped down his arm. "Don't let him bait you," he said. "He wants your blood."

"And I want his," Jasan said.

Caden's gaze flickered back to Mr. Bellows's scissors. Mr. Bellows and Rath Dunn had seemed friendly on the lawn. Lest Caden forget, it wasn't only Jasan's blood Rath Dunn sought. He also wanted magical locks. Caden understood. He wanted Brynne's hair.

At this moment, it wasn't Jasan who was in danger. It was Brynne. Caden gripped his brother tighter. "We must keep them from getting Brynne's hair."

Mr. Bellows had stepped closer to her. Tito stepped beside Jane. There they faced each other—Tito, the future Elite Paladin; Jane, the enchantress and future Elite Paladin;

and Brynne, the sorceress—against the evil English teacher with the scissors.

Brynne looked livid and terrified. She glowered at Mr. Bellows. "Touch my hair and I'll make you regret it, necromancer," she said, and none of the fear in her eyes could be heard in her voice. It didn't quaver; it didn't shake.

At that moment, Caden truly believed she was the most dangerous person in the room.

It seemed Tito agreed. "Dude, don't come closer. She means it."

Jasan glanced to where his and Caden's arms were locked, at the small bit of blood dribbling from under Caden's sleeve. He said nothing, then pulled Caden nearer to Brynne and her chair. He raised his arm. "Be still," he told her.

Brynne's eyes widened. Then, with an incredibly fast and tight blow, he knocked the back off the chair. Tito dived and caught it, then raised it so Brynne could straighten her head. She grabbed it from him and tucked it to her chest protectively, hair still glued to it.

Jane looked between them. "I'll call Rosa."

Rath Dunn didn't move. Then, with a smile and a shrug, he stepped back. "Best be careful," he told Brynne. "Sometimes girls lose their heads when they lose their hair."

Rath Dunn guffawed and disappeared out the door. Mr. Bellows hurried after him, scissors tight in hand and gaze never leaving Jasan. It seemed the chair display had made an impression on him.

It seemed it had also made an impression on Brynne. Her snarl at Mr. Bellows morphed into a dopey smile when she turned to Jasan, her cheeks turning rosy. Which made no sense. She'd met Jasan many times before. Jane and Tito watched Jasan, too. Truth be told, they'd gone a bit rosy cheeked as well.

Jasan, of course, stared after Rath Dunn like he was about to chase him down and attack.

Brynne stepped closer to Jasan and cradled the chair seat to her chest. "Thank you, Your Highness," she said in the common tongue, and in a sincere, annoying manner she never used when addressing Caden.

Jasan glanced back at her. He kept to the royal tongue. "Be more careful." Then he pulled Caden to the side of the classroom, near the window, and spoke in quiet, quick words. "Rath Dunn, the tyrant, is the same as me, trapped by this Ms. Primrose?"

That's right. It wasn't time for Caden to be annoyed. Quickly, he explained about the vials. "And he moves against her," Caden whispered. "And he wants Brynne's hair, and Ms. Primrose's perfume. And your blood. You must be careful, too."

Jasan didn't look careful. He looked reckless and ready to challenge Rath Dunn to a fight to the death. He looked like he'd discovered new purpose in the middle school.

"Don't fight him. Even if you win, Ms. Primrose will devour you for killing her favorite teacher."

"I don't care," Jasan said, and sounded like he meant it.

"You should care," Caden said. "I care."

Jasan let go of him and moved away. "Until you can get home, just stay safe. Keep away from me, and keep away from Rath Dunn."

That wasn't possible. "The tyrant teaches my math class. I've got a quest and—" Caden started, but Jasan was gone in an instant. The alarm stopped flashing. There were the sounds of doors opening and students returning to the building.

Tito leaned against the doorframe. He, of course, spoke in the local tongue. "I don't know what he said, but he didn't sound happy."

"He's never happy," Caden said.

Brynne walked up beside him. "He's just intense." She'd tucked the seat back under her arm. The soft smile remained on her face. "And you're right. We must save him. And you." She glowered down to where her hair was stuck to the seat back. "I hope Rath Dunn and Mr. Bellows are connected to that gas accident. They deserve to be eaten."

"And Ms. Jackson," Jane said.

"Certainly," Brynne said. "That goes without saying."

9

VILLAINS IN THE CAFETERIA

osa picked up Brynne early and promised to find something to unstick her hair from the seat back. She took Jane home, too, as Brynne claimed to need her for support, and Rosa had a soft spot for Brynne. Tito and Caden were left at school, each with detention slips, Tito for pulling the fire alarm—which apparently could have brought him much worse trouble than detention—and Caden for being late to his morning class a second time. Once again, he'd forgotten to get a note.

Mrs. Belle's science class had been relocated to a corner of the cafeteria. Caden, Tito, and the rest of her students crowded around two lunch tables. Scents of roasting ham and apricot crumble wafted from the kitchen. Caden leaned over to Tito. "Let's question Mrs. Belle."

"After class, bro," Tito said, and arranged his colorful

pens. "I need these notes." He held up his thumb and first finger. "I'm this close to the seventh-grade science award at the end-of-year ceremony. I need it to win the overall."

"These awards aren't as important as my quest," Caden said.

"Bro, these awards are my quest. They're important to me," Tito said. "I've worked all year for them."

It was true Tito worked hard. But no one would get eaten if Tito failed to get his awards. Caden left that unsaid. Although Caden found it challenging, he was beginning to learn when not to say things. Truly, his skills in speech were growing.

Halfway through the cafeteria science class, Mr. Bellows walked in. On the far wall, he taped up a poster for the spelling bee, then another.

Mrs. Belle stopped her lesson on the moons, stars, and the once-and-future planet Pluto. "Five minute break, ladies and gentlemen." She tapped her bloodred-painted nails against the table. "Then we'll have a quiz."

Derek groaned and asked Olivia to share her notes with him. Tito turned to his notebook. He would "cram," as he called it, until the quiz was in front of him. Caden doubted there was much any of them could learn in five minutes. He got up and walked over to Mrs. Belle.

It was from her room that the gas had originated, and Mr. Bellows had been skulking near the locked door yesterday. Caden motioned to Mr. Bellows. "He tried to steal my friend's hair," he said. "What's the reason for your anger?"

Mrs. Belle turned. Her scowl disappeared, and she smiled. "I'm sorry?"

"You're glaring at Mr. Bellows," Caden said. "Why?"

"I dislike the distractions."

"Is that all?" he said. "Do you suspect he was involved in the gas explosion? I saw him trying to get into your room."

Mrs. Belle's fingers froze midtap. Carefully, she said, "The police said that was an accident, Caden."

The police could call it that, but Caden wouldn't. He was certain it was a not-accident. An incident. An act of sabotage. "I don't think so."

Mrs. Belle's smile faltered. "Don't spread that type of rumor," she said. "I might get blamed." She lowered her voice. "You'd be smart, prince, to stop attracting notice. Now wait, quietly." She shuffled a stack of papers on the cafeteria table and called to the class. "Three more minutes."

Caden stepped from the corner area to the empty cafeteria. Mr. Bellows moved near the serving area. From the kitchen, Ms. Jackson, the lunch witch, strode out toward him.

Her lush brown hair, smooth skin, and sparkling eyes were beautiful. Her chef's uniform was sleek and midnight black. Two red bands were wrapped around her upper arms—symbols of her vows to avenge her lost brother and sister. Beside her, Mr. Bellows looked like a gray-skinned, dull-eyed, talking corpse.

They were whispering.

Caden moved closer, but Ms. Jackson took notice of him. She left Mr. Bellows to his posters and stalked Caden's way, straightening chairs and tables as she approached. Once she was within an arm's distance, she said, "You destroyed my family, young prince."

Caden saw Tito and Mrs. Belle watching from the back corner. "They took Jane," Caden said.

Ms. Jackson brushed a pencil shaving from his coat. So close, she smelled like baking bread and sweet spices. "Well, now I'm going to destroy yours."

With the exception of Jasan, Caden's family was a realm away. They were noble and powerful Elite Paladins. But her threat sounded real. And Jasan was banished. "I see," he said. "And how are you going to do that?"

"It's a surprise." She started to laugh. "Maybe your brother will help me."

"None of my brothers would help you."

She leaned closer. "Don't be so certain."

"Caden!" Mrs. Belle waved to him from the converted classroom area.

Caden turned away, but Ms. Jackson grabbed his arm. Her gaze skidded to the other students. "After your family breaks into shambles, I'll drain all you brats. You, dear prince, second to last. Right after Tito and right before Jane. I'm saving Jane for last."

"All you'll do," he said, "is continue to serve cafeteria food."

He walked back to the converted classroom area. Behind him, he heard Ms. Jackson laugh. It started as a pleasant giggle but devolved into a cackle. The sixth graders who had first lunch began to arrive. Caden pushed through them, passing by Ward and Tonya in the crowd. He nodded at his allies, then took his seat beside Tito.

Tito pointed his blue pen toward Ms. Jackson. "What was that?"

"An empty threat."

Mrs. Belle walked over and motioned for him and Tito to sit farther apart. She placed a quiz in front of Tito, then Caden. She'd written out Caden's in the common tongue. No other teacher did that for him. "Be careful of Ms. Jackson," she said quietly. "She's very old. And very cruel."

At second lunch, Caden and Tito were released from the converted classroom area into the cafeteria proper. Ms. Jackson served roasted ham and apricot crumble to a long line of salivating students. Tito returned from the serving line with a double helping.

"Mr. Rathis is on ham-carving duty back there," Tito said. He dropped his voice. "He and Ms. Jackson seemed pretty happy with themselves. No idea why, though." He held up a piece of ham. "Maybe because the food is so darn good today. I mean it—it's like heaven."

"The witch probably cooked someone. For all you know, you're eating a classmate," Caden said.

"A delicious classmate," Tito said. He scanned the lunchroom. "Too bad. Derek's over at the front table. Guess it's not him."

In the Greater Realm, there were beings that would cook and eat people. Especially children. It was hardly a joking matter. Caden sighed. "Why do you take Rath Dunn and the lunch witch's food, Sir Tito?"

"Why shouldn't I? It tastes good. I see what they're up to. And it bugs them that they can't get inside my head."

Caden wasn't so sure about that. "They could get inside it if they had an ax," he said.

Tito peered at him for a moment, like he was considering explaining something. Finally, he said, "Good point," and ate a forkful of the crumble. "But they're messing with you. You've got to pretend like they're not getting to you. You've got to relax. Like me."

Caden leaned back in his chair. "I don't pretend," he said. "Or relax."

"That's your whole problem, bro."

"My problem is an Elderdragon is going to eat me and my brother if we don't find evidence that the gas incident was sabotage," Caden said, and crossed his arms.

"Yeah," Tito said. "That, too."

In math class, Rath Dunn seemed to be in good spirits as he boomed out a lecture on death rates and decimals. Caden's attention wandered from the board to Rath Dunn's desk. To the drawer where Caden had found the vials labeled "Tear of Elf," "Magical Locks," "Blood of Son," and "Essence of Dragon." Why was he collecting such things? For that matter, why would anyone sabotage the science room?

When the class finished, Caden gathered his things. He and Tito had detention—he for his second tardy, Tito for his alarm pull. Caden felt sure he could talk Mr. McDonald into letting them walk the halls. They would make detention useful and search the school.

Rath Dunn, however, blocked Caden from the door. "You and Tito stay," he said.

The other students rushed out.

Tito stepped up beside Caden. "We have detention," he said.

"I know. With me."

"With Mr. McDonald," Caden corrected.

The three of them were now alone in the room. Rath Dunn reached to the door and locked it. His smile could have chilled a flame spirit.

"I switched weeks with him," Rath Dunn said. "You should be grateful. He doesn't know much about punishment. Or math."

As school was over, Tito pulled his blue sparkly cell

phone from his bag. "I'm calling Rosa."

"No need," Rath Dunn said. "I called her this after-noon and told her I'd use detention to tutor you. You should thank me, son of Axel. I always go the extra mile for my students." His eyes flickered to Tito. "I have some enrich-ment work for you as well, boy."

Tito looked at the screen and frowned his lopsided frown. "Rosa texted and said Mr. Rathis will drive us home."

Rath Dunn opened his arms wide. "See, that's my way. Above and beyond."

Caden and Tito exchanged a look. "We're not going anywhere with you," Caden said.

"Whatever," Tito said. "I'm calling her. I'll tell her you're scaring me."

Before Tito could punch a key, Rath Dunn snatched his phone and put it in his red blazer pocket. Caden's fingers twitched. His phone was in his pocket.

Rath Dunn seemed to guess his thoughts. "Give me your phone, too, prince," he said, "or I'll break your hand."

One thing about Rath Dunn, he was honest. He kept his deals and he made good on his threats. The pink stones on the case glittered as Caden handed it over. "What do you want?"

"Some hair, some blood, some perfume. Not much, really." In a cruel voice, he added, "But I already got the tears I needed." He went to his desk and sat. "That vial was particularly fun to fill. Took a while though."

"What did you say?" Tito said.

Rath Dunn repeated his words, then held up his red marker. "Now it's time to learn some math." His gaze shifted to Tito. He tossed a paper his way. "There's some enrichment for you." Tito bent down to pick it up but he didn't take his gaze off Rath Dunn or Caden. "You go sit in the back, Tito."

Caden nodded at Tito to do as he was told. Tito sat one row back. His whole body looked tense.

Rath Dunn, on the other hand, looked delighted. He grabbed Jane's desk and dragged it so that it was edge to edge with Caden's. Jane had carved the elvish word for "mother" on top of hers. It looked like it had been crushed under Rath Dunn's fist. The desk screeched against the tiles like it hurt.

Rath Dunn placed a problem sheet between them. "Now, sit, prince." The sides of his eyes crinkled, but he didn't fully smile. "I've made you a special worksheet, one even you can understand." He picked it up and began to read. "One brother dies by the hand of another." He held up his finger. "Now, listen carefully. For one month their father mourned, after two months he vowed justice, at three months he suspected, at six he—"

"This is fiction," Caden said.

"It's a math problem, a series. Answer the question." With dramatic flair, he raised the paper once more. "How many months until the king dies?" He then waited, as if he were a patient tutor and not a terrible villain. His line of sight shifted over Caden's shoulder. "I'm certain Tito knows."

Yes, Tito was good at math. So was Brynne. Jane was decent at it. Caden swatted at the paper in front of him. He was capable enough with numbers. "What is your point?"

Some cruel glee returned to Rath Dunn's expression. "Sometimes, I need some fun. One day, when I'm in control, you'll see how bad that could really be for you." He tapped the desk. "Now, what's the answer, son of Axel?"

The day Rath Dunn gained control would be bad for all of them. Caden forced his shoulders square. It was important not to show fear. It was important not to play this game. "The answer is never."

"Wrong." He wrote a giant red X on the paper.

Rath Dunn snorted. "Next question. Ten Elite Paladins are impaled onto spikes. Fifteen are thrown into the fire. Twenty-five drown. Forty—"

"I'm not answering these questions," Caden said.

Rath Dunn wrote another large X on the test. "But we're just beginning. Question three."

Two hours and many taunts later, Rath Dunn abruptly ended his lesson. "Time to go." He got up, put Jane's desk back in place, and opened the door. The hall looked deserted.

Slowly, Caden got to his feet. "We can walk home."

"Yep," Tito said.

"No need for that." Rath Dunn grabbed Caden's arm. Quick as wind, he grabbed Tito's as well. "Like I said, I'll drive you," he said. "I have permission."

Bad things were about to happen. Caden felt it deep in his gut. Bad things were about to happen, and the crimson-dressed despot in front of him was the reason.

Rath Dunn dragged them to the parking lot. There was only one car left. It gleamed red like an elfish ruby, and looked as fast as an Autumnlands firefox.

Near the car, Rath Dunn released Tito but kept Caden gripped tightly and pulled out a key. Tito stepped back. The red car's lights flashed, and the car door clicked and unlocked. "My Audi," Rath Dunn said, and Caden could tell he liked the car. "Get in."

Caden pulled against him. "We won't get in that car with you."

Tito stepped farther away. "Give us back our phones."

The long spring shadows stretched between the school and the mountain and over the asphalt. Rath Dunn laughed and began to drag Caden toward the car. "You can stop fight—"

Caden punched him in the gut. Hard enough that he loosened his hold. Caden pulled free and kicked at Rath Dunn's knee. The kick, Rath Dunn blocked. Mostly. He grimaced, though, and Caden jumped two strides back.

Rath Dunn straightened up. He motioned for them to come back. "Don't make me run you boys down."

Caden was fairly certain Rath Dunn could catch one of them. His skill in battle was great. Yet Caden would rather run than surrender. He nodded to Tito and they dashed in opposite directions.

Rath Dunn grabbed Caden before he'd run a stride. He whacked him in the temple, which made Caden a bit dizzy, and dragged him to the car. "Behave," he said, and tossed him into the passenger seat. "I'm taking you home. That's all." He paused and turned back to the parking lot and spoke in a loud voice. "That is, I'll take you home if Tito gets in the car. Otherwise, I'll toss you down the rocky side of the mountain."

"And if I get in, you won't hurt us?" Tito sounded like he was halfway across the parking lot. "Why should I believe you?"

Rath Dunn sounded offended. "I don't lie, boy."

In some ways, it made Rath Dunn more treacherous. It gave people confidence when striking deals with him. Even Caden had once fallen prey to his honesty. It seemed now Tito had as well, as he was throwing his backpack in the backseat and slowly getting into the car. Honesty and honor, Caden was beginning to believe, weren't always the same thing.

Before Caden fully regained his senses, Tito was in the backseat, the doors were locked, and Rath Dunn was zooming from the parking lot. Caden hurried to buckle his seat belt. Rosa insisted they always wear seat belts. He rubbed his temple. His arm throbbed. He felt a bit carsick from the twisting, turning road.

"You boys should be grateful," Rath Dunn said in his pedantic teacher's voice. "I'm teaching you a lesson today."

Tito leaned forward. He, too, looked pale. "What lesson is that? How to be a maniac?"

Rath Dunn grinned. He took a sharp turn, and the force slammed Caden against the door and Tito back. "That when I decide to kill you, I can." He shrugged. "And will."

Caden felt his heart racing, his stomach turning. "That's against Ms. Primrose's rules."

Rath Dunn turned to look at him. "For now," he said. Truly, he should keep his eyes on the twisting road before them and not on Caden. "You'd be wise to be useful," Rath Dunn added, "but it seems you're too foolish for that."

Caden rested back against the leather seat. Though not the appropriate reaction of an eighth-born prince nor a future Elite Paladin, he felt like he was going to throw up. The thought of how his father would crinkle his brow in disappointment if he did so helped him keep down his lunch. "You'd be wise to slow down," he managed to say.

Rath Dunn growled at him in such a way that Caden worried he might change his mind and kill him in the passenger seat of the red Audi. "Next time I get you alone, son of Axel, you'll suffer. Tell your brother that for me."

Caden wouldn't tell Jasan that. Tito, however, was also his brother. Mostly to irritate Rath Dunn, he turned and said, "I'll suffer next time. Did you get that, Sir Tito?"

"Huh?" Tito said. "Oh yeah, sure." He sounded distracted. With Caden's life being threatened, he could pay a bit more attention. Also, "yeah, sure" was hardly an appropriate response to Caden's future torture.

Rath Dunn took another sharp turn. His eyes flashed, and he glanced into his rearview mirror. "What are you doing back there?"

"I'm going to tell Rosa you threatened us."

Rath Dunn returned his gaze to the road. His scar tugged at his mouth, and a slow grin spread across his face. What type of game was he playing to want Rosa's fury? Surely, he wasn't so foolish. "Go ahead." He chuckled. "From what I've heard, Caden has already complained many times."

"Yeah, but she thinks I'm sane," Tito said.

"Does she now? You're her foster kid, right? What does she really care?" Before Caden could challenge those words, Rath Dunn slammed the brakes.

Caden lurched forward, the seat belt pinching his neck. Tito cursed. Rath Dunn began to drive carefully. Slowly, he turned into Rosa's drive. The door locks flipped up. Caden doubled over and promptly threw up on the red floor mat. He certainly wasn't telling Jasan about any of this.

Tito scrambled out the back door.

Rath Dunn stared at the mat. He seemed unable to comprehend.

Perhaps Caden's nervous stomach wasn't so bad. Rath Dunn might kill him one day, and Caden's fathers and brothers might be embarrassed by his mess on the mat, but the action had distracted his enemy. Caden used the moment to jump out.

Rath Dunn rolled down the window. He spoke near a whisper. "Who knows, though? Maybe your brother won't care. Maybe he'll want to kill you himself."

"Jasan wouldn't hurt me."

Rath Dunn reached in his pocket and tossed Caden's and Tito's cell phones to them. "We'll see who hurts who," Rath Dunn said. He slowly pulled down the drive, turned, then sped down the road like a spray of red blood.

Caden stared after him partly in shock, partly still nauseous. He felt unnerved that the tyrant knew of Rosa and her house, worried he could hurt her as well as Tito, Brynne, and Jane. At least Caden had thrown up on his floor mat. It wasn't the noblest of things, but it would require Rath Dunn to clean.

Suddenly, Caden couldn't catch his breath.

Tito patted Caden's back. "Bro, you okay?" He also sounded a bit shaky.

Caden wasn't okay. Rath Dunn was going to kill him. Also Tito. The math problem about the brother replayed in his head, as did Ms. Primrose's words: "Heroes aren't sent here, dear." The royal Winterbird had been stripped from Jasan's uniform. How could he have been banished? How could anyone believe Jasan would hurt Chadwin? Unlike Jasan's feelings for Caden, Jasan liked Chadwin. Certainly, the king knew that. He had to know that. How could their father let this happen?

A gentle hand on his shoulder startled him. It was Rosa. "Are you all right? How was the tutoring?"

"He drove like a madman," Tito said. "Caden's right. He's crazy."

She looked at Caden with something between concern and sorrow in her expression. "Go inside and get something to eat."

Caden's hands felt shaky so he put them in his pockets. "I've told you, Rath Dunn is my enemy, he's the enemy of all good peoples." Rosa looked skeptical, like usual. "He is also a danger to Brynne and Jane."

Rosa crossed her arms. Her face was iron. "He's not your enemy, Caden. He's your math teacher."

"He's both," Caden said. "You shouldn't have given him permission to drive us home."

She frowned at that. "I'm sorry, Caden. I didn't realize it would upset you so much. Go inside and calm down." Her voice was kind but stern. "We'll discuss this later," she said, and went to tinker with her metal flowers.

In the living room, the girls sat on the green couch. Jane was dressed in her pink training clothes. Brynne had a yellow towel around her neck. Her hair hung in long, dark strands past her shoulders.

Caden reached out and touched a strand. "Rosa has saved your magical locks."

"For now," Jane said.

Brynne's face turned red. "For always. No one better touch my hair."

Smartly, Caden let go of it. "He'll try again," he said. His head and stomach still felt as if they were spinning. "At least we know what he wants from you. We must plan to protect both you and your hair."

Brynne started to braid her damp hair. "I'll protect me," she said. "He comes near my hair and I'll fling him against the wall. I got rid of those assassins that way." She looked at Caden. "Remember?"

Caden did remember. Telekinesis mind magic. Brynne rarely talked about that day when they were just children. But people had died. Caden's guard Luna had fallen. If not for Brynne, Caden would likely have also.

However powerful Brynne was, though, Rath Dunn was a tyrant. He'd easily caught Caden. He was fast, and he was their math teacher. He had power over them. And Rosa, as protective as she was, didn't see it. Even if Rosa wanted to keep them from school, Caden had a sinking feeling Ms. Primrose had ways of stopping her.

Jane scooted over so Tito could sit beside her. "If Brynne can fling him against the wall, I'm in favor of that." She smiled at Brynne. "Or just take out Ms. Jackson. She's the master of ritual magic. Rath Dunn needs her to do the spell. The ingredients won't matter without her."

"If he had to, he could cast it himself," Caden said. "He seems meticulous enough. And he's conniving enough to have alternate options."

"But it would make it more difficult, right?" Jane said.

"Ritual magic takes time, even after all the ingredients are collected," Brynne said. "What might take a master weeks or months to set up could take a novice years or decades to do."

"So it would be smart to get rid of her."

Tito nudged Jane with his elbow. "You've got a bit of a dark streak, you know that," he said, then glanced at Brynne. "No wonder you and Miss Destructive get along. You're both beautiful and scary."

Jane blushed, but this wasn't the appropriate time for what Tito had explained to him was flirting.

"It would be foolish for us not to prepare for Rath Dunn's next attack," Caden said. "But flinging him against a wall would likely end in Ms. Primrose eating Brynne." He glanced at Jane. "And 'taking out' Ms. Jackson would be just as difficult and yield a similar result."

Tito looked over at the door as if checking for Rosa. Then he leaned farther over and peeked out the window.

Jane's blush had faded, and she seemed to be thinking seriously. "We need to do something."

Tito shrugged. "If you want to prepare, then we need to know why Rath Dunn wants Brynne's hair and Caden's brother's blood."

"Does evil need a reason?" Caden said.

"Usually," Tito said. "It's called motive." He reached for his pack. "I found something interesting in his backseat. These mean something." Tito handed a paper to Jane and one to Brynne. The third he kept. "Mr. Rathis had a box full of them. They slid from under the car seat when he took one of the curves."

Caden held out his hand.

"You can't read it, bro," Tito said.

True, but Caden didn't like feeling left out.

Brynne crinkled the paper in her hand. "It's a complaint against the school. Signed, Anonymous."

"Mine claims the buildings aren't properly cleaned," Jane said.

"This one says Ms. Primrose is too harsh on students," Tito said. "It's signed by Ms. Elise Hicks, esquire."

That name sounded familiar. Well, not the esquire. The Elise Hicks.

Tito handed Caden the paper. "That's Derek's mother. The scary lawyer."

Caden scrunched up his brow. "What does Rath Dunn gain from that?"

"How would I know?"

There were steps on the porch. The door creaked. Caden turned and hid the paper behind his back. It rumpled behind him. Jane stuffed hers between the sofa cushions. Caden had no idea what Brynne had done with her letter, but it was hidden.

Rosa looked at them for a long moment. Finally, she said, "Time for dinner."

11

THE MEANING OF WORDS

The next day was Thursday. On Sunday, Caden would be cursed. On Tuesday, he and Jasan would be eaten if he failed his quest. As each day passed, Caden's troubles increased.

The weather seemed unaware of their impending fate. The sky was bright, the sun warm. The air smelled of cut grass.

Caden rode in the front of Rosa's pickup. He was royalty. Until he was dead, it was his proper place. He'd explained this many times to the three nonroyals in the backseat, and still they kicked the back of his seat. He turned around sharply.

Brynne, Tito, and Jane smiled at him.

"This isn't the behavior of future Elite Paladins," he informed them.

Brynne looked over at Jane and Tito. "No future Elite Paladin did that, prince."

"It was you, then."

"Maybe," she said, and Tito and Jane laughed.

When they arrived at school, Rosa had them wait a moment. "Be good. Work hard. Bring home that spelling trophy." She reached out to Tito, then Brynne. "I'd be there if I could, but the sculpture installation has been scheduled for months."

"Yeah," Tito said, and shrugged. "It's okay."

Brynne opened the rear door. "Don't worry, Rosa. I'll certainly win."

"Dream on," Tito said.

Caden unbuckled his seat belt. "If there were weapons involved, I'd be more impressed." He had a quest to complete, a saboteur to unmask, and an Elderdragon to please. A sword would help with all those things. "When can I have my sword returned?"

Rosa's cheek twitched. "I've told you," she said. "No swords in the house."

"One day you'll reconsider."

"Go to school, Caden."

Once in the building, Tito and Brynne went to prepare for the spelling contest, but Jane walked with Caden to his locker. Unlucky twelve-four was smudged. Truly, it was cursed with muck. There was another note inside—a pink one, not one from his brother. The locker was also cursed with pink notes. He put the note with the stack.

Beside him, Jane rummaged in her backpack. She was dressed in the colors of spring—pale yellows and greens. Her hair was combed over her ears as if she wanted to hide their slight elfish points. She pulled a small kitchen whisk from her pack. It looked suspiciously like the one Rosa used to make her eggs. "I enchanted it."

He grabbed his reading book from his locker. "So you've moved from the office to the kitchen?"

She handed the whisk to him. In his left hand he held his reading book, in his right, the enchanted whisk. His right fingers started to tingle.

"It's who I am," she said.

True, enchanters enchanted. That was why they never lived long. Caden had hoped the discipline and rigor of the Elite Paladin path might help Jane control it, but that hope was dimming.

"Don't worry," Jane said. "The smaller the enchantment, the less life force required." She looked proud. "Brynne and I figured it out."

If anyone knew about lack of control, Caden supposed it was Brynne. Still, Brynne's magic worked differently from Jane's. "You don't know that for certain," he said.

"I'm mostly certain," she said. "And this way it's measured. I won't accidentally enchant something like Tito's necklace again. I won't burn myself out."

The power in the whisk felt more intense than Caden's

magical chain of paper clips, more intense than Tito's necklace of protection. He frowned and offered it back to her.

"Keep it for now," she said. "The enchantments work better when I give them away."

"Are you certain it's a small enchantment?"

"More powerful ones are harder to detect."

He swished it in the air. Nothing happened. "What does it do?"

"It mixes things."

Jane seemed more impressed by the item than he was. Still, it was enchanted. Caden deemed it magic item one hundred and thirty-one, the Enchanted Whisk of Mixing, and stuck it in his inside pocket. Now he had three magical items. No one had three magical items. He stood up a little straighter.

A group of eighth graders walked by them. He heard a girl say, "Did you see the new gym teacher?" One of the boys added, "He keeps killing the basketballs." They broke into giggles and whispers.

Caden looked down at the floor. The tiles looked gritty and needed to be mopped. How could Jasan have been banished? Rath Dunn said his brother was a traitor. The dagger that had killed Chadwin was here, and Jasan had denied nothing.

Jane touched his arm. She seemed to have guessed his thoughts. "The lunch witches used my memory of my mother against me," she said. "Don't let Mr. Rathis make you doubt your brother, Caden. Mr. Rathis is the villain." She glared at a short, stout teacher opening a classroom door. "Don't trust any of them."

"I don't," Caden said. He got out his cleaning cloth and wiped the fingerprints from the locker door. When he next spoke, he kept his voice low. "I don't understand how Jasan could have been banished."

She stared at him for a moment, then nodded. "Then talk to him. He could help us with the quest."

If Jasan knew Caden had taken such a quest, he'd be furious. He might lock Caden away and try to fight Ms. Primrose. "Perhaps," he said.

"If it'll help, you can give the whisk to him."

So that was why she'd handed it to Caden. It was a present, possibly a peace offering, for Caden to give Jasan. "A kind offer," he said.

Although Jane was intent on revenge against the lunch witch, she was often kind and brave. Truly, Caden should have knighted her. It was a terrible oversight. With Jasan in Asheville, however, Jasan was the topmost Razzonian royal. Jasan would have to do it and Caden wasn't sure if he would. He wasn't sure of much these days.

"Let's find him," Caden said.

When they turned the corner, however, Ms. Primrose stood in front of them, a stern expression etched into her features. She shifted her gaze from Caden to Jane, and her stomach rumbled. She didn't laugh it off.

"You know the rules, dears," she said.

Jane shivered as if cold breath had touched her neck. "We know," Jane said.

Ms. Primrose tapped a timepiece on her wrist. "Don't be late. Punctuality is important."

Well, Caden could only agree with that. Still. "We're not late yet."

"But you will be in ninety-four seconds."

That seemed somewhat exact.

"Ninety-three," she said. As she said it, her teeth looked bright white, pointed, and like they could rip flesh. She noticed him looking and covered her mouth. "It's impolite to stare." She narrowed her cold, pale eyes. "Ninety-two."

She pointed Jane toward the English classroom, and Jane smartly hurried to it. Then Ms. Primrose grabbed Caden by the elbow—he was tired of people and old dragons doing that—and led him to the reading room.

The light in the hall turned as blue as a snow tortoise shell. Ms. Primrose stopped in front of the classroom door. Her skin shimmered with scales. Her hair, her shadow, everything about her seemed reptilian. Her gaze lingered on Caden like he was a tasty bit of roasted rabbit.

"Dear," she said, and her tone had an edginess that was unfamiliar. "Have you completed my quest yet? Do you have proof? Two days have passed."

"I have five more," he said. For the first time since he'd taken the quest, he wondered if it helped Ms. Primrose keep herself under control. After all, she'd said even she was bound by the agreements made in forgotten tongues. "Until my time is up, you can't eat me, Jasan, or any other student or parent." He spoke softly, the way he talked to Sir Horace when Sir Horace was spooked. "This was our contract."

"If you neglect your studies and break my rules, I can still punish you," she said. "I can turn you into a cat, keep you in my office, and eat you when your time runs out."

Could she turn him into a cat? Well, she'd turned herself into an old lady, so it seemed possible. He eyed her. There was something he'd often wondered. "May I ask you a question?"

She huffed a bit and checked her watch. "Thirty-three seconds. I suppose I can answer one question," she said.

In the legends about the Elderdragons, they were described as young and beautiful. But Ms. Primrose always appeared as an old lady. "If you can transform yourself into anything you wish," Caden said, "why an old lady?"

She bristled, but she had given him permission to ask. "I can appear as a human, but I transform into my version of a human. I'm old in any form I take. If I were to turn you into a cat, you'd certainly be a loud, yowling kitten. Another question like that, and you'll see firsthand."

"I understand," Caden said.

"You had better. And you had better find who dares embarrass me, so I can have someone for dinner. If not,

I'll eat you and your brother." Some of her power seemed to pull back. She ran a gnarled hand over the door and knocked. "Above all else, my school is my most precious treasure."

Mr. McDonald opened the door just as the late bell rang. Ward and Tonya sat at their computers. When Mr. McDonald saw Ms. Primrose, he blanched. Truth be told, he'd been acting odd recently. Some days, although not many, he'd actively taught Caden reading. He'd been working with Tonya on her stuttering, and he'd tried to engage Ward in conversation at least twice. His fear of Ms. Primrose seemed to be exponentially increased.

"His reading is improving," Mr. McDonald said, and it sounded like a plea for mercy.

"It better be," Ms. Primrose said, and Caden saw the sharp glint of her teeth again. "You need to start doing your job. My school's reputation is everything to me." Her stomach rumbled. "Otherwise, I'll eat you."

Ward and Tonya both looked up at that.

Mr. McDonald seemed ready to cower behind the nearest computer. "Yes, ma'am."

After she left, Mr. McDonald remained shaky. "We're going to watch the spelling bee today." He was taking deep breaths. "It's required." He looked from Caden to Tonya to Ward. "If you have any questions, ask me."

The auditorium was a large space. Two aisles divided thirty rows of creaky wooden seats into three sections. Mr.

McDonald directed Caden, Tonya, and Ward to a middle row on the left side.

The ceiling was high. Exposed oak beams stretched from side to side like the giant growth limbs of wood elementals. In the rear, exits led into the school's back hallway. In the front, there was a podium and stage. On each side of the stage, exits opened to outdoors. Future Elite Paladins always noted exits.

A few parents sat in reserved seats in the rear. Students fidgeted in the rest of the rows. As Mr. Bellows was moderating, his English class—including Jane—sat with Mrs. Belle and her morning science students. Caden leaned back.

A spelling contest was a waste of his royal time. He didn't understand the purpose of a competition that included no swords, spears, or horses. And he had a quest to complete.

At the podium, Brynne ran fingers through her long hair and glared at Mr. Bellows. It was as if she was daring him to try to cut it again. Her clothes were shades of purple, and her eyes shone silver under the stage lights.

A slight smirk tipped Mr. Bellows's thin lips. He hissed the first word. "Fratricide."

Caden felt his face heat. He knew the word. He was gifted in speech; he knew most words. "Fratricide" meant brother killing brother, but he'd no idea how to spell it. The word seemed to hang like a dagger from the beams above.

Three rows up, Rath Dunn turned, caught Caden's gaze, and smiled.

One day, Caden would bring them to justice. He looked away. When he did, his breath left him. Jasan sat in a back left seat. It seemed he'd also been told to watch the spelling bee.

The other teachers had been in Asheville longer than Caden. They'd had time to learn the language, and Caden suspected had used charms, tricks, and magic to speak and read it. Jasan had been here mere days. And he wouldn't use tricks to learn the language. Elite Paladins didn't deceive. As Ms. Primrose would say, it wasn't in their natures.

As such, Jasan didn't react to the word—he didn't understand it—but his gaze slid from Rath Dunn to Caden and turned as cold as ice-covered rock. Jasan was being taunted in a language he didn't understand, and in a land in which he didn't belong. There was nothing fair or just about that.

Then again, maybe it wasn't Jasan being taunted. Maybe it was Caden. After all, Caden understood the hard-to-spell words.

On stage, Brynne looked caught between terrified and livid. She twisted her hands together. Her gaze darted from Jasan to Rath Dunn to Caden, and finally to Mr. Bellows at the front. "Fratricide," she said, and it sounded like the word tasted foul on her tongue. "F-R-A-T-R-I-C-I-D-E, fratricide."

In contrast to Brynne's sleek beauty, Mr. Bellows was worn looking. "Correct," he said, but there was nothing correct about fratricide.

As Brynne returned to her stage seat, Tito shuffled to the podium. Caden needed to clear his head. He wanted to keep thoughts of fratricide far away.

Caden relaxed his hands and concentrated on the sounds around him—students whispering, teachers shuffling papers, a soft buzzing of activity. He listened more carefully. Buzzing? He sat up straight.

Something was actually buzzing.

It sounded like a bee—the stinging Ashevillian equivalent of a Greater Realm crater wasp. Caden held back a shudder. When he'd been seven, he'd fallen into a crater wasp nest. The resulting fourteen welts had hurt for weeks.

Rosa had assured him that there were no actual bees in an Ashevillian spelling bee. Though why the odd people of this world would call a spelling contest a "bee," Caden had no idea. Perhaps the buzzing was part of the show? He turned toward Ward and Tonya.

Ward scowled at Caden. Obviously, Ward wanted him to keep quiet. Caden, however, didn't want to keep quiet. "Do you hear that buzzing?" he said.

Ward ignored him. Tonya huddled down in her chair and set her notepad in her lap. Onstage, Brynne was in her chair still glancing from Jasan to Rath Dunn and chewing on her bottom lip. If she heard the buzzing, she showed no indication of it. For his part, Jasan had turned his glower upward and was tracking something in the rafters.

Caden followed Jasan's line of sight and felt his eyes go wide. A single bee zigzagged near the ceiling. Truly, Caden hated bees. Matter of point, he hated all creatures that stung. He nudged Tonya with his elbow. "There," he warned.

Tonya looked worried, but before Caden could comfort her, Mr. McDonald leaned forward from the row behind and thumped Caden with his book. "Quiet," he said.

Caden did keep quiet. He mustn't show fear of insects while Rath Dunn, his great enemy and math teacher, sat just a few rows in front of him. Rath Dunn was the one to fear, not the bee. One bee Caden could shoo away or, if necessary, squash beneath his boot. Besides, he needed to support his foster brother, Sir Tito, and his ally Brynne by paying attention to the pointless contest.

From the front, Mr. Bellows's cruel voice echoed. "The word," he said with reverence, "is 'sedition.'"

Sedition. Pertaining to treachery, subversion, and treason. No doubt a word Rath Dunn enjoyed. The meaning was clear enough, but like most words, Caden had no clue how to spell it. Truly, English was more complicated than the wiggly written language of the gnomes.

Tito didn't spell the word right away. Instead, he said, "Can you use it in a sentence?"

"Among royal heirs, sedition is common," Mr. Bellows said.

"Um. Okay," Tito said.

Tonya wrote the word on her paper. At the podium, Tito spelled it with the same letters. She was good with words. If she had more confidence, and was not embarrassed by her stutter, she would be on stage competing. She saw him look at her notebook, and turned the ripe red of an Ashevillian apple.

"Correct," Mr. Bellows said.

Although Tito had strictly forbidden Caden from cheering, clapping, or "any other weird thing you think about" as support, Caden felt the need to show solidarity. The villains wouldn't win. They would be stopped. Caden nodded his approval and raised his fist in victory. Nodding and fist raising weren't cheering, clapping, or weird. From the stage, Tito gave him a withering look.

From the back of the auditorium, Jane clapped. As Tito returned to his chair, he smiled. It seemed Jane was allowed to clap. In the brief silence that followed, Caden heard more buzzing.

A second, more devious-looking bee flew overhead. He nudged Tonya, and he snapped his fingers to get Ward's attention. "Two bees." One bee was not such a problem. Two bees was the beginning of one. Once there were three, he'd have too few feet to squash them.

Caden turned, caught Jasan's gaze, and pointed to the

insects. Jasan was allergic to stinging things. Best he be aware of the double danger.

Jasan stared for a moment, then stood and stepped out the back exit. It was the smart thing to do. They should evacuate. Caden told Mr. McDonald.

"It's springtime—bees will get in sometimes. Sit and listen. I don't want any trouble from you today."

Caden sank into his seat and tilted his head back. He closed his eyes. He wouldn't look at the bees or Rath Dunn's round shiny head. He wouldn't think about his brother Chadwin lying warm but unmoving with a dagger in his back. He wouldn't think about Jasan or the two bees flying around, or the fact that he and Jasan might be devoured in five days.

Then something landed on his forehead.

Beside him, he felt Tonya fidget. "C-c-caden?" she said. "There's a b-b—"

A bee. There was a bee on his forehead.

12

THE SPELLING BEE SWARM

With great care, Caden opened his eyes, raised his hand, and flicked the bee away. He looked up. His heartbeat quickened. The number of bees had multiplied. They darted from backstage, in and out of the beams, and crisscrossed in short, heated paths.

Others in the auditorium were looking up now. Students pointed. Rath Dunn shielded his eyes with a paper and peered at the swarm. On stage, Brynne looked surprised, and Tito looked irritated. Mr. Bellows released an angry screech at the disruption of his spelling contest.

Caden pulled Tonya and Ward down to the gritty auditorium floor. He could hear Rath Dunn shouting orders. "Stay calm," he was saying. "Move toward the nearest exit. Slowly, people. Calmly."

Typically, Rath Dunn was drama and threats; he was

machinations and scheming. The tone he used now was different. It was a general's tone. It was a tone to be followed. Those two sides of Rath Dunn were why he was so dangerous and why he'd almost conquered Caden's home of Razzon.

Caden peeked over the row in front of him. Rath Dunn directed students with a slight smirk. Tito, Brynne, and the other spelling bee finalists were out of their chairs and shuffling toward the left front exit. Across the auditorium, Mrs. Belle was leading Jane's class out the auditorium's back door at a quick clip.

The large room was halfway empty when the swarm became unnatural. It became so dense it darkened the room. Faces seemed to form from the cloud of swirling insects—faces Caden knew. First Mr. Bellows. Then Rath Dunn. Mr. McDonald. Finally students: Derek, Tonya, Caden, more.

Suddenly, as if controlled by an unseen master, the swarm dived at Mr. Bellows. He swatted bee after bee dead, then held out his hand. A rotten aura surrounded his bony fingers. The fallen bees reanimated and surrounded him like a protective shield. He was using necromancy—the forbidden art of death and reanimation. Even crouching rows away, Caden smelled the corpse-like scent of it.

By the right front exit, Rath Dunn ushered students out. He crushed the insects foolish enough to come near him. His mouth was twisted in a feral smile. His fists were fast and sure. He seemed to be enjoying himself.

Caden, Ward, and Tonya needed to escape. Caden turned so that Mr. McDonald could tell them what to do, but Mr. McDonald was gone. Caden spotted him running out the rear exit without so much as a glance back. It seemed Caden, Ward, and Tonya were on their own. Mr. McDonald zoomed out the door just as part of the swarm dived at him.

Suddenly, Caden understood. He'd seen the faces of Mr. Bellows, Rath Dunn, and Mr. McDonald in the bee swarm, and they'd been attacked. The swarm faces were targets. That meant Caden was a target. Tonya huddled beside him. So was she. They would be attacked next.

He grabbed Tonya's hand with his left and Ward's hand with his right. Ward tensed. It was obvious he didn't like unannounced contact, but he didn't argue. "We must go."

It felt as if Ward wanted to pull away, but he didn't. Instead, he nodded. Tonya squeezed Caden's hand. Her eyes were saucers.

The right front exit was closest. Together, they dashed to it. Rath Dunn saw them and motioned them to run faster. Just before they got to him, he stepped out and shut the door. Caden shoved on the door, but it wouldn't open. Someone—no doubt Rath Dunn—held it shut from the outside.

Beside him, Ward grimaced and swatted a bee from his forearm. Caden rammed the exit with his shoulder. Still it didn't budge. He looked around. Everyone else was gone.

Caden and Tonya were the only targets left inside.

The swarm was thick. The buzzing vibrated against the walls. They needed to get to another exit right away. Toward the rear exit, the swarm was so dense Caden couldn't see the back wall of the auditorium. Between them and the left front exit, the bees were still numerous, but there were fewer. It was their best hope of escape.

Tonya seemed to be thinking the same thing. She pulled Caden's hand in that direction. "We have to get out," she said. But the only way out was through stinging, angry insects.

Quickly, Caden catalogued his possessions. He had his coat. It would offer some protection, but not enough, and not for all three of them. His compass and paper clips were in one pocket, his cell phone and the whisk in the other. The compass wouldn't help. The paper clips were supposed to hold things together, but right now he needed to break through the bees. There wasn't time to call for help with his cell phone. He pulled out the whisk.

If nothing else, the whisk could act as a projectile. He hurled it. It tumbled through the swarm and landed on the floor in front of the stage. "Run, now!" Caden said.

The bee swarm began to swirl in long, dark ripples, like Rosa's eggs in the mixing bowl. Maybe the Enchanted Whisk of Mixing deserved more respect than Caden had realized?

Although the swarm had been broken, stray bees still

attacked. Caden, Tonya, and Ward had made it halfway to the exit when Tonya collapsed. Ward knelt beside her. His face was red with two stings. Tonya only had one bee sting that Caden could see, but it was swollen badly. Her cheeks were flushed. She looked like she couldn't catch her breath.

"She's allergic," Ward said.

Like Jasan, Caden thought, as he felt a bee land on his cheek.

Ward laced his arm around her to help her up. Caden did the same and reached down to snatch the whisk as well. Something sharp and needlelike plunged into his neck. He slapped at it and felt another sting on the back of his hand. A third landed on Tonya, and Ward reached out and knocked it away with his thumb. She looked at the door, determination etched in her red, swelling face.

Around them, the bees were reforming into a dense swarm. In the rear, the dark wall of bees started to roll toward them. With no time to lose, he pointed the whisk upward, and the bees began to swirl again. Then he pointed it away from them, and the bees moved, as one, in the opposite direction. The air was clear—for now. There was only time to run.

Between them, Tonya wheezed.

The door in front of them slammed open. Jasan ran inside. He seemed to have little trouble dodging stray insects using his gift of speed, though his eyes went large at the rolling swarm that was about to overtake them. He grabbed for Caden, but Caden pushed Tonya toward him instead. "Take her first!" he yelled in Royal Razzon.

With a nod, Jasan picked her up. Caden saw her slump in his arms, and they ran out and into the Ashevillian sun. Caden pulled the left exit door shut behind him.

The side and front lawns were crowded. Jasan laid Tonya on the ground. Ward, often so quiet, yelled loudly for help. Soon a large woman in a paramedic's uniform jammed a giant needle into Tonya's thigh. Her breathing started to improve.

The Ashevillian paramedics loaded Tonya, Derek—who Caden disliked but mostly didn't want dead—and another young student into an ambulance. The teachers darted furtive glances at one another. Students huddled in small groups, many nursing bee stings, while the school nurse flitted from group to group like a bee herself. Jasan moved to the side of the crowd, then farther away.

Towering above everyone, Ward's father, Manglor, strode toward them. He held his mop like a scepter. His hair fell in dark braids. Caden didn't know who Manglor had been before he was banished from the Greater Realm, but Caden felt more and more certain that Manglor—and by lineage, Ward—was royalty.

Manglor glowered at Caden. "Move, child," he said. Caden stepped back. Manglor put his large hand on Ward's small shoulder.

Trusting Manglor would keep Ward safe, Caden jogged

after Jasan. Jasan needed to know Caden believed in him. Caden caught up with him by a large rhododendron bush. "Wait!" He reached in his pocket, pulled out the whisk, and held it out.

Jasan spun around and grabbed his wrist. "I told you to be careful," he said in Royal Razzon. He looked at the whisk and his frown deepened. "What's that?"

At least the whisk was getting Jasan talking. "The Enchanted Whisk of Mixing. A gift. For you." Caden pointed toward where Jane stood in the crowd. "It would be rude to refuse."

With a huff, Jasan snatched the whisk. Then his gaze lingered on Caden's cheek. "Go get your injuries treated."

Caden touched the sting on his cheek. It felt hot. His face was swelling. "They're minor."

That seemed to annoy Jasan. "Then you're lucky." He pointed to the auditorium. "That was an attack."

Caden knew magically controlled attack bees when he saw them. He didn't have to be told. "I know."

"Then you know you should have taken refuge sooner. You're not that slow that you'd be last out."

Jasan was not gifted in speech like Caden, but he knew how to goad him. Caden wasn't slow at all. Jasan just was faster than everyone. There was a difference. Caden bristled. "You'd have me leave my allies in a bee swarm?"

"I'd have you save yourself."

Jasan had run into the auditorium to help. He'd carried

Tonya out. "You didn't do that. You ran back into the attack, and you're in the most danger. You're allergic. Rath Dunn wants your blood, and Ms. Primrose is hungry."

Jasan didn't look like he cared. His nostrils flared. He looked at the crowd, from one teacher to the next, his expression growing colder with each shift. Finally, he looked at Caden. "I'm different. My life doesn't matter now."

Caden felt like he'd been punched. His brother wasn't even trying to survive happy, villain-filled Asheville. "It matters to me," Caden said. He had to sound certain when he next spoke. He held his brother's gaze. "And I know you were wrongly accused."

"Do you?" Jasan snorted and ran his hand through his hair. "You'd say that about any of us, any of your brothers."

Was that a bad thing? Caden wasn't sure how it could be. And doubting his brothers was what Rath Dunn wanted. Still. He wasn't saying it to all of them. "I'm saying it to you."

Jasan was stubborn, surly, and difficult, but if he understood how much Caden needed him, he'd be less reckless. He'd agree to work with him. Caden just needed to be persistent, charming, and equally stubborn.

"We're brothers," Caden said. "We must work together. We have enemies here."

The pink-flowered branches swayed, and Jasan swatted one away with the whisk. Pink petals fluttered into the spring air. They swirled in a small whirlwind above the bush. "You're my half brother," Jasan said. He walked away but seemed to hesitate. He turned back. "And sometimes brothers are enemies. Remember that."

The words felt like another burning sting. "You're not my enemy," Caden said, but Jasan had disappeared into the crowd. Only the rhododendron blossoms heard him.

These days, Caden felt that he spent as much time standing on the lawn as sitting in the classroom. Tito and Jane stood beside him. The spring day had turned cold. Parents started to arrive to pick up students.

Tito scrunched up his nose and pointed at Caden's cheek. "Ouch," he said.

Stinging things seemed to especially dislike Caden. It was fortunate he'd no allergy or he'd be dead many times over. "It's sore. Nothing more." He smiled at his friend. The spelling contest was important to Tito, and the bees had ruined the bee. "I'm sorry you weren't able to win your award."

"Yeah, whatever," Tito said. He kicked at the ground. "I can still sweep the grade awards. And beat Derek. He didn't win either."

"He was taken away in the ambulance. That's the opposite of winning."

Tito frowned, and his mouth turned lopsided. "Yeah. I almost felt bad for him." Then a slow smile spread across his face. "Maybe he'll miss a few days and fall behind."

"Doubtful," Caden said.

"No one misses many days here," Jane added. "Rosa sent me back the week after I was rescued. But I know you can still win."

And Derek wasn't Tito's only competition. Brynne also got excellent grades. "You also must beat Brynne," Caden said.

Tito grinned. "She's not eligible. She's been here only four months."

"That's fortunate for you."

"I'd still beat her."

Caden wasn't as sure. "She's a sorceress. Studying is one of her greatest skills. Besides, she magics herself before each quiz." Caden felt his brow crinkle. "Where is Brynne?"

"I'm here," Brynne said from behind him. "I thanked Prince Jasan for saving Tonya."

Caden turned and frowned at her. He should demand that she make her presence known *before* she snuck up behind him. She could text him a smiley face or the like. "I helped save Tonya, too." He turned his head so that she could better see his swelling cheek. "And I was injured."

"You always get stung by things. You look puffy but fine."

Tito snickered.

There was nothing funny about a puffy prince. With a huff, Caden motioned to the auditorium. Now that Brynne was here, they needed to discuss the bee incident. "That swarm was no accident." When he spoke, he could see his breath. The temperature was dropping.

Brynne shivered and nodded. "The bees were controlled."

"There are magic bees now?" Tito said.

That was a silly question. Caden raised a brow. "Of course not, Sir Tito," he said. "But there are dangerous creatures that can control bees. And not only bees but other things that swarm." This bee swarm was another not-accident. Another embarrassment for the school. He was failing in his quest for Ms. Primrose.

Caden scanned the crowd. Ms. Primrose stood near the drive talking to a paramedic. Three parents surrounded her, and none looked happy. There was no doubting that the dangerous chill in the air was because of her. She saw Caden and glared. The chill spread. Students huddled together. He understood the meaning of the cold, the meaning of her glare: find out who is sabotaging my school or become my dinner.

Even the sunlight was tinted the cold blue of an angry Elderdragon. He tugged his coat tighter. "This is another act of sabotage. We must search the school and find out who's responsible."

Of course that was when Rosa drove up. She jumped out of the pickup and spent several minutes frowning at Caden's stings. Once she seemed content that he wasn't seriously injured, she said, "Get in the pickup. I'll take you all to lunch."

Caden sat in the front seat. Away from the school, the air turned warm again. People strolled on the downtown sidewalks. Two women played string instruments while begging for coins. A man walked by with a small fluffy white dog under his arm.

Caden's thoughts of bees dimmed at the sight of the dog. Truly, he hoped the dog was a pet, and not food for one of the local eateries. Some of the food sellers included hot dog on their menus. Rosa insisted hot dog wasn't made of dog, but as she couldn't explain what exactly it was made from, Caden feared for the fluffy white dogs of Asheville.

He pointed at the man and dog. Before he could speak, Rosa said, "I've told you, Caden. There are strict guidelines about what we eat and how it's prepared. There are sanitation rules. We don't eat dogs."

Caden wanted to believe her, but the Ashevillians ate all form of strange things: round meats, square fish, round grains and milk. Officer Levine had once offered to bring him pigs in a blanket as a snack. Caden didn't eat pigs. In the Greater Realm, farrow pig flesh had hallucinogenic properties. As for blankets, Caden didn't eat those either.

Rosa parked, and they walked to a sidewalk café just north of the bookstore, the chocolate shop, and an art gallery. The table had a wooden top with an attached red umbrella. Nearby, sidewalk street performers played twangy guitars. The air smelled fresh, but each time a car passed on the nearby street, the fresh smell was mixed with exhaust.

The restaurant served vegan food, which Caden liked, and hamburgers, which he didn't. He stared at the menu and felt his cheeks heat. Despite his hard work in the literacy class, he couldn't understand much of it. Also, something red, either ketchup or blood, was smeared on the side. He showed Tito.

"Lick it," Tito said. "Then you'll know."

Eighth-born princes didn't lick strange menus in foreign lands. Caden tossed the menu aside. His plate looked smudged. He polished it with his napkin while the others ordered.

The waiter wore thick-rimmed glasses, a black T-shirt, and an apron. The outfit was far simpler than the ornate silver and gold trimmed costumes the Winter Castle butlers sported. It was also far less interesting. When it was Caden's turn to order, the waiter tried to sell him on the hamburgers. In the Winter Castle, the servers knew better than that. "We're famous for 'em. All our beef is grass fed and locally raised," the waiter said.

Caden wasn't clear what Ashevillian steers ate if not grass. "Is the beef round?"

"Actually, our chef makes the patties square."

"How is that better?" Caden said, and peered at him. "It's not made of dog, is it?"

Rosa placed her hand on his. "Give him the vegetarian special," she said. "Please."

Proper food would help him prepare for the turmoil of

the next five days. "I suppose that will do," he said.

While they ate, Jane recounted the bee swarm. "Mrs. Belle led us out right away. No one in our class got stung," she said.

Caden considered. Mrs. Belle's class hadn't been attacked, and her face hadn't appeared in the swarm with the others. That was definitely interesting.

About the time the food arrived, Officer Levine joined them and ordered a square burger. Tito glanced between him and Rosa. "Why are you here?" he asked. "None of us have done anything illegal."

Caden thought it was obvious. "Officer Levine is wooing Rosa," he said.

Officer Levine choked on his water and cleared his throat. "The important thing is that you kids are all right."

It was a change of subject, but not one Caden minded. "For now," he said, and forked his greens. "There is danger at school. First gas, now bees. These not-accidents"—Caden would call them what they were—"are the work of a villain."

Officer Levine picked up his hamburger. "Why do you think that?"

Neither Rosa nor Officer Levine believed Caden's accounts of the villains at school or of the Greater Realm, but Caden wouldn't hide who he was or his royal heritage. He wouldn't keep quiet when there was danger. "Ms. Primrose gave me a quest to find the culprit. She's going to eat me if I fail."

Rosa reached out and squeezed his hand. "No one's going to eat you, Caden."

"Not if I succeed, no," he said. "But if I disappear in five days, I want you to know why." He turned to Tito. "And I'll bequeath my confiscated sword to you, Sir Tito."

"It'll be better than that mop," Tito said, and bit into his grass-fed square burger.

Then Caden smiled at Jane. "And I'll leave you my compass, enchantress."

She smiled. "Thanks, but I know you'll succeed."

Rosa seemed less than amused. She peered first at Tito then at Jane. "I've told you two not to encourage these stories. I meant it." She turned to Caden. "And that's enough. I've told you, no more stories about dragons or other realms."

"No more truth, you mean," Caden said.

"Son," Officer Levine said, "you need to learn when to be quiet."

"Actually, I've been practicing that."

"Then practice it now."

"I will," Caden said.

Tito snickered.

Caden opened his mouth to say something to Tito about that, then changed his mind and took a bite of his beans. Officer Levine pulled Rosa away from the table for a moment. They stood near the sidewalk. His face was flushed, so Caden suspected his words were of love.

Tito watched them with a frown.

Suddenly, Brynne kicked Caden under the table. Hard. She arched a brow. "But what about me?" she whispered. "What do I get?"

Should Caden leave the sorceress something? He wasn't sure she deserved it. She'd thanked Jasan and not him. She had cursed him. And the curse would overlap his quest. Caden set down his fork. Suddenly, he wasn't hungry.

Questionable morals aside, Brynne was his closest ally. "Fine, you can have my coat." Brynne at least understood its value. His words seemed to make her happy. "But only if I'm devoured," he added, which seemed to make her less so.

13
THE GREEN CURTAIN

That night, Caden dreamed of giant crater wasps with stingers made of jagged knives. They snatched away his brothers, one by one, and dumped them into their glass hive. Chadwin fell first. Then the wasps stabbed Valon and Maden. Maden's large frame fell to the ground hard enough to crack it. Next fell Lucian, Martin, and Landon. One by one, they all collapsed. Jasan was faceup in the middle, staring with dead eyes. Caden's father pounded on the hive with sword and scepter but couldn't break the shimmering walls.

When Caden awoke, it was warm, and he heard *plink, plink, plink* as rain hit the roof. He put on his red T-shirt with the picture of an eagle. An eagle wasn't an imperial Winterbird, but it was a bird. In the months he'd been stranded it had turned from cold February to warm June.

He, however, still wore his coat.

Tito came out of the bathroom with his hair wet, his jeans and T-shirt on but wrinkled, and a towel around his neck. "Yeah," he said, and motioned to Caden's coat. "Unless that thing is enchanted with air conditioning, you're going to have to take it off come summer or you'll melt."

Ice mice and frozen prairie prawns melted in heat. Razzonian princes didn't. "Nonsense. I'll always wear my coat."

"Say that after you've gone through a North Carolina summer."

At school, Tonya was absent, but Ward was there. As was Mr. McDonald, who had left them to the bee swarm in an act of *sedition*. The coward sat in the back corner behind a giant book. He didn't attempt to help Caden read or engage Ward.

Caden felt his cheeks redden and his eyes narrow. He put on his earphones and turned to his computer. On his screen a new word flashed: F-A-M-I-L-Y. The magic voice in his earphones said, "Family." Family was important. Caden needed to unmask the true culprit before he or she succeeded. He would save Jasan, and he'd find out Rath Dunn's scheme. More words flashed—first "father," then "brother." Truly, the magic voice seemed to understand Caden's thoughts.

Ward lifted his red earphones off his ears and motioned

Caden to do the same. "Your brother is staying next door to us," he said in a soft, low voice. Ward was quiet but he missed little. "If you come over this weekend, you might see him. Pa doesn't like you, or him, but Ma does."

"Why doesn't he like us?" Caden whispered back.

Ward looked at his computer screen. He didn't say anything at first, but Ward was succinct with words, and he seemed to need extra time to choose those he used. Finally, he spoke again. "Pa doesn't trust new people, especially from his world. And he thinks your brother's angry."

A valid concern. Jasan was often angry. Still. "He controls his temper well enough."

Caden didn't think Ward would say any more, but he was wrong. Ward's gaze shifted to Tonya's empty seat. "Your brother— he's okay." That was right. Ward had seen Jasan save Tonya. "I'll tell Pa that."

Ward didn't believe Jasan was a villain. That made one person. Caden would convince others, and he'd find a way to convince his family they had made a mistake, too. First, though, he had to complete the quest and save his and Jasan's lives. In schoolwork and in quests, Elite Paladins prioritized.

"Then Saturday I will visit you," Caden said, but Ward had already lost interest and was now playing a computer game.

Caden's computer was flashing "mother," but he'd had enough of the voice for one day. He needed to investigate.

To do that, however, he needed permission to leave class. If he had permission, it wasn't skipping. It was within the rules of the hungry Elderdragon. And Brynne had advised him on how to get permission.

Caden stood, walked up to Mr. McDonald, and tugged the book down so he could see his face. "I need a pass to visit the bathroom," he said.

Moments later, Caden clutched his bathroom slip and ducked down the side hall that connected to the gymnasium. He did a quick check for Jasan. Sadly, Jasan wasn't inside. Then he hurried to the boys' bathroom—the rarely used one beside the basketball court—and called Brynne.

She didn't pick up. He texted her a frowny face. Soon after, his phone buzzed with the awful wasp-like noise that meant someone was calling him. He poked the Answer button.

"You need to learn to text more than frowny faces, prince," she said, and sighed. "If I'd been caught using my cell, I'd have been sentenced to detention."

Caden was working as best he could at texting, reading, and writing. "But you didn't get caught," he said.

"Of course I didn't. I said I might throw up. Like you did in Rath Dunn's car."

"You and Tito need to stop telling people about that." She should have used a different excuse, but it was good she was free from class. "Meet me in the boys' bathroom. The one by the gym."

Brynne, ever difficult, refused. "Eww. I don't want to meet there," she said.

"Just do it, sorceress."

"No."

He could feel her irritation. She didn't like it when he ordered her about. It was fortunate he was beyond her physical reach. Now that he considered it, he should have all conversations with Brynne over the phone.

She sounded amused when she next spoke. "You meet me," she said, "in the girls' bathroom, the one in the west hall."

Caden felt his annoyance grow. He did not see how her bathroom was better than his, but he feared neither girls nor the girls' bathroom. "Very well," he said, and pushed the End button.

Caden's third-born brother, Lucian, was gifted in stealth. He'd advised Caden on how to sneak, how to move without being noticed. Caden used those skills now. The halls were cold. When he listened, he heard a rumbling from the direction of the long hall. He went the opposite way.

He passed the science room. Mrs. Belle stood by the door. There was a piece of toilet paper stuck to her shoes. Her morning class had built pointless paper flying contraptions. They tossed them down the hall while she leaned against the door. Like Mr. Creedly the day before, she seemed to be guarding it. In the next hall, Caden avoided

Ms. Jackson. She cackled as she carried a large witchy pot toward the cafeteria.

When he arrived at the girls' bathroom door, he paused. His instinct was to push the door open and stride inside. Proper decorum meant he didn't. He stopped, composed his royal person, and knocked.

Brynne threw the door open and pulled him inside by his coat sleeves. "Quiet."

Caden shrugged her off and looked around. In his royal opinion, the girls' bathroom was nicer than the boys'. One, the doors on the stalls were a regal pale pink and not a dull bluish-gray. Two, unlike the boys' bathroom, all the stalls had doors. There was a faint fruity scent intermingled with the bathroom smell. It was still small and plain compared to the ornate tiled baths of the Winter Castle.

Brynne watched him with her silvery eyes wide and her hands outstretched. She bit at her bottom lip. "Now what?"

While the girls' bathroom was cleaner than the boys', it needed wiping down. Caden traced his finger across the sink. "Mrs. Belle guards her classroom. I doubt we can get inside. But we should check the auditorium before too much time passes. The incidents seem related."

"Agreed," Brynne said.

The halls that led toward the auditorium were empty, but Caden sensed a powerful presence. It was like walking into the blue-tinted belly of a beast. He mentioned the atmosphere to Brynne. "Ms. Primrose is hungry. You can feel it in the whole school."

"True, but she won't eat you for four more days." She grabbed his hand. "And I won't let you get eaten. I'll help you complete your quest." He was about to thank her when she added, "And I'll help save Prince Jasan."

The auditorium doors were locked and sealed with yellow tape. With Brynne's magic and thieving skills, they made it past both quickly. Although the door she magicked cracked in half.

He looked at her.

"It didn't blow up," she said, and sounded pleased. "And it didn't crumble to dust."

Indeed, it was an improvement from her typical lock picking. Inside, the large room was quiet, the rows of seats empty. Caden dragged his boot across the aisle. It was tidier than it had been before the incident, and the fallen bee bodies had already been removed.

Above him, several of the beams seemed to have small cracks. He didn't remember seeing them the day before. Of course, the day before he'd been dealing with his brother, a spelling contest, and a bee swarm. He'd been thinking about quests and Elderdragons. Truth be told, he was still dealing with all those things.

He pointed to the stage. Someone had put up a new banner, this one likely for Tuesday's awards ceremony. "The first bee flew from that direction," he said. They looked there first. Except for a creaking floor, there was nothing interesting. "We should go backstage."

Brynne pushed him toward the dark curtain separating the front of the stage from the back. "You first, prince."

He'd no problem with that. "It is the leader's duty to enter first."

"Fine," she said, and stepped up beside him. "We'll go in together."

Backstage was cluttered and dimly lit. Three rickety chairs sat in the middle of the space, one turned on its side. On the floor, set backdrops painted with mountains and thunderclouds were stacked. There was a pile of puddled green curtains near the back. A cracked mirror leaned against the side wall.

Brynne walked to the mirror. She was reflected twice, once on each side of the split. Caden stood beside her and saw his reflection also doubled. She smoothed her long hair over her shoulder. She had been very protective of her hair lately.

Caden had an idea. "Maybe you should shave your head and destroy your hair," he said. "Then no one would be able to steal your locks."

Both of her reflections narrowed their eyes. "I don't think so."

"You're overly concerned with it."

"You trim yours every two weeks."

Caden did trim his hair every two weeks. But that

wasn't for vanity. That was to keep it Elite Paladin regulation length. "Then we must make sure no one else cuts your hair."

"If someone does, he or she will regret it."

He didn't doubt that.

Beside the mirror, there was dust and trash. Something red and glistening peeked from under the mess. Caden bent down and picked up a broken bloodred fingernail. He held it up.

"Mrs. Belle paints her nails this very bloodred color."

Brynne scrunched up her nose. "Do you think it's hers?"

He took his blue bathroom pass and folded the broken nail within it. "It might mean something," he said, but he hoped it didn't. Mrs. Belle actually seemed to like Caden. He'd prefer that she wasn't involved.

Something squeaked and skittered by the far wall. Caden pointed in that direction. "Check that out," he told Brynne.

"Afraid there might be rodents?"

"No."

"Well, I'm not either." She walked over and placed her ear against the wall. "And what will you do?"

"I'll investigate the curtains," he said.

Something about the way the fabrics fell reminded him of a bird's nest. They looked messy but not random. He used his foot to push the mound over.

Like dirty water breaking over green rocks, a flood of cockroaches gushed out. Each was as long as Caden's finger. He jumped on one of the rickety chairs—not because he was scared, of course, but because in battle it was advantageous to be above your foes.

Brynne gasped. She fell into a defensive stance and put her arms up to protect her face. Caden could tell Brynne was trying hard not to scream. She might not fear rodents, but she definitely feared roaches.

Through her arms, she said, "I'd hoped those foul creatures didn't exist in this realm."

"As did I." Caden grimaced, though truly it was because he was losing his balance on the chair, and not because of the bugs.

As quickly as they had swarmed, the roaches scampered behind the backdrops and into the dark corners of the room. It was quiet once again. Brynne lowered her arms. She looked at the green velvet curtains with disgust and slight confusion. "Strange," she said. "None of those roaches spit at us."

In the Greater Realm, roaches were bright red and known to spit stinging excrement upward of ten strides. These local roaches hadn't done so, but they were also three times bigger. Caden regained his balance on the chair and scanned the room. It was better to be safe.

Like bees, roaches were creatures that swarmed. They were creatures that could be summoned and controlled by monsters. But the roaches weren't attacking like the bees. He looked up at Brynne. "What do you think?"

She bit her lip. "If someone summoned bees, the roaches might be attracted to the residual magic where the spell was cast. Or another attack could be planned." Brynne glanced at him atop his strategic chair. "Frightened?"

Protecting his royal self from swarming roaches was smart, not cowardly. He took in Brynne's raised brow. It seemed he needed to prove his courage. He hopped down.

Around the green curtains, there were no signs of magic. There were no words carved into the floor or painted onto the green velvet. There were no lingering smells of incense and spices like those used in ritual magic. There was nothing sour in the air as from harmful sorcery. There was nothing dead or sacrificed. Nothing he could see anyway.

He crouched so that he could investigate the area between the broken mirror and the wall. A roach huddled in the shadow like it feared Caden would crush it if it moved. Truly, it seemed an innocent, if not disgusting, creature. Caden granted it his royal mercy.

The wall behind the mirror was also cracked. Within it, he could see wriggling termites. He heard squeaking that sounded like mice or rats. But there were still no runes. No signs of ritual magic. Not even any lingering scents of sorcery.

"There is no evidence of ritual magic here," he said.

Who could have controlled the bees? Without signs of ritual magic Caden doubted Ms. Jackson was responsible. Ritual magic was her weapon. Maybe Mr. Bellows? But he'd been distraught over the disruption, and the bees had been alive, not reanimated. Rath Dunn was a menace who was collecting ingredients for a sinister spell—could he have done it somehow? Yet Mr. Bellows and Rath Dunn had both been targets. Why would they target themselves?

Those three had seemed so gleeful after the gas incident. Caden had felt almost certain they were involved with the school's not-accidents. Now, he wasn't as sure. After all, evil beings delighted in suffering, even in suffering not caused by them.

And there was still Mrs. Belle. She hadn't been targeted. Her students hadn't been hurt in the swarm. The broken fingernail seemed to burn in his pocket. Of all his teachers, Mrs. Belle seemed to like teaching the most. Why would she do such a thing? As Sir Tito had wisely said, this type of evil had to have a motive.

Caden stood back up.

The floor creaked. In and near the walls, the skittering of rodents resumed. He didn't want to fight rats, and Brynne wouldn't want to fight roaches. Not to mention, they'd soon be missed in their classes. Bathroom passes only excused a student for so long. Caden caught Brynne's gaze.

She nodded and grabbed his hand. "We should go now," she whispered.

They sneaked from backstage through the auditorium and to the rear exits that led into the school hall. He squeezed Brynne's hand. "But we should return later," he said.

A grin flirted with her face. "When the school is closed? And locked? And empty?" she said.

"That would be ideal," Caden said.

Her smile turned dazzling, her eyes bright with mischief. "This is the best idea you've had since I've known you, prince."

14
THE SCHOOL AT NIGHT

At lunch, Caden briefed Tito and Jane about their time in the auditorium. Tito looked disgusted as he shoved rosemary mashed potatoes into his mouth. "So, in your fantasy world cockroaches spit excrement?"

"You're missing the important part."

"That is the important part," Tito said. He pointed his mashed potato–covered spoon at Caden, then at Brynne. "The fantasy world is my world. You—weirdo and sorceress— live with me." He motioned at the teachers. "The fantasy world villains are my teachers. And the head of this school is an Elderdragon. Odds I run into some spitting cockroaches or carnivorous rabbits seem pretty high to me. I see a half-size bright red cockroach, I know to step on it first, ask questions later."

Jane had been casting her daily death stare toward Ms.

Jackson in the serving line. She paused to turn and smile at Tito. "And if you see a giant fanged rabbit you know to run."

"That's just good sense," Tito said, and motioned to Caden. "I knew that even before his craziness."

Caden sat back and crossed his arms. "This is serious."

Jane seemed to reconsider. She turned back toward Ms. Jackson. "I still think it was her."

Brynne swiped some of Tito's balsamic glazed carrots. "The likelihood she's responsible is low. There were no signs of ritual magic. None," she said. "We checked."

Jane looked annoyed.

"Well, we did," Brynne said.

That night, once Rosa was asleep, Caden climbed from his bed and rushed to dress. He kicked Tito's bed to wake him.

Tito blinked slowly. "What?"

"We're going to search the school for clues," Caden said.

Tito pushed up to his elbows and checked his phone. "It's two a.m."

"We won't miss class, and Ward told me his father has Friday nights off. It's a good time to investigate."

"It's a better time to sleep."

"You wanted to help," Caden said. "I'm letting you." He tossed Tito's backpack to him. Tito was good at packing things Caden didn't always know existed. "Sir Horace will take us."

Tito put his forearm over his eyes. "The school will be locked."

Caden pulled out his phone. It was true, he didn't know many words to text, but he was learning. He hit the z. Then he hit it thrice more. Zs had something to do with sleep. He added a frowny face because he liked frowny faces, then hit Send to Brynne. "Brynne will come and handle the doors." A moment later, Caden's phone buzzed. It was a text of a smiley face. He pulled Tito's arm from his eyes and showed him. "See," Caden said, "she's already ready."

"I've got no idea how you two manage to communicate like that," Tito said.

Caden yanked Tito's arm and pulled him up. "I have only until Tuesday to complete the quest. Time grows short. Get up, Sir Tito. We must find proof of the true culprit lest I and my brother be devoured, lest the guilty villain causes more not-accidents."

Tito groaned, but he got dressed. He frowned as he helped lower down the escape rope. "If Rosa finds out about this, she'll blow her top."

Tito often worried about Rosa blowing her top. Caden put his hand on Tito's shoulder. "After which she'll ground us and send us to counseling." He smiled. "Neither of which is true punishment. Not compared to Winterlands ice shard immersion. It's—"

Tito held up his hand. "Yeah, I don't want to know what it is," he said. "Look, I know counseling isn't awful, but it's not fun either. Some of us don't want to talk about every-thing."

Caden leaned closer. "The gnome people of the lower Springlands force people to talk by cutting out their tongues and using ritual magic to make the tongue talk." He pointed to his mouth. "If they find you innocent, they use the spent blood to magic it back. It takes several weeks, though."

Tito scrunched up his nose. "You can't help it, can you? You told Rosa that one yet?"

Rosa found Caden's knowledge of Greater Realm pun-ishments distressing. He opened the window. "I'm waiting for the appropriate time," he said, which would most likely be when Rosa was about to take Caden's phone for texting emojis with Brynne at dinner.

A few moments later, Caden and Tito stood at the edge of the woods, Tito with his backpack, Caden with his magi-cal coat, compass, and pocketful of paper clips. Soon after, Brynne ran up to them with moonlight shining in her hair and silvery eyes.

"Jane said she'll cover if she hears Rosa get up." She looked between them, seemingly excited. "To the school?"

"The royal weirdo wants to break into it."

Brynne beamed. "An excellent idea."

"We're not breaking in, we're investigating. We are on a mission given to me by the principal. We are doing so to protect the school, not steal from it."

"We could steal a little," Brynne said.

Caden didn't dignify that with an answer.

He whistled for Sir Horace. His noble steed should be near. He often came to check for the snacks Caden left him this time of night.

The clouds cleared, and the moon appeared. It was over half-full—a waning gibbous moon according to Tito. Brynne stood beside him.

In two days, Caden would again be cursed. He'd be at the mercy of any command given him. His brother needed him, he'd a quest to complete, and Brynne's careless magic could destroy Caden's ability to help him.

"You said you'd break my curse."

She shifted on her feet. "I am trying, prince," she said. She bit her bottom lip and looked up again. "I have one idea. . . ."

From the gentle slope of the mountain, Caden heard hoofbeats. He felt them pounding the ground as he waited for Brynne to tell him some reasonable way to break the curse. She twisted her hands together, then reached them out as if to gather the moonlight. "We could destroy the moon." She smiled, unsure. "No moon, no curse."

Tito laughed.

Caden glanced back up. "I'm not sure that would be honorable. Although," he said, and reconsidered, "Mrs. Belle once claimed the moon is a hunk of uninhabited rock. Destroying it wouldn't be much different than crushing a stone."

Brynne's face lit up. "I know," she said like she was

thrilled Caden was in favor of her scheme. "But I'm not sure how to destroy something so big and far away."

"You once blew up Mr. Rathis's door from afar." No one would suffer at the destruction of a moon. He met Brynne's gaze. "I believe in you. You can do it."

Tito stopped laughing. "No, bro, you and Miss Magic here can't blow up the moon."

Brynne seemed a bit insulted. "I might be able to do it."

"No, we need the moon," Tito said. "It controls the tides and other important stuff." He looked between them. "No destroying the moon."

A moment later, Sir Horace poked his mighty muzzle from the trees. At Caden's command, he knelt by the yard's edge. They climbed on his back, Caden in front, Tito in the middle, and Brynne tail side. Tito shifted as if uncomfortable. "If we get caught," Tito said, "you're the one who's going to have to explain why we snuck out."

Brynne laughed. "Like you could stop him, Sir Tito."

That also made Tito laugh.

More jokes about Caden being chatty. No matter, he would simply explain to them why they were wrong on the ride to the school. Sir Horace stood, pawed the ground, and released a mighty whinny. He was a Galvanian stallion ready to run through the night, and he got them to the school faster than Rosa's pickup ever had.

Except for circles of light from the lampposts on the roadway and walk, the campus was dark against the Ashevillian night. The moon, a mere two days from half full, backlit the mountain.

"Let us be careful now," Caden said as Sir Horace cantered up the drive.

They approached the side of the building, and Caden felt Sir Horace tense. Sir Horace knew of the danger here, of the villainous teachers and the Elderdragon. Caden often talked of it on their nighttime rides. "Easy, friend," Caden said, and patted his neck.

At the side door near the gymnasium, they stopped, and Brynne hopped off. Sir Horace snapped at her shoulder as she walked close to his head. She looked indignant and spoke in hushed tones. "Control that beast, prince."

"He's being playful." Caden also spoke in a low voice. "It was meant as an endearment."

To prove Caden's point, Sir Horace nipped her long hair.

"Ow," Brynne said.

"See," Caden whispered, "he's warming to you."

Behind him, Caden felt Tito moving about. Caden looked back and watched as Tito scooted backward, then slid roughly down Sir Horace's majestic gray rear, and caught his nose in Sir Horace's tail. It was a dangerous dismount, indeed. Sir Horace also watched, obviously dismayed.

Once on the ground, Tito moved away and looked up at Caden. He frowned his lopsided frown. "What?"

Caden hopped from Sir Horace with ease. "You need riding lessons."

"I really don't," Tito said, and pulled two flashlights

out of his book bag. He handed one to Caden. The other he switched on and shone at the lock.

Brynne crouched in front of the door and pulled a pin from her hair. It shimmered gold in the yellow light of the flashlight. Caden bent down to better examine it. It was an extremely nice-looking hairpin, much finer than seemed possible. It had a shimmery aura around it. Enchanted, no doubt. As Jane had given Rosa a magic-looking stapler earlier that day, which Caden had deemed enchanted item number one hundred and thirty-two, the Enchanted Stapler of Stapling, the pin would be number one hundred and thirty-three, the Magical Hairpin of Unlocking.

Between Brynne's magic and thieving skills—not to mention her enchanted hairpin—the lock clicked open almost immediately. Nothing exploded, cracked in half, or crumbled. She grinned at Caden, then pushed open the door.

She and Tito crept inside first. Caden tried to lead Sir Horace into the hall by his mane, but Sir Horace didn't want to enter. Also, he was too big to fit through the door.

"Maybe you should leave Sir Horace outside," Tito whispered.

Sir Horace edged back.

Caden supposed Sir Horace was more suited to outdoor adventure. "Stay near," he told Sir Horace. "We will be back soon enough." Then he let the door softly click shut.

The hall was long, dark, and deep. The tiles seemed to

disappear into shadow. The classroom doors were black voids between rows of dented lockers. It felt cold and quiet like a crypt. They kept their voices as low as possible.

Although Caden couldn't see Tito's face, he could feel his frown. "It's not supposed to be this dark," Tito said. "Or creepy."

"It's night," Brynne said. "Night is dark." She had her cell phone out. It made her face glow, and she looked like a beautiful ghost. She pushed a few buttons—updating Jane, no doubt.

"Schools usually keep one or two emergency lights on all the time," Tito said.

At the foster prison, Rosa insisted they turn off all lights whenever they left a room. She said it saved money and the planet. Still. Tito did know more about schools than Caden, and it was odd to see the school encased in darkness. Usually, it was only the long hall that felt so like the Winter Castle catacombs, and even the catacombs had torches kept alight with fairie fire.

The school at night was not the same as the school during the day. It was almost unrecognizable.

Caden switched on his flashlight. Brynne stepped so that she was shoulder to shoulder with him. She switched her cell phone to its flashlight mode. "We should look in Mrs. Belle's classroom," she said. "That's where the first accident occurred."

The science classroom was locked, but this time no one

lurked about and kept them from finding a way inside. Brynne opened the door with the Magical Hairpin of Unlocking, and Caden shone his light inside.

Broken beakers and toppled shelves lay wrecked on the floor. On the front counter, three lone flasks were lined up like Mrs. Belle had put them there for a class that never happened. The door to the chemical cabinet in the back hung open. The shelves were empty, the contents missing.

The classroom smelled bad. It was a different bad smell than the green gas, however. It wasn't deep and rotten like the fruits of a fartenbush. This bad smell was like decaying flesh, like dead mammal.

Tito closed the door behind them. He shone his light on the window, but there was no glass. A thick piece of wood was placed in the frame like a false exit. "Well, this is fun and smelly," he said. His voice sounded muffled. Then he shone his light in Caden's face. "What are we looking for?"

Caden squinted and shone his flashlight so that it was Tito who was blinded. Tito had his shirt pulled up over his nose.

"Anything odd," Caden said.

Tito spoke through his shirt. "Well, there's the smell...."

Brynne stepped between them and pushed both their flashlights toward the floor. "We found bugs and rats in the auditorium. Look for other swarming things. Ants, maybe? Or birds."

Tito pointed his flashlight toward the ceiling as if

checking for some murderous bird swarm.

"Birds don't swarm," Caden said. "They flock."

"Close enough," Brynne said. Her cell phone flashed a message. She held it up and kept her words low. "Jane wants us to look for signs of ritual magic."

Near Caden's boots lay a pile of broken glass. It was as if it had been left where it had fallen. Most of the room looked like that, like no one had entered since the accident. It felt like a ruin and not the lively space where he had learned about atoms and cells. He'd seen Mr. Creedly and Mrs. Belle guarding the door. Were they trying to keep people out? And if so, why? He reached out to pick up a glass shard and his blood-dagger wound pinched.

Caden set the shard of glass back in the pile. He needed to keep his wits as sharp as the broken glass and figure out the culprit. He'd save himself and Jasan. And if possible, he'd connect Rath Dunn to these evil actions. To do that, he needed to be brave and smart like the Elite Paladin he would be once he found a dragon to slay.

"Huh," Tito said.

Though the word was simple, Tito sounded thoughtful. Maybe he had similar thoughts. "What is it, Sir Tito?" Caden whispered.

Tito shone the light at Caden's face again. "If there was evidence lying around the science room, Ms. Primrose wouldn't need you to investigate. The police wouldn't have deemed it an accident."

That, too, had crossed Caden's mind. "The police don't understand Greater Realm magic. They don't believe in lunch witches and ritual magic. If we know what happened, and who did it, we can build an Ashevillian case against him or her."

"Yeah," Tito said. "How do you expect to do that?"

Caden rubbed at his arm. It was stinging. "Maybe we can convince Officer Levine and Jenkins to investigate with Ashevillian tools."

"Bro, I don't know," Tito said. "They're busy policing spring tourists right now."

Brynne moved over to the side of the room and held her glowing phone near the sink. "Or we can trick them into confessing," she said. "That works, doesn't it, Sir Tito? That's what the detectives do on the television." She opened the door under the sink and shone her phone around inside.

Tito moved to the back and started looking in cabinets. "Yeah. Maybe."

Caden doubted any villain would confess. He looked at the desktops. When he got to Jane's desk, he saw that someone had used a sharp edge to cut through her sketch of the Great Walking Oak. He traced the gnashes with his thumb. The Walking Oak was the protector of elves, magic users, and plants. While Caden felt the Winterbird was superior to the tree, it was disrespectful to strike out the image.

From the back of the room, Tito swore. Then he said, "Oh gross."

Caden and Brynne hurried to him. Caden shone his flashlight at Tito. Truly, Tito looked as if he'd seen something icky.

"In the third cabinet," Tito said.

Caden peeked over Brynne's shoulder and rubbed at his arm. It hurt more this night than most. That was odd. His wound only reopened in the proximity of Rath Dunn's blood dagger, and Rath Dunn and his blood dagger were nowhere near the science room. The school was empty.

Brynne used her phone to light the space.

Inside, there were seven dead and dried-up rats.

"You wanted rats," Tito said. "I found you rats."

"Dead rats," Caden said.

That didn't seem right. The creatures in the auditorium were skittering in the walls, and the spelling bee swarm had been after the gas incident. These rats looked many days gone. The fur seemed brittle. It was more skeleton than anything. Yet the smell was intense. Like necromancy, Caden realized.

Tito shone his light back into Caden's face. "We had rats once at the house. Jane talked Rosa into using humane traps." Then he had to explain what a humane rattrap was. "You, like, catch the rat in it, then let it go in the woods. Live and let live, I guess."

"That would never work with Greater Realm rats," Brynne said. "They'd just return to the building and eat you." She picked up a stray pencil and poked at the rat closest to her. There was something under it—a fabric bag wrapped with a length of gray hair. She reached in and grabbed it.

Caden stepped back. "What is it?"

Undeterred by the ick factor, Brynne untied it and dumped it out. Chalk-white bones—like that of small animals—tumbled onto the floor. "Bones," she said. "Dead things. These, and the smell, are definite signs of necromancy." She looked up at Caden. "The only villain I've seen who appears to be a necromancer is Mr. Bellows."

"He killed the poor rats?" Tito said, and Caden wondered if it was truly Jane who'd talked Rosa into the humane traps.

"Necromancers don't kill so much as collect and use the dead," Caden said.

Brynne gathered the bones and retied the bag. "He probably just dug them up somewhere. Or found them in the walls. Who knows?" She scrunched up her nose. "Strange that he'd animate rats, though."

"You're saying these were zombie rats?" Tito said. Now he sounded more amused than repulsed. "That's what you're saying?"

"Somewhat." She stood, let the cabinet close, and put the bag on the floor. Then she stomped on it until everything within was likely a fine dust. "There. If he wants more zombie rats, he'll have to make a new one."

What purpose was there in reanimating rats? Caden

crossed his arms. "The bees were living, not undead."

"Then the necromancer controlled the rats but not the bees," Brynne said. She shone her phone under a desk, then tilted her head. "There's something here."

Caden ducked down, but he didn't see anything. "Where?"

Tito crouched beside him. Like Brynne, he turned his head to the side. "There are weird symbols. The light has to hit it right to see them."

Caden tilted his head. Then he did see runes and ritual magic signs scribbled under the desk. He checked another. It was the same.

"What's that mean?" Tito said.

That meant Jane would be as happy as a crypt wraith in a plague. Caden furrowed his brow. "It means, unlike the auditorium, there are signs of ritual magic here, and ritual magic is always connected to the place it's cast," he said. He pointed toward the rats. It seemed the rats and runes were connected. As were the lunch witch and the necromancer. "And such evil requires sacrifice."

In the glow from her phone, Brynne looked oddly impressed. "Maybe they mixed their magics. The lunch witch used some of the school rodents to fuel her spell, then the necromancer animated the dead." He could sense Brynne's mind dancing with possibilities. "I've only heard whispers of such things."

"If so, they did it for an evil purpose. It's not a good thing."

"I didn't say it was, prince. But it's an interesting thing."

"Not as interesting as the zombie rats," Tito said.

In the back corner of the room, Caden shone his light on the remains of a small potted palm tree Mrs. Belle had kept in the room. It looked withered and dead. He considered the plants that had died around the school—the azaleas, the dead forest downslope of the cafeteria.

"Maybe the plants were sacrifices, too." The wound on his arm was really stinging now.

"Possibly," said Brynne. Her fingers moved surely as she sent Jane a message. "We should check the auditorium again. And the cafeteria, as it is the lunch witch's domain."

Caden wasn't really listening though. Dead rats and runes weren't proof enough. He doubted proof of ritual magic or reanimation would be useful by Ashevillian standards. Maybe he should try to get those responsible to confess? After all, he was gifted in speech.

Suddenly, the ache in his arm turned to a slashing pain. It bled. It felt like it did when he walked into math class and Rath Dunn sat behind his desk. It felt as it did when the blood dagger was close. As he stood there, the pain got bad. His realization was worse. His stomach dropped.

They weren't alone.

15
THOSE WHO WALK ABOVE

$\mathcal{I}$f the blood dagger was near, so was Rath Dunn. Caden signaled to the others.

Tito shone his light at Caden. "Bro, what's wrong—"

Caden mouthed, "Quiet." He flipped off his light. Tito did the same. In the dim glow from her phone, Brynne looked wide-eyed and worried. Then she turned it off, too, and the room went black.

The darkness felt like a solid weight pressing in on Caden. The only sounds were the quiet rasps of his, Brynne's, and Tito's breaths. None of them moved.

Between breaths, Caden heard the shuffle of footsteps, the sounds of feet outside the door. He felt blood pool around his bandage. Brynne sucked in a quick breath. He reached out and grabbed her hand, then reached out with the other to grab Tito's.

Someone turned a key. Then the jiggling of the key stopped abruptly—as if the person was surprised the door was unlocked. Caden heard the doorknob turn slowly.

He, Brynne, and Tito crouched in the dark. They weren't hidden per se, but they weren't standing up. It was too late to move to better cover. All they had was the dark and the desks.

Two figures entered. A glow came from the larger one's hand—a cell phone—but the light didn't reach the back of the room. The ache in Caden's arm intensified. The figure moved the cell phone near some of the rubble, then to the flasks lined up on the counter, like he was interested in the destruction. When he chuckled, there was no doubt it was Rath Dunn.

Caden kept as still as the dead. If the tyrant found them alone, he'd hurt them. Likely kill them. Then he would hide their bodies, and they'd be labeled runaways like Jane had been before they'd saved her. Or worse, he'd give their bodies to Mr. Bellows to be reanimated.

The second figure stood near him. "One of my more interesting spells." It was Ms. Jackson, the lunch witch, the mistress of ritual magic. She was a criminal returning to the scene of her crime. She held a box under her arm. "They'll suffer for taking my brother and sister."

"Patience, beautiful." His voice was like velvet. "Take whatever you like." With great care, Rath Dunn picked up the large flask on the counter, one of the few surviving pieces of Mrs. Belle's glassware, and offered it to her. "From me to you, with my utmost admiration."

She took it. Under his phone's dim light, her skin seemed to glow. Her hair looked soft and thick. Her eyes were bright. Her terrible beauty was the reason Jane's mother was lost. "What I truly want is the little half elf."

Tito pulled his hand away. At first Caden feared he'd attack or do something else foolish. Then Caden saw a soft, shielded glow from Tito's direction. He'd taken his cell phone from his pocket. Caden glanced to the front worriedly. This was a bad time for a text message.

Brynne squeezed Caden's hand tighter. Tito's breaths became faster.

Ms. Jackson strolled toward the back of the room. Rath Dunn held up his phone to light the way. The dim light stretched across the floor inches from Caden's boot. It was lucky that they'd moved away from the rat cabinet. Ms. Jackson opened it. She grabbed two of the dead rats by the tails and set them in a box. "For my porridge," she said, and cackled. She sauntered back to the front. "I want that chatty prince, too," she said. "He's the reason my siblings are gone."

"That's not part of our deal," Rath Dunn said. He pulled something from his vest—an envelope—and left it on the front counter. "And I've already promised him to his brother."

Had Brynne not been holding his hand, Caden would

have sprawled over. What did that mean? But Rath Dunn and Ms. Jackson had grown quiet, like they sensed another presence, like the math tyrant and the lunch witch knew they were not alone.

Brynne was squeezing hard enough to hurt his hand now. Tito was breathing far too loud. Caden held his breath. They would soon be discovered. In the middle of the night, in this dark school, who knew what these two villains would do to them.

Rath Dunn didn't shine his phone toward them, though. He shone it toward the door he and Ms. Jackson had left open, then turned the light upward by the ceiling. Near the top of the doorframe, two eyes flashed green—the type of eyes that could see in darkness. Whatever creature possessed them watched Rath Dunn. In the glow of phone light, it looked like it had long, spidery limbs stretched out on all sides.

Rath Dunn chuckled. "Stop creeping around," he said to the shadowy figure. "It's uncouth. And you wonder why the students call you Creepy Creedly."

As Rath Dunn spoke, Brynne whispered in his ear, "Breathe, prince."

Caden inhaled, though his heart was pounding. There were now three villains in the front of the room, villains he feared would hear his heart beating and attack them. Elite Paladins didn't panic, though. They slayed dragons and fought evil, and they did so bravely. Caden would also be brave as soon as he caught his breath.

If his great father, King Axel, were here, he'd say, "Rely on your training. Don't let emotion hinder you," and he'd be right. Caden breathed slower. He peered to the front of the room, to the figures visible from the soft glow of Rath Dunn's phone.

The creature on the ceiling seemed to rotate so that it was standing on the floor. It spoke in a hiss. "You don't belong here." Now Caden could see that it was, in fact, Mr. Creedly. "This isn't your room."

"We came to pay our respects," he said. "Nothing more." He grabbed another flask and gave it to Ms. Jackson. "For your special brew," he said.

Mr. Creedly crept closer, his green eyes set on Ms. Jackson. She cradled a flask in each hand, the box closed and tucked beneath her arm. The shadow of Mr. Creedly's limbs looked like a net. "This isn't your room," he repeated. "Or your flasks, old one."

Ms. Jackson seemed to bristle at the "old." "They're my flasks now." There was something cold and cruel in her words. "And it's not your room either."

"Now, now, Ms. Jackson," Rath Dunn said. "Mr. Creedly and Mrs. Belle are friends. He's trying to look out for her." He sidestepped Mr. Creedly. "Besides, you'd be better served worrying about that Elite Paladin who is going to teach gym than getting in our way. I'd bet that one knows your kind, and like me, knows how to kill you."

"You and the necromancer destroyed this room, old one," Mr. Creedly said.

"Oh, you think so? And you caused the bee swarm," Ms. Jackson said.

"Yes," Rath Dunn said. "Thank you for that."

Mr. Creedly cocked his head. "I'll destroy you. I'll destroy those who aren't loyal to her. Those who annoy her. I serve her. No one is as devoted as me."

"Is that why you attacked those she favors more than you?" Rath Dunn said. "You'll have to do better than insects next time. Well, Bellows was upset about his spelling bee getting interrupted. He'd planned it for weeks," Rath Dunn said, and chuckled. "But your little stunt was helpful. I've collected several complaints." He leaned nearer to Mr. Creedly. "Now move."

"This isn't your—"

"I go where I please," Rath Dunn said, and it was a threat.

Rath Dunn seemed to stare into Mr. Creedly's shining green eyes for a long moment. Then he held the door for Ms. Jackson as if she was merely a beautiful lunch lady, and not an evil youth-stealing lunch witch, and strode out after her. The door slammed shut behind them. Their footfalls faded down the hall in the direction of the cafeteria. The pain in Caden's arm began to wane. Without Rath Dunn's phone, and with Tito's hidden by his hand, the science room returned to stifling darkness.

Still, Caden, Brynne, and Tito stayed crouched. The smell of necromancy irritated Caden's nose. The darkness pressed down on him. The muscles in his thighs began to ache. He dared not move. He dared not think of what he'd just heard. Mr. Creedly was still in the room.

An eternity seemed to pass. Then: "I hear your heart-beats," Mr. Creedly said.

There was a skittering above, like tapping on the ceiling. Caden glanced up. In the black above, he felt something looking down.

"I see you, young ones."

There was no more hiding. Caden flipped on his flashlight and shone it at the ceiling. Shiny green eyes stared back down at him. Brynne gasped. Tito jumped up. In one hand, he held his cell phone, in the other, he brandished his unlit flashlight like a club.

"And we see you," Caden said as calmly as he could.

Sometimes, it was important to feign bravery.

16

CREEPING CREEDLY

r. Creedly's strange green eyes glowered down at Caden. His lips were set in a snarl, his teeth fanglike. The rest of him seemed devoured in shadow.

Then the shadows shifted, and soon Mr. Creedly was standing—feet on the floor—in front of Caden. In the closed room, with only the flashlights to see by, it looked almost as if there were spider legs crawling under his skin. He seemed the embodiment of swarming bees and skittering rodents, like something that would nest with the auditorium roaches.

Tito kept his flashlight at the ready. He had his phone in his other hand. Brynne was as motionless as the darkness and looked ready to flick Mr. Creedly away with her telekinesis magic or incinerate him with her pyrokinesis. Truth be told, her magic was likely too strong for an enclosed space like the wood-windowed science room. Better she unleash her power as a last resort.

"You don't belong here," Mr. Creedly hissed.

"We'll go," Tito said, and took a step toward the door.

Mr. Creedly held out a long arm and blocked his way. His eyes flashed green as they caught the light. "You'll stay, young one. You're trapped in my shadow."

Caden was unsure what that meant, but it couldn't mean anything good. All Caden knew was that the long-limbed creature was possessive of Ms. Primrose and seemed oddly friendly with Mrs. Belle. He couldn't think of two more opposite people than Creepy Creedly and sweet Mrs. Belle. Caden cleared his throat. "She"—he emphasized the "she" so he knew he spoke of the Elderdragon—"won't be happy if we aren't in class Monday. If three students go missing from her school, it will be an embarrassment. Someone will get eaten."

"She understands my kind. It's in our nature. We will envelop you." Mr. Creedly folded his arms in and out and twisted until his strange eyes locked on Caden. "She likes you," he hissed.

That Caden couldn't deny. It seemed Mr. Creedly loathed anyone who was competition for her favor. And the longer Caden kept Mr. Creedly talking, the longer Mr. Creedly wasn't attacking, and Caden would much prefer if his enemies fought among themselves and left him and his friends alone.

Caden took a deep breath. "It's true. I amuse her," he said, and Mr. Creedly crept closer to him. Caden spoke slowly and clearly. "But it's Rath Dunn who is her favorite."

"Rathis," Mr. Creedly hissed, but he kept his eyes focused on Caden. "First you, young one, then him." As his anger seemed to grow, so did the sounds around them. The quiet was replaced with squeaks and the sounds of tiny feet in the hall. Dark shapes squeezed under the gap between door and floor.

Tito stepped toward the front counter. "Bro, those are rats. And not dead ones."

Brynne lifted her hands. She pushed like she was using all her power to drive Mr. Creedly into the whiteboard behind the front counter. Caden had seen her use telekinesis magic to move men and women who were more solid than Mr. Creedly. "Get away from us!"

Nothing happened, but Brynne was breathing hard from the effort. Mr. Creedly turned to her. "Magic affects but one," he said, and he extended one of his long arms out and around her. "And I am many."

So Mr. Creedly was more shadow and swarm than man. He was too many pieces and places for Brynne's magic to target, and whatever small speck she flung away was replaced with more darkness and insects.

Brynne looked ready to light the room on fire. Tito was about to charge with his flashlight. Tonight, they would fight. But how would they win against an enemy made of shadows and darkness, an enemy whose weakness—and powers—they didn't know?

One of Mr. Creedly's spidery shadow arms snaked itself around Tito's calf. Another crept along the floor toward Caden's boots. Brynne dodged a dark shape slithering toward her neck.

Caden didn't know exactly what Mr. Creedly was, but he seemed to be made of insects, spiders, and vermin—a sentient swarm whose true form could only be seen at night. Caden, Brynne, and Tito needed to get away from him. To do that, they needed a distraction. And Mr. Creedly hadn't seen what was in Ms. Jackson's box.

Caden squared his shoulders. He kicked open the rat cabinet. Five still remained. "Your kind have suffered here," he said, "but not by our hands."

Mr. Creedly widened his eyes. His web of shadows drew inward, then moved toward the dead creatures. He gathered them to him. They absorbed into his chest. Ants scampered down his cheeks like meandering tears.

Then Mr. Creedly turned his focus to Caden. His jaw seemed to dislocate and unhitch from his skull, and he let out an unearthly scream. It was a loud, hollow, high-pitched sound. The last intact glass beaker shattered. Vermin squeezed under the plywood window.

They had their chance.

"Run!" Caden yelled.

Tito and Brynne darted for the door. Brynne waved her

hand. The door flew from the hinges and slammed up and into the ceiling. Caden plowed through the rats and ran after them for the hall. As he did, Mr. Creedly's screams stopped, and Caden heard skittering footsteps following. Mr. Creedly hunted them.

They ran down the hall for the side door that led outside. Caden glimpsed back and saw Mr. Creedly running across the ceiling. He reached for Caden with his shadowy arms. Caden ran faster, but Mr. Creedly latched on to his wrist. It knocked Caden off balance and—*clank*—he crashed face-first into an open locker door.

His left cheek stung. It felt as if hundreds of small, sharp needles pierced the skin by his wrist. Without thinking, he brought the flashlight down and smashed Mr. Creedly's arm. It dissolved into a fluttering mass of termites, ants, and wasps. Mr. Creedly screamed. He lunged at Caden with five long shadows.

Brynne turned. "Caden!" She looked like she was going to run back.

Tito was at the side door. He had opened it. He turned back as well.

"Keep running!" Caden yelled. "Don't stop!"

The flashlight was no sword, but it was heavy. It had smashed the one arm well enough. Caden dropped into attack stance seven. Attack stance seven was for multiple opponents, and Mr. Creedly claimed to be many.

Caden had to be fast—fast and sure like his brothers

and father had trained him. He smashed the next arm with a downward strike. Insects screeched out. Then he spun around. He kicked through arm three and drove the flashlight through arm four. Arm one was starting to reform. He slammed the light into arm five. He was left in a cloud of insects, but already the insects were morphing back into shadow.

Caden dashed for the door.

Brynne and Tito were running back toward him.

"I told you to run away!" Caden said.

Tito skidded to a stop and switched directions. Brynne did the same. They zoomed through the side door to outside. The spring air felt soft on Caden's skin.

Tito slammed the door shut behind them. They ran down the drive, and Caden whistled for Sir Horace. His mighty horse charged from the night like a cavalry of one and knelt before them. They were galloping away when Caden heard the side door crash open. The night was filled with Mr. Creedly's high-pitched, terrifying screech. When Caden chanced a look back, he saw a spidery form with long limbs and reflective green eyes watching from the side of the school.

Caden turned and faced forward. Instead of directing Sir Horace through the creature-filled forests, he let his steed run on the empty night roads, cautious to look for cars and to stop at the colorful intersection lights. Soon they were in Rosa's sculpture-filled yard.

Caden and Brynne climbed down from Sir Horace. Tito fell off.

Caden petted Sir Horace's mane. For now, they were safe.

"So," Tito said. He brushed off his jeans, got to his feet, and reached into his pack. "Look what I grabbed out of the drawer." He waved an envelope in the air, the one Rath Dunn had planted in the room.

Brynne beamed in the moonlight. "Sir Tito, you're becoming a regular thief!"

While Caden was glad Tito had grabbed the envelope, he didn't think thieving skills were such a good thing. He pointed at Brynne. "You've been training him."

"So?" Brynne said. "You've been training him, too. Why can't I?"

"I'm training him to become an Elite Paladin, not a thief."

"Actually, I'm going to be an architect," Tito said. He fiddled with the envelope. "It's already been opened."

The back door creaked open. They all held their breaths. A moment later, Jane stepped out. She was dressed in her nightclothes and her feet were bare. "Did you find anything?"

"Loads of creepy crap," Tito said. He held up the envelope. "And whatever this is. Mr. Rathis put it in the science room."

"How do you know?"

"He was there," Tito said. He pulled out the contents and used his flashlight to read them. "It's a service call for the fume hood. Or a printout of one." He flipped over the envelope. "This thing was stamped last year."

Well. Caden didn't know what that meant. He felt his brow crease. Brynne was looking at the sky. Obviously, she didn't know what it meant either.

Jane touched his arm. "It shows the school hasn't done what it's supposed to do."

"I see," Caden said. But he didn't. "What does Rath Dunn gain?"

Brynne glanced back at him. "I don't know, but it's similar to the complaints, right?"

"Sort of," Tito said.

Sir Horace whinnied and nudged Caden's ear with his wet nose. Caden petted his soft gray hair. In the undergrowth, a cricket croaked.

"I'd feel better inside the house, bro," Tito said. "I've had enough bugs for one night."

Caden agreed, but he first needed to speak with Sir Horace. He scratched his stallion's nose. "Be safe, friend," he said. "Especially this night. Don't fight without me. If there's danger, run away."

"He can't understand you, Caden," Brynne said. "He's a horse."

Caden knew Sir Horace was a horse. And he couldn't allow Sir Horace to be insulted. "He's a Galvanian Snow

Stallion, deemed the eighth finest in the land." He raised his chin. "He understands perfectly."

Although . . . now that Caden considered it, Sir Horace was of the Greater Realm. And he wasn't gifted in speech like Caden. He might not understand the local English. To be safe, Caden repeated the command in Royal Razzon.

Brynne and Tito glanced at each other, wearing expressions similar to Rosa's and Officer Levine's when they thought Caden unhinged. "I don't know if he understands English," Caden explained.

Sir Horace leaned over to nuzzle Jane.

"Either way, he should understand now," Jane said.

Caden patted Sir Horace once more and nodded.

On the second floor, Rosa's light came on. Tito pointed. "Ah crap. Hurry."

Brynne and Jane rushed inside using the back door. Caden and Tito climbed the escape rope, as the attic steps creaked. Then they stored it under Caden's bed.

A few minutes passed in silence. It appeared they'd gotten back to their room without Rosa knowing. Tito flicked on his bedside lamp. Orange light streamed across the slanted walls. "Might as well keep it on. Otherwise, I'll think Creepy Creedly is up there creeping around."

"A good plan." Caden was restless. He sat on his bed and replayed the night's events in his mind. He looked at Tito. After battle, it was important to analyze actions. "Why did you turn on your phone while we were hiding?

It seemed foolish. And you're rarely that."

Tito grinned. He pulled out his cell phone and sat beside Caden on the bed. "We need proof, right?" he said. "Asheville-type proof, too, not crazy fantasyland proof."

"We do."

Tito swiped his finger across the phone a few times. "Listen," he said. A moment later Ms. Jackson's voice played: "I want that chatty prince, too. He's the reason my siblings are gone." Then Rath Dunn spoke. "That's not part of our deal. And I've already promised him to his brother." After a while, he heard Mr. Creedly's voice. "You don't belong here."

"I recorded them," Tito said. "How's that for proof of misdeeds?"

Had they said anything truly damning? "Do you have the rest?"

"It's muffled after that. But cool, huh?"

"It's good," Caden said. "We need more, though."

"Well, it's a start," Tito said.

It was a start. A smart start at that. Truly, Tito would make a formidable Elite Paladin. "We should collect more evidence with phones," Caden said. "And we need to get into the cafeteria."

"Okay. But not until Monday. Sneaking over there again would just be dumb. Give me your phone. I'll send you the audio file."

After Caden had it, he played the message again. Rath

Dunn's voice sounded menacing.

"And I've already promised him to his brother."

What did that mean? "My brother wouldn't hurt me."

"Bro, I hate to say this, but your bro didn't seem so friendly." Tito stood up and went to his messy side of the room. "Are you sure he wouldn't do anything?"

Caden was sure, wasn't he? Lest he forget, Jasan had saved Tonya. He couldn't be a traitor, could he? "None of my brothers would work with Rath Dunn." But he didn't feel as certain as he wanted. He leaned back on his pink-and-orange quilt.

There was more bothering him. Rath Dunn knew it hadn't snowed the night Chadwin died. How could he have known that? Rath Dunn was banished years before. As far as he knew, the only ones with recent contact with the Greater Realm were Caden, Brynne, and Jasan.

"Rath Dunn knows things I didn't tell him. Jasan, Brynne, and I were the only ones brought to Asheville recently. Who else could tell him such things?" Caden took a deep breath. "I don't understand."

"Huh." Tito was quiet for a moment. Then he said, "You know, there was this foster kid, Dwayne, who lived here before you. He went to college in New Zealand. That's like being a realm away. It's too far for him to come back and visit."

Caden stared at the ceiling, at the orange lamplight across it. "Your point, Sir Tito?"

"He and Rosa still email at least once a week."

It seemed Tito had no relevant point. "We've no email in the Greater Realm."

Tito was quiet for a moment. Then he said, "Yeah, but you got a bunch of freaky magic stuff. Are you sure there's no way Rath Dunn could send a message? There's no way he could talk back and forth, especially since he doesn't care how it's done or who gets hurt?"

Was it possible Rath Dunn had made contact? It would be unwise not to consider the possibility. And it seemed convenient and terrible that Rath Dunn needed Jasan's blood, and it was Jasan who had been accused and banished for Chadwin's death. "Anything is possible, especially with Rath Dunn."

Caden leaned back. His bed felt warm and soft, but there would be no restful sleep this night.

In the morning, Caden's left eye was tender from where he'd slammed into the locker. He'd slept a hard, short sleep and woke feeling confused. Mr. Creedly was more mon-ster than man. He'd caused the spelling bee swarm and attacked Rath Dunn and Mr. Bellows at it because they plotted against Ms. Primrose. He'd attacked Derek because he annoyed Ms. Primrose, and Caden because she liked him. But why had Mr. Creedly attacked Tonya?

On the other side of the room, Tito was sprawled across his bed, asleep and drooling. Caden tossed a pillow at his head. Then he asked Tito's opinion.

Tito stumbled out of bed. "She started taking college-level math classes. She showed me her textbook. That means she's mad smart. And I don't say that type of thing lightly." He yawned. "Ms. Primrose probably likes her, too."

"But she's in my morning class."

"Because she stutters," Tito said sleepily. "Not because she's not smart."

Ward had once told Caden that Tonya was smart as well. Caden thought about his classmates. Ward seemed attuned to the computers. Jane was a rare enchantress. She seemed to prefer art to other classes, but she also brought back high grades. Derek, unlikable though he was, scored almost as high as Tito on tests, and was his main competition for the grade award. Truth be told, the only student at the school who Caden had seen fail a test was Caden himself.

Were all of Ms. Primrose's students exceptional? Caden wouldn't be surprised. She did collect people. And Ms. Primrose had once called Tito her favorite jewel. Just how smart did that make Tito? As smart as Brynne?

Caden considered. "You are to receive the grade award this Tuesday?"

Tito still had his eyes partially closed. He pulled a black T-shirt from a pile of clothes next to his bed. "That's the plan. That's the completion of my quest."

Caden peered at him. "So how mad smart does that make you?"

"Super mad smart," Tito said, but he hunched his shoulders. "And, well, I study all the time. That's the main thing."

"Brynne studies constantly as well," Caden said, and headed for the tiny Ashevillian bathroom. "It only adds to her talents."

Once in the bathroom, Caden looked in the mirror. His cheek was bruised, his eye slightly swollen. He had been running fast when that locker door hit his face. The swelling flesh was a testament to his speed. But if he failed his quest, speed would do him no good against an Elderdragon.

Now he knew Mr. Creedly had caused the bee swarm. And thanks to Tito, Caden had a nice recording of Ms. Jackson and Rath Dunn acting suspiciously. They needed proof, though.

After he washed in the tiny bath, he trimmed his hair. It was Saturday; they were visiting Ward today. Jasan was supposed to be housed next door. It was important for Caden to look like a future Elite Paladin when he saw his brother.

Jasan should see that even stranded among cars, cafés, and villains, Caden followed the noble path of the Elite Paladin. Then Caden would ask him about home, about their brothers and father. He rubbed his cheek once more. He'd ask him what he knew of the monster that was Mr. Creedly, and he'd play the recording of Ms. Jackson and Rath Dunn. He'd see how he reacted to the line "I've already promised him to his brother." Although Caden would have to translate it.

The bandage Caden kept wrapped around the blood-dagger wound was pink and needed tending. He changed it, pulled on his freshly washed horse T-shirt, and fixed the sleeves so they covered the wound. Rosa would be unhappy if she noticed it.

Tito was more awake when Caden returned from the shower. He blinked slowly, then pointed at the left side of Caden's face. "That side of your face is bruised up."

"I ran into the locker."

"Yeah, I remember," Tito said. "Let's not tell Rosa that." He took another glance at Caden's face, then flopped back down on his bed and groaned. "She's going to suspect something. Why'd you have to go and get beat-up looking?"

The worst Rosa would do was take away their phones. "Even if she finds out, she won't send us away."

"You're right. If she finds out we broke into the school, she'll kill us. There'll be nothing left to send away." Tito sat back up. "Don't tell her about last night, got it?"

Rosa would ask about his bruised face and Caden couldn't lie. Lying was against the Elite Paladin code. Not even commoners in the Greater Realm lied.

"Got it?" Tito said again.

Caden touched his face and frowned. "I understand."

Tito seemed to sense that was not a full agreement. "I

wish it was Sunday. Then I could just order you not to tell."

"Luckily for me, it's Saturday. I'll do what I please." Caden was growing frustrated with his friends making light of his time of the month. It was not funny. It was life threatening. "My curse is no joke. I have to complete my quest and endure orders from whosoever speaks to me." He felt his cheeks heat. "It could cause my death and the death of my brother."

Tito looked contrite. "Sorry, man," he said. "It's just you don't know when to lie."

That was untrue. "I know never to lie."

Tito grabbed his clothes and trudged toward the bathroom. "See, that's what I'm worried about."

THE GARDEN GNOME

Tito was right about one thing: Rosa was highly suspicious of his bruised face and blackening eye. As he and the others sat around the kitchen table eating round grains and milk, she examined him with great care. "It didn't look like that yesterday night," she said.

"No," Caden said. "Not until this morning."

"Tell me how that happened." There was iron in her tone.

Jane watched with an even expression, Brynne with wide eyes. Tito looked terrified—much more so than after they'd fled Mr. Creedly and his swarms. A future Elite Paladin was truthful, though. Caden hoped his friends would understand.

"I knocked him with the sparring mop," Tito blurted out.

Caden was taken aback. Tito had lied. Not only that, he'd lied to Rosa. Jane also looked surprised. Brynne seemed impressed, but mischief often impressed her.

Rosa turned her no-nonsense stare to Tito. "Is that so?"

Tito looked sicker than when he'd pointed out the dead rats.

Brynne broke into a grin. "A knock with the mop could certainly cause a black eye. Right, Caden?"

She wasn't technically lying, but there was no reason for her to be so happy about the deception in her question. Caden glared at her, then at Tito. If he shared the true story now, it would be worse for them all. Still. Caden wouldn't lie. "I suppose a knock with the mop *could* cause a bruised face."

Jane lifted her spoon to her mouth. "I thought it would look worse," she said.

Rosa looked at them, and her cheek twitched.

"Sorry," Tito mumbled, and he didn't meet her gaze.

They finished the breakfast in silence. Rosa seemed suspicious and rightly so. Caden had greater concerns than his foster mother's disappointment, though. He needed to see his brother and talk to him in private.

Once Caden got Tito and Jane alone on the porch, he chided them on their easy untruths. "And Jane still has to be knighted. Jasan has to agree to it. As future Elite Paladins, you must be honest."

Jane shrugged. "Rosa wouldn't understand the truth. Not now."

"Not ever," Tito said.

The breeze rustled the leaves on the trees and brushed against Caden's skin like soft wool, but it didn't comfort him. "Future Elite Paladins don't lie. It doesn't matter if she understands."

"It matters to me." Tito ducked from the wind. "This future Elite Paladin doesn't want to be kicked out of his best-ever foster home because he broke into his freaky school with weirdoes from another dimension."

The screen door creaked open and shut, and Brynne stepped out. "I'm no weirdo, Sir Tito."

"You hang out with Prince I-must-slay-a-dragon-and-never-utter-an-untruth," Tito said. "So you're a little weird."

Rosa followed a few moments later with her truck keys dangling from her fingers. She looked at them and didn't smile. "Be on your best behavior today at Ward's house," she said. "Get in the pickup."

They piled into the truck—Caden in front, the other three in the back. Rosa started the engine and looked in the rearview mirror—seemingly right at Tito. "Maybe you'll have something to tell me when I pick you up."

"Doubtful," Caden said.

She slid her gaze to him, and her cheek twitched again.

"I'm just being honest," Caden said, and Tito kicked his seat.

Ward lived with his parents in a townhouse near the Trader Joe's and Harris Teeter stores where Rosa sometimes shopped. His home was painted a pale pink with white trim. The door was painted green like a forest, and there were beds of blooming white and yellow daisies in front. In the middle of them stood a strange smiling figurine with a tall pointed hat.

It made Caden uncomfortable. It seemed to be looking at him. "What is that?"

"A garden gnome," Tito said.

"That isn't a gnome." He turned to his friend. Gnomes were small creatures with bad breath and pointed teeth. "Gnomes are smaller. And meaner. And they don't wear hats, because they wouldn't fit over the horns," he said. "And they only smile before they attack."

Tito shrugged. "Asheville-type gnomes are happy, ceramic, and have tall pointed hats."

Caden glanced at the garden gnome again. "I don't like it."

Tito sighed and pulled him toward the door. Caden kept the gnome in his sight, though. He didn't trust it. Why did it have such a tall hat?

The townhouse to the left was pale yellow. The one on the right was pale blue. Both had similar white trim and flower beds. Likely Ms. Primrose wanted her teachers in pretty, polished places, like her other collectibles. According to Ward, Jasan was living in one of these townhomes.

Rosa knocked at the green door, and Ward's mother, Desirae, welcomed them inside. She was tall with an athletic build and wore a bright pink sundress. Caden had seen her at the social services building once or twice when he'd met his counselor. Manglor towered behind her. Caden greeted him, but Manglor just turned and went up the stairs. One day, Caden would make him smile.

"I'll be back at three to pick you up," Rosa said.

Desirae stepped outside to speak with Rosa while Caden and the others met Ward in the living room. He sat on a white leather couch with a game controller. At the other end of the room, large windows overlooked a small, flower-filled yard. There were more suspicious tall-hatted garden gnomes out there.

Tonya also sat on the couch. It was a good omen to see their fallen colleague returned. Caden felt a grin break across his face. "You look well, ally."

"I'll go b-back to school on Monday."

"You have been missed," Caden said, and he meant it.

Soon, Desirae brought in food. In Caden's royal opinion, she seemed nervous. He wondered if she knew her husband was from another world. "Is there anything else you need?" she said.

A prince must always be gracious. He took her hand. "We are grateful for your hospitality and for Ward's friendship."

"Um . . . thank you, Caden," she said, and returned to the kitchen. Ward turned red.

Once they were alone, Brynne eased onto the couch. Jane and Tito sat on the floor with a bowl of strange orange puffs. Caden remained standing. One, a prince didn't sit on the floor. Two, they were here first to see Jasan, then to play games and eat weird orange food.

Indeed, Ward was a good friend, for he paused his game and said, "He's in the yellow house."

"Thank you," Caden said.

Ward turned back to his game. "But he doesn't answer the door."

"I see," Caden said, but certainly Jasan would open the door for Caden. Still. Their noble father had once told Caden that it was better to be overly prepared than unready. He looked to Brynne and her glimmering hairpin.

She arched a brow. Her face flushed. "I could go with you."

"Good, I may need you."

Brynne stood up and stretched like a wind cat. "You often do, prince."

While the others played games, he and Brynne slipped out the back door, through the garden, past the creepy gnomes, and out the back gate. In the area outside the gate to the yellow town house's garden, Caden spotted hoof-prints. Familiar-looking ones. He bent down.

"What?" Brynne said.

Caden pointed to them and smiled. "Sir Horace has been here."

"Why would he come here?"

"He explores. He must have seen Jasan and followed him."

As Jasan had trained both Caden and Sir Horace in

riding, Sir Horace seemed to consider Jasan a close friend. Truth be told, Sir Horace listened to Jasan's commands as much as Caden's. There was no way Sir Horace would have such love for a traitor.

Caden and Brynne walked to the back of the yellow town house and peeked into the rear window. Except for a small tan couch, a cushioned chair, and a coffee table, Caden saw little inside. He pounded on the back door. No one answered.

"Maybe he's not home?" Brynne said, sounding disappointed.

"Then I'll wait inside until he is."

Brynne seemed fine with that. "I'll wait with you." She pulled out her hairpin and smiled brightly. "You're ever so lucky I'm a sorceress and a thief."

She didn't have to be quite so thrilled with the prospect of seeing Jasan. Caden frowned at her. A moment later, they were inside.

The yellow house's living room was a mirror image of Ward's living room, only with different furniture. There was a small booklet on the coffee table. It looked a little like Tito's booklet of hard-to-spell words. It was tattered as if it had been passed from person to person. He picked it up and showed Brynne. Half the words he recognized as being of the common tongue of the Greater Realm. He couldn't read as many of the other half, but he knew their English letters.

"He needs to learn some English to teach here," she said.

There were also papers nearby written in the Royal Razzon language—plans for the fitness class. He'd drawn quick neat sketches of exercises and fighting stances. It seemed Jasan planned to use the pictures to teach. If he'd prepared so much, it meant he wasn't completely ready to throw away his life. At least, that was what Caden hoped.

"I suppose I could magic him for you," Brynne said. She sounded quite thrilled with the idea. "I'd have to do it each morning, though."

No Elite Paladin would use magic to enhance an ability, and such spells would drain Brynne even more than she already drained herself. He set the papers back down. "No, I'll teach him some words. And he has his sketches."

"We'll see," said Brynne.

Just as in Ward's house, the kitchen was in the front. A window with soft blue curtains let in sunlight, and the daisies outside framed the bottom of it. Unlike Ward's house, the sink was loaded with dishes. The Enchanted Whisk of Mixing sat beside the sink, dirty with dried eggs. The countertops were smooth, pale granite. A clear box with a cell phone in it sat near the edge, and there were candy bars stacked beside it.

Brynne reached around Caden and pocketed two bars. Then she smiled like she was daring him to speak. Truth be told, Jasan shouldn't be eating candy bars. They were not proper food for an Elite Paladin, so Caden ignored her thieving.

He opened the refrigerator. It was filled with fruits and eggs—those were okay—and what he recognized as fast food containers. He picked one up and sniffed. Some kind of poultry fried in heavy, unhealthy batter. He put the container back and poked at a box on the bottom shelf that said "Pizza." Inside was a round slab of dough covered with melted cheese and greasy meats. Caden made a face. Pizza, fried fowl, and candy bars weren't approved by the Elite Paladin dietary guidelines.

"Eeek!" That was Brynne.

Caden spun around, one hand ready to strike, one hand still on the refrigerator door.

Jasan stood in the kitchen entrance. He wore a fitted gray T-shirt and loose black sweatpants. His hair was damp like he'd just gotten out of the shower. He looked weary and not at all happy to find Brynne in his candy and Caden in his refrigerator. He held Brynne's wrist.

She was turning bright red. "Your Highness," she said. She spoke in the common tongue. "I didn't think you'd mind if I took the candy. I hope—"

Jasan glanced at Brynne like he wasn't concerned, and he released her. He spoke in the elegant tongue of Royal Razzon. "Keep it."

Caden also spoke in Royal Razzon. "We need to talk." He nodded at Brynne to leave. "Alone."

She sighed like it was a great imposition. "Fine. I'll wait next door." She smiled at Jasan. "I can spell you to speak English if you need me to, Prince Jasan."

Caden waved her away. "Just go," he said.

After she left, Jasan leaned against the granite counter. He seemed annoyed, like when their father had ordered him to help Caden with swordplay or riding. "I told you to stay away from me. It wasn't a request."

Caden had no intention of staying away. He wanted to sound calm and collected, but his words sounded more hurt than anything. "I'm not going to do that."

Jasan clenched his jaw and took in a deep breath. That was good. Jasan wasn't fond of solving things with conversations, but his controlled breathing meant he was going to talk, and not just yell or speed away somewhere. "Caden," he said. "My enemies here are many. You need to understand. You could get hurt."

Perhaps Caden had been stung more by Jasan's words in the gym and after the spelling bee than he'd admitted. He felt unsure. "So you do care then?"

"Sometimes."

That was more than Jasan normally admitted. Caden felt a small smile form on his lips. His confidence started to return. "All times, you mean."

"Don't push it," Jasan said.

Jasan's eyes seemed weary. Dark shadows filled his face. Caden looked down. The floors were a limestone tile.

They badly needed sweeping.

"Look at me," Jasan said, and Caden looked back up. "Listen. If you and that little sorceress can't leave the school yet, then keep quiet and guarded until you can. Sit quietly. Don't draw unnecessary attention. The villains are dangerous, and Rath Dunn won't hesitate to hurt you."

Caden was aware. "He's already explained that to me."

Jasan's face darkened. "Has he, now?"

He pulled up his sleeve. "See for yourself."

Jasan inspected the wound and set his mouth into a tight line. Likely, he was planning Rath Dunn's demise. "He did this with that dagger of his?"

At least Caden now had his attention. He needed to convince Jasan they had to be unified against Rath Dunn. He pulled his phone from his jeans pocket. "There is something I need to ask you. It's about Rath Dunn. He knows details about our family that I didn't tell him." Caden took a deep breath. "And I overheard him say something else troubling." He explained about Tito's recording. "Listen."

He played the audio file just as Tito had showed him. Jasan wouldn't understand the words—the villains tended to keep to English in Asheville—but he'd recognize Rath Dunn's voice. "He speaks to the lunch witch. She's a master of ritual magic."

Jasan peered at the phone. "What are they saying?"

Caden translated. He hesitated as he got to the part about himself. "He said he already promised me to my brother." His voice cracked. "Who is he talking about?"

Jasan's face was turning red. He gripped the counter behind him so tightly Caden expected it to crumble under his touch. But it didn't. "Maybe he's talking about me. Did you consider that?"

"I did," Caden said truthfully. Jasan had saved Tonya. He'd been surprised to discover Rath Dunn in this happy Land of Shadow. Jasan wouldn't kill Chadwin. Sir Horace wouldn't visit a traitor. Wherever Rath Dunn was getting information, it wasn't from Jasan. Nor was it Caden or Brynne. Caden held his brother's gaze. He had to sound sure. "I know it's not you."

Jasan gritted his teeth, then pushed away from him. He clenched and unclenched his fists as if wanting to hit a memory. "You're the only one who thinks that."

Caden could tell Jasan's control of his temper was reaching its limit. "Then we'll have to show the others they are wrong," Caden said. "If it takes years, so be it. I'm alive, that's proof enough." In the following silence, Caden heard the rumble of engines as cars parked in the spaces out front. The refrigerator hummed. What was it his counselor had said? "People make mistakes. Father will realize that soon. The Greater Realm Council will—"

Jasan released a harsh, hurt-sounding laugh, and his quick temper seemed to spike like a raging kiln fire. He grabbed Caden's shoulders and pushed him against the refrigerator. The door was cold against his back. "I don't care what Father realizes now, Caden. And the Greater Realm Council doesn't admit mistakes. My portrait will hang in the Hall of Infamy beside the likes of Rath Dunn. Do you understand at all? There is no going back for me."

Jasan was hurt. He was lashing out. He'd no real gift with words, other than to spew them out quickly and without much thought.

"You're wrong," Caden said.

Whatever was happening was part of something terrible, something that was interconnecting in horrible and unknown ways.

Caden pulled away. "Rath Dunn wants your blood. Maybe he's communicating somehow with the Greater Realm." He shifted on his feet. The words came out shaky. "If you didn't . . ." Caden couldn't say "Kill Chadwin." Not out loud. He just couldn't. He looked back up. "If you didn't do what they said, and you're not the brother he promised me to . . . who is?"

Jasan turned back to him. He looked troubled.

"I'm unsure."

The night before Chadwin was killed, Caden and his brothers had gathered with their father in the Great Hall. The table was forged from giant bluebirch, one large and smooth piece of wood that stretched across the room. The imperial Winterbird was engraved into the tabletop and inlaid in gold and silver metals. The table legs looked like wings.

King Axel sat at the table's head in a chair finished in dark velvets, at the place of honor. Valon, Caden's first-born brother, sat to the king's right. Second-born Maden to his left. Then sixth-born Chadwin beside Valon, and seventh-born Jasan beside Maden. The others, third-born Lucian, fourth-born Martin, and fifth-born Landon, were on a diplomatic mission to the Summerlands. Caden sat beside Jasan.

They were quiet, so Caden told them of how he'd spoken to a rock spirit in the garden.

Maden, the size of a small frost giant and with hair the color of straw, chuckled. "Rock spirits don't speak."

He was wrong, of course. "Rock spirits don't speak the common or royal tongues. But they do speak, they are sentient." Caden kept Maden's gaze. "The one in the garden wanted to be chipped into two."

"It doesn't sound so bright," Maden said.

"It wanted a twin."

Valon, first born, peered at Caden. Of all Caden's brothers, he looked most like their father. His hair was dark blond, his build powerful. His brow always seemed creased with worry. Caden had never seen him laugh, and Caden caught his attention even less than he caught their father's. Now Valon looked at him with a calculating expression. "His gift seems particularly strong." Then he looked at the king. "We should utilize all our assets, Father."

It was rare that any of Caden's brothers did more than tease him about his gift of speech, and his gift seemed to make their father uncomfortable. Caden sat up straighter. True, he could translate anything spoken to him.

Maden chuckled. "Hmm," he said, "we may wish to talk to the garden rocks."

Caden frowned. That was a more typical response.

Valon seemed unperturbed. "Such an ability has its uses."

The king raised his hand. They quieted immediately. "Caden's your brother; he's not an asset," he said. "Remember that."

Caden, however, had no qualms with being a useful asset. His life goal was to be an Elite Paladin like his older brothers, to slay dragons and defend the king and kingdom. Being useful would only help him with that goal. "I can be both," Caden said.

Valon nodded. "I agree."

Jasan leaned forward. "I don't."

Chadwin looked at Valon and Maden and Jasan with a strange expression. He'd been watching them like that often in recent days. "Nor do I," Chadwin said. "He's barely twelve turns."

"He's sitting here," Caden said, "and he's capable enough."

Chadwin turned to him and smiled. "Of course," he said. "And when you are older we can serve the kingdom together. But for now, you are still too young, little brother."

Only Chadwin ever called him little brother. It always

caught Caden off guard, and made his cheeks flush and his heart twist. All he wanted was to be useful. To be an Elite Paladin, like his heroic brothers.

Chadwin turned toward the king. "Don't you agree, Father?"

King Axel surveyed the group. "Caden will concentrate on his studies and his riding," their father said. Then he turned to Caden. "And he'll also stop talking to rocks."

That had been the last night all his brothers had been alive. The next morning, Chadwin was dead. And Caden would never serve with him.

Caden looked at Jasan. In Rath Dunn's taunts about a traitorous brother, he'd never specified Jasan. Caden had five more surviving brothers. Chadwin had trusted them all. No matter what he'd suspected, it wouldn't have been a dagger in the back.

If Jasan was innocent, and if Rath Dunn were to be believed, one of Caden's other brothers was guilty. But that night, Caden's three middle brothers had been away. The only ones who could've turned traitor were Valon, first born, or Maden, second born.

Caden heard a bird happily chirping outside the window. Slowly, Caden gathered his courage. He said what he didn't want to say. "Valon and Maden were there that night. They were there that morning. And they've both seen my favorite sword enough times to have a similar one made."

Jasan said nothing. He never made anything easy.

Caden couldn't bring himself to ask if Valon or Maden had killed Chadwin. Instead, he asked something that likely meant the same thing. "Could one of them have framed you?"

"I don't know," Jasan said.

Caden raised a brow. Jasan did know. Caden knew it. It was time to accept that one of their loved ones was a traitor, was capable of *fratricide*. It was time to say it aloud.

"It is no accident it was you who was framed," he said slowly. "It is your blood Rath Dunn needs—the blood of the seventh-born son—and someone made sure you were sent here so he could get it. Someone was communicating with him. There is a traitor in our family."

"And?" Jasan said.

This wasn't so hard to understand. Caden threw up his palms. "And we need to warn Father, and Lucian, and Martin, and Landon, and whoever else doesn't know."

Jasan leaned forward. "Lucian, Martin, and Landon aren't my concern. Nor is the king."

"It's your duty to protect them and to protect the kingdom," Caden said.

"Not anymore." He grabbed one of his candy bars from the counter like he was going to eat it. "Don't ask me to protect those who sentenced me to death for killing my own brother."

"They've been tricked," Caden insisted. Their father

would have never banished Jasan otherwise. "Do you want Lucian or Martin or Landon to die like Chadwin? Do you want Father to die?" If Jasan wouldn't protect the kingdom, he'd still protect them. "We're family."

"Again—not anymore."

That wasn't true. Jasan couldn't say that. Caden felt his insides knot. "Always."

When Jasan looked mad enough to punch someone, he often hit the wall. There were holes throughout the Winter Castle's lower training room—fist marks that crushed right into the stone. He looked that angry now.

The punches came with words, not fists. "No one considers you family except Father," Jasan said.

Caden felt his body start to shake. "Chadwin did."

"Not really."

It was as if Caden really had been hit in the eye with a sparring mop. He reeled back. Some of Jasan's anger seemed to drain. "I didn't mean . . ."

Knock. Knock. Knock.

Someone was at the door. Like Ward had said, Jasan made no move to open it. At the castle, a servant or guard would have done so. Maybe Jasan didn't understand how doors worked since there had always been someone to open them for him.

Caden remained against the refrigerator. Blood rushed to his cheeks, and he felt acid drip on his tongue. "But they know I'd never betray them."

Tap. Tap. Tap.

The knocker was at the window now. It was Rosa. She stood outside among the flowers, peering inside at him. She looked a little worried, a lot furious, and was at least two hours early to pick them up. That couldn't be good. Caden wasn't sure he could take anyone else being upset with him today. But he didn't want to be in this kitchen any longer.

Caden hadn't told Jasan of the quest. How would Jasan respond if he did? Maybe he'd say he didn't care if they both died. Maybe he'd lock Caden away and attack Ms. Primrose. If Jasan did that, he'd be devoured. They'd both be. Caden wasn't sure which scenario was worse. He turned away.

"I've got to go," Caden said.

Jasan started to reach out to stop him but then didn't. "I don't care about any rules. I don't care if I'm eaten. Stay away from me."

Caden almost said, "I don't care if you're eaten either" and "I also don't consider you family." He wanted to say that. He wanted to say many things. But he didn't. He couldn't. A future Elite Paladin was always honest.

18

TRUTH AND CONSEQUENCES

Rosa trampled a yellow daisy as she came to meet Caden on the front step. Her pickup was parked in the space in front of Ward's house. Brynne, Tito, and Jane were in the truck's backseat. Jane and Brynne were watching. Both looked shamed, although he guessed Brynne was faking it. Tito was between them with his hands pressed to his cheeks. Ward's mother stood on the sidewalk.

"You're early," Caden said.

At that point, Jasan came outside. Rosa looked at Jasan. She stared for an instant. Then she reached for Caden's arm and nodded to Jasan. "Who's this?" she said in English at the same time Jasan said it in Royal Razzon.

Desirae spoke up. "He's a new teacher at the school."

Maybe she did know Manglor was from another realm. Maybe she knew Caden, Brynne, and Jasan were as well.

From the way she'd jumped into the conversation, he suspected it.

Rosa looked between Caden and Jasan. Was there any family resemblance? Jasan looked like the first queen. Caden had a different mother, but there were similarities— same nose, same-shaped eyes.

Caden pulled away and glared back at Jasan. He should say Jasan was his half brother. But what did it matter? Jasan wouldn't understand his words anyway. Looking back at Rosa, he said, "He's my brother. He's been banished for crimes he didn't commit."

Instead of grimacing or telling Caden to stop with his stories, Rosa seemed sad. "Get in the truck, Caden," she said.

He started to move forward, but Jasan grabbed the back of his horse T-shirt and stopped him. "I asked you a question," Jasan said in Royal Razzon. "Who is this person?"

Caden jerked from his grasp and answered in the royal tongue. "Someone who does consider me family," he said.

Rosa reached out and pulled Caden to her. "Don't grab him like that." She looked at Jasan with blatant suspicion. "What language is that? How do you know Caden?"

"He doesn't understand English," Caden said to Rosa. To Jasan, he said, "She's my guardian in this strange land." Then, in English, he added, "He's speaking Royal Razzon."

Jasan glared at her. Rosa glared back but didn't seem to know what to think.

Desirae laughed nervously.

It seemed Jasan had had enough. "Just go, Caden." His voice seemed to crack on the name. "Keep away from me." He went inside. A moment later, the front door of his picturesque yellow town house locked with a click. It seemed he did know how to work the door after all.

"What did he say?" Rosa said.

"He said to leave."

Caden looked at the pickup. In the backseat, Brynne pointed at Rosa, then made a face like she was screaming in fear. As if Rosa sensed it, she turned. Immediately, Brynne closed her mouth, closed her eyes, and sank back into her seat. Caden began to think they were in great trouble with their foster mother, and he wasn't entirely sure he wanted to go home with her.

"Then let's leave," Rosa said. "Now."

Maybe this wasn't a time to be rebellious. Although not cursed for another day, Caden complied. "As you wish," he said, trudging to the pickup and climbing in the passenger seat.

Rosa remained outside for a moment. She seemed to be apologizing to Ward's mother and kept motioning to the truck. By the yellow town house's front window, Jasan peeked through his curtains, eating a candy bar, his gaze moving from Rosa to Caden to Brynne in the backseat.

Brynne leaned forward. "He looks upset."

"You took his chocolate." Caden buckled his seat belt.

"And he's been banished." Although he was as upset as he'd ever been with his brother, Brynne should know Jasan wasn't a traitor. In a small voice, he added, "They think he killed Chadwin. He's innocent, though."

"Of course," she said. "Rath Dunn wants his blood. That's why he's here. Prince Jasan is honorable and brave." Then she smiled. "He's looking at me, too."

Caden was tired of her talking about Jasan. He didn't want to hear it.

Having the gift of speech wasn't all about speaking languages and charming people. It was about knowing what to say to get the desired response. Right now, Caden wanted Brynne to stop talking about his brother. He turned to her. "If he finds out you cursed me, he'll be furious."

Her smile faded. "Don't tell him, then," she said. Brynne was quiet for a moment. Then she said, "He's especially protective of you."

"Not really."

Jane had been looking out the window. "Rosa's coming back," she warned.

Brynne glanced out, biting her bottom lip as she saw Jasan. "It's just—" She twisted her hands together. "Look, prince, he might get really angry if he finds out. . . ."

"I suspect so."

She took a deep breath. "Don't tell him. He'll never forgive me, Caden," Brynne said. "For doing that to you."

"I suspect he won't."

Rosa was standing beside the driver's door. She had her head down like she was breathing deeply and counting.

"Please," Brynne said.

Rosa was opening the door.

Brynne quickly added, "Don't tell him. Not until I've fixed it. I'll break the curse or destroy the moon. I'll figure something out. I promise. Please."

Rosa didn't say much when she got in the car. Nor did she look at them. When Caden opened his mouth to speak, she held up her hand. "I don't want to hear a word until we're home."

Caden wasn't sure why she was so mad. People would often answer a question when asked even if they didn't want to do so. "Why?" he said.

Rosa, however, was of strong mind. She didn't answer. Someone in the back kicked his seat. From the arrangement of people behind him, it was likely Jane this time. Which meant the kick was a warning, not an idle tease.

When they pulled up to Rosa's house, Officer Levine's patrol car was parked in the drive. He and Jenkins stood on the porch. They were in full uniform. An official visit, it seemed.

Rosa put the truck into park. "Inside. On the couch. All of you."

This was a bad development.

They squeezed on the green interrogation couch—Jane on the flank, Tito and Caden in the middle, then Brynne on the other side. Brynne was leaning back and closing her eyes. Feigning sleep was her typical strategy when in trouble.

Jane looked worried, and she grabbed Tito's hand. Tito was bouncing his leg up and down, up and down, in an unconscious tic. He looked like he might be sick at any moment.

They should worry less. Rosa's punishments consisted of long talks and reduced computer and phone privileges. Her punishments were nothing like the fiery flogging of the Autumnlands, or the hard and often bloody labor of the elvish ruby mines. Her punishments were unpleasant, not torture.

Well, Rosa's disappointment might amount to torture for Tito. Tito didn't seem to understand Rosa would never send him away. Caden believed Rosa loved Tito most of all of them. Not that Tito could see it.

Rosa stood in front of them. She wore a green camouflage top and a long yellow skirt. There was nothing happy in her expression. Officer Levine stood beside her, but his expression had more compassion. Jenkins stood to the right with a tablet.

Officer Levine sighed. "There was a break-in at your school last night."

Tito flinched, and Caden saw Jane squeeze his hand.

Rosa peered at them, each in turn. Her gaze paused on Brynne. "Eyes open, young lady."

Brynne squirmed but did as told.

"There was a considerable mess made in the hall."

Caden raised his brows. "We caused none of it. And I don't like messes."

Officer Levine nodded. "Is that so?"

"It is."

He peered at Caden. "All right."

Jenkins looked up. His red hair looked dark indoors. "The secretary reported seeing three kids running from the school." He pointed his pen at Caden, then Tito. "Two boys," he said, then flip-flopped his pen slowly to each end of the couch. "One girl."

Rosa was fuming. Caden could imagine steam rising from the floor on which she stood. She zeroed in on Tito. "Did you go to the school last night?"

"No," Jane said.

Rosa made a motion to indicate she wanted everyone silent. "I'm asking Tito," she said.

She was a skilled interrogator, indeed. Neither Jane nor Brynne looked ready to break. Caden was an eighth-born prince. He was solid as a stone. Also, he didn't care too much. His mind kept wandering back to Jasan, to the accidents, to other things of importance. Tito, however, was close to talking. Disappointing Rosa was his weak spot.

Tito didn't look at her. His hand looked limp in Jane's. "Yes, Rosa," he said.

"You lied to me," she said.

Tito, who had stood tall while threatened by villain and vermin, looked terrified.

"We vandalized nothing. Matter of point," Caden said, "we were attacked by Mr. Creedly and his rats."

Officer Levine frowned at him. "Uh-huh," he said. "Was it your bright idea to break into the school?"

The others might keep silent, might keep their intent and motives close. Caden wouldn't. He would tell them the truth until they believed him. "Ms. Primrose ordered me to find the cause of the gas accident. She's going to eat my brother and me on Tuesday if I fail."

"That's pretty specific, son," Officer Levine said.

"It is."

Rosa was looking at him now, too. Some of her anger seemed to have dimmed. "Phones on the table."

Tito and Jane immediately put their phones on the coffee table. Caden tossed his down as well. Brynne hesitated. Truly, she loved her phone. She seemed to love all Ashevillian tech.

"You have until the count of five," Rosa said. "One."

With a huff, and a defiant expression that meant she'd just steal it back later, Brynne complied.

"You three," she said, and motioned to Jane, Tito, and Brynne. "Upstairs. Now. You can stay in your rooms until I decide what to do with you." She pointed to Caden. "You, don't move."

It seemed Caden was in the most trouble. Once Caden

heard the girls walk into their room and Tito's slow footfalls on the creaky attic steps, Rosa sat down next to him. "This is serious, Caden," she said.

"The school may press charges, son," Officer Levine said. "Against all of you."

Caden looked from her to Officer Levine. That sounded different from Rosa's grounding. A good leader protected his people. "Jane wasn't there."

Jenkins scribbled on his tablet. "You sure about that, kid?"

"I tell the truth," Caden said.

They were speaking softly. It was an odd shift, as Rosa was obviously furious with the others. If anything, she should be most angry at him. It made his stomach twitch. He still didn't understand the strange culture here, and "press charges" was an odd phrase.

In Caden's mind, charges brought up images of Sir Horace barreling down a mountain, but it must have had another meaning. Many English words had multiple meanings, and sometimes Caden's gift of speech only helped him with the literal one.

Would he be crushed by a stone, or charged by a horde of beasts? Punishments like those seemed rare in this land. Besides, he didn't need to know what it meant. "Ms. Primrose won't press charges." Of this, he was certain. "She gave me my quest."

Officer Levine stared at him a moment, then said, "Son,

you were seen at the school last night, and last night the school was vandalized."

"I damaged nothing," he told them. "You think too lowly of me."

"Kid," Jenkins said, "you've got to learn to shut it."

Caden most certainly did not need to learn to shut it. He turned back to Officer Levine. "Mr. Creedly was there. He caused the bees to swarm during the spelling bee." He thought back to the dark science classroom. "Rath Dunn and Ms. Jackson were there, too, skulking around in the dark. They are the ones you should question."

Rosa took his hand. "Why do you think that, Caden?"

Caden looked down at their hands and raised a brow. "I don't think that. I know that."

Officer Levine and Rosa exchanged a look. It was a sad, concerned look that Caden didn't at all appreciate. "Caden," Rosa began.

"I have proof," Caden said. "Hand me my phone." Reluctantly, Rosa handed it back to him. He played the audio file. "Can you tell me that wasn't threatening?"

For a moment, she seemed lost for words. "No," she said finally, "I can't. But that doesn't mean he's a tyrant from another realm. And I don't know when you recorded that, or in what context."

"I just told you when and where." He held her gaze. "And Rath Dunn is a tyrant, and he is from the Greater Realm."

"I know you believe that, Caden," Rosa said, but it didn't sound as if she did.

Officer Levine sat down on his other side. "Son, we are trying to help you."

Caden straightened his posture. "You still believe I'm crazy."

Rosa squeezed his hand. "We don't think you're crazy, Caden."

He pulled away from her. "Brynne and Tito also were there. Ask Manglor, Ward's father—he knows." He stood up. "Ask my brother. Actually, go ask Ms. Primrose."

"And if I do, and they remember things differently?"

"They won't."

"We should talk about this later." Rosa took a deep breath. "Go upstairs. For now, you're grounded."

Caden wasn't quite ready to go upstairs. He felt incredibly uncomfortable under their scrutiny and had to remind himself to keep his shoulders square. He looked at each of them and over to Jenkins. "You also thought me wrong when I said Jane had been kidnapped. But I was right about the lunch witches."

"You were right that Jane was taken by some troubled people," Rosa admitted. She seemed to neither be agreeing with him nor challenging him.

"Yes, troubled lunch witches." He crossed his arms. "You should consider that I'm right about this, too. You need to open your eyes to the reality of my school before someone else is hurt. It is dangerous. No one should go to school there."

Jane had been kidnapped at the school. The science room had exploded. The spelling bee had turned into a disaster. Caden frowned at his thoughts. Why hadn't Rosa taken him, Jane, Brynne, and Tito out of the school? Why hadn't any of the parents done so? Caden hadn't thought about leaving the school before, either. It was an unsettling realization.

Caden and Ms. Primrose had agreed to the unbreakable terms of his quest in a forgotten tongue. She made her teachers sign contracts in blood. Hadn't Rosa filled out paperwork when Caden had enrolled? Maybe the parents and students were bound to Ms. Primrose, too.

"It's a good school," Rosa said.

"And a dangerous one." Caden turned and went toward the steps. He looked back. "Jane is alive because of me."

"I know," Rosa said.

When Caden got to the attic room, Tito was crouched in the corner by the floor vent. When he saw Caden he put his finger to his lips—a signal for silence—and waved him over. Caden knelt beside him. He could hear Rosa's voice filter up through the house.

"These paranoid stories of his are affecting the other kids," she started. Her words were muffled, but if he strained he could understand. "Jane's still in recovery. Tito has never gotten into trouble like this before. He never had trouble with Mr. Rathis before. And goodness knows Brynne needs no encouragement. Half the time, I think they believe him. Sometimes, I almost do. He's a good kid, but he's a bad influence."

Truly, Caden was taken aback. His royal personage wasn't a bad influence—especially when compared to Brynne. "Brynne's the bad influence, not me," Caden whispered.

"Quiet," Tito mouthed.

Officer Levine's voice was kind. "What's his counselor say?"

"That Caden believes what he says. Every word of it." She laughed, but she didn't sound happy. "Harold"—that was Officer Levine's first name—"I'm worried the counselor might believe him, too."

"We'll find another counselor, then."

Caden wasn't liking what he heard through this vent. Also, his counselor wasn't supposed to talk to other people about their conversations. During their next session, Caden was going to have to address that betrayal. There was the sound of movement. He heard the front door open and shut. Quickly, Tito cracked open the attic window.

Their words became clearer. Then: "I don't know what to do. And I don't know what to think about the scene with the new gym teacher."

"What do you want to do?"

When Rosa next spoke, her voice was more solid, more

even. She sounded like a general who had made a difficult choice. "I've got three other kids to think about. I've got to protect them." Caden moved to the window. Their voices became fainter as they stepped off the porch. "Maybe if he went into treatment for a few weeks. I could apply to get him leave from school."

Maybe Caden was wrong. Maybe students could escape the school.

Then Rosa added, "He could come back if he got better." Then again, maybe not.

The words left him more unsettled than Rosa and Officer Levine's gentle demeanor. If they believed him a bad influence and vandal, they should be angry at him like they were at Tito, Brynne, and Jane. He turned and looked at Tito.

Tito was wide-eyed and his mouth agape. "You've got to convince them you're not crazy. They're going to send you to the nuthouse."

Despite the name, the "nuthouse" was not a storing place for Ashevillian pecans and walnuts. It was Tito's term for a terrible place with wailing people and padded cells. It was worse than "juvie," apparently. Caden wasn't sure what "juvie" was either, but the way Tito talked about it, Caden assumed neither place was somewhere he wanted to go.

Tito started talking again. "They think your crazy is causing problems for the rest of us, so you have to convince them you're getting better."

Caden looked at him. "I'm not crazy."

"Yeah, but they don't know that."

Caden leaned against the wall. "No matter what I say, they don't believe the truth."

"Then tell them what they want to hear."

What they wanted to hear wasn't true. Caden had little of his homeland—just his coat and Sir Horace, a trouble-making sorceress, and a brother who wanted him to stay away. And his honor. He wouldn't compromise it for comfort and the easy way out. All future Elite Paladins were tested. He wouldn't fail in his noble path because Rosa wanted to get rid of him.

"I'll prove I'm sane. I'll unmask the villains for what they are."

Tito shook his head. "I got an idea," he said. "Just pretend you're a normal messed-up kid until you can do that. Tell Rosa you're sorry, and you won't say weird stuff anymore."

"I don't say weird stuff. I point out facts."

Tito's frown was lopsided, his eyes concerned. "Bro, this is a good place. You don't want to be sent somewhere else. Trust me on that. I'll help." His voice cracked. He was truly worried. "I'll tell her it's a game, and . . . I don't know. We'll figure something out."

Tito rattled on.

So Rosa was sending Caden away. To protect everyone

else. That was what she'd said. It wasn't her fault she knew nothing of the Greater Realm. She was doing her best. He wouldn't hold any ill will toward her. He thought of his family. His father had sent him away. An inner voice added, "To protect you," but it wasn't so convincing. Jasan wanted him to go away, and Chadwin apparently had never considered him truly a brother.

Tito was saying something about "abandonment issues." "You can play that up. My old case worker always went straight for that when I got upset and . . ."

Outside, the sun was low. Tonight, the half-moon would rise and he'd be cursed once more. If he was ordered to go away, to go somewhere where they would lock him up far from his friends, from the school, he'd have to go. He'd not be there to unmask the saboteur and save his brother, nor be around to find a way to help his family. Ms. Primrose would find him and eat him.

"You've got to be smart here, you understand?" Tito said.

Caden sat on his bed and put his chin in his hands. He understood. Most people liked him. Of this there was no doubt. The ones he loved just didn't want him around.

19

THE ORDERS OF FRIENDS

Caden awoke early the next day. He sat up and swung his legs to the floor. At once, his arms felt tingly and his limbs strange. It was the curse. His will was no longer his own. Until the half-moon waned on Tuesday night, he was bound to do as told.

Likely, he'd be eaten by then.

Outside the window, thunderclouds hung low near the mountaintops. It was supposed to rain today. The weather in Asheville was like that—always changing.

In the Greater Realm, the weather shifted some, but not like it did here. The Winterlands were always cold and snowy, although sometimes they were colder and snowier. It was the same with the Summerlands. They were hot and dry or hotter and drier. The Springlands were warm and pleasant, and the Autumnlands cool and crisp.

Across the taped line that divided the room, Tito sat up in his bed. He had dark circles under his eyes. His face looked pinched. Caden didn't mention the weirdness of the weather to him. Tito thought the weird weather was normal the way Caden thought nonweird nonchanging weather was normal.

Instead, Caden said, "I'm the one who needs to convince them to let me stay. You needn't worry."

Tito picked at his purple quilt. "Bro, I'm going to worry."

It was Tito's nature to fear for things that had not yet passed. Caden was still here. They still had villains to draw from the shadows and plots to uncover. "Sir Tito," Caden said, "they haven't sent me away yet."

Tito wiped his arm against his face. "It just blows, man."

Caden didn't understand that phrasing, but it wasn't always necessary to understand someone's words to get their meaning. Caden knew what Tito meant. "We will overcome, no matter what happens."

If he collected Ashevillian proof of sabotage, his quest would be completed and he could show Rosa and Officer Levine the true natures of the villainous teachers. Then they would have to accept he wasn't crazy. The not-accidents would be shown for what they were. Ms. Primrose wouldn't eat Jasan. Rosa wouldn't send him away. That would solve his problems. But how could he prove something magical in a way that someone nonmagical would understand?

He'd find a way. "I'll prove to them I'm not crazy."

Tito forced a smile. "Yeah, that sounds like what a crazy person might say." He shrugged. "I know you're telling the truth, and I think you're a little loco. Maybe we should come up with a better plan."

If it came to it, Caden was trained in survival. "If I have to, I can always return to living in the woods."

"The woods, huh?" Tito stood up and grabbed one of his black T-shirts. "You know, I think that cements it." He cleared his throat. "You're a werewolf."

"A what?"

Tito explained.

Caden was nothing like a werewolf. "I'm no man-beast that feasts on flesh."

"You're bound by the lunar cycle," Tito said. "Admit it, you're a werewolf."

What did this have to do with anything? Still, that was an order. Caden was under the power of the curse. He admitted it. "Because of my unrelated lunar issues, I'm a werewolf," he said. "Although I don't fit the werewolf description at all."

"I knew you'd agree," Tito said.

"It's not funny."

"Yeah, I guess it's not," Tito said. When he looked up, he seemed determined. "I could order you to tell Rosa you made up everything."

"No," Caden said. His honor was the one thing that

was truly his. "That would be a lie."

"But if I ordered you," Tito said, "it wouldn't be your fault."

Would Tito do something like that? Nothing was more important to Caden than becoming an Elite Paladin, nothing. To do that, he needed to slay a dragon, fight evil, and always act with honor. It was terrifying enough that the villains might find out and order him to do something that would jeopardize his honor, his life, or the lives of others. He shouldn't have the same worry about his friend.

One thing about Tito, he didn't do well with disappointing people. Mostly Rosa. But Caden suspected those feelings also filtered down to others—Jane, Brynne, even Caden.

"If you order me to lie," Caden said, "we'll never be friends again."

Tito frowned. "Never is a bit harsh, don't you think? Especially if I do it to help you."

Maybe. Caden stood up, but suddenly felt conflicted. Had Jasan vowed something similar to their brothers, their father, when they wrongly banished him? Didn't Caden want Jasan to find a way for them to be family again one day?

Caden changed into his daytime T-shirt. This one sadly had no magnificent horse or soaring bird; hence, he saved it for nonschool days. It did, however, have interesting blue-and-green stripes, and was better than the black T-shirt

Tito was wearing. "Don't make me lie, Sir Tito. Please."

Tito frowned at Caden as if Caden were the unreasonable one. "Whatever." His brow creased. "Yeah. Okay. I won't order you to lie. You'd just go all freaky on me, anyway." He bent over and laced up his sneakers.

"Good, then we can stay friends."

"Don't forget that," Tito said.

That was an order. Combined with the guilty look falling over Tito's face, it was also one that worried Caden. He stood at alert. "Why not?"

"'Cause I got an idea," Tito said. "Listen, until your curse is done, don't say anything to Rosa or Officer Levine about the Greater Realm. And don't say anything to anyone else when they can hear."

Caden was taken aback. "What?"

"Bro, you won't have to lie." Tito looked like he wanted Caden to agree badly. "This way, you're less likely to say something too crazy."

"Sir Tito," Caden said, and he felt fury building. "You shouldn't give me orders at all. I should get to choose what I say. No one else."

"Yeah. I know. I'm sorry," Tito said, but he didn't take back his words.

And an order was an order.

At breakfast, Caden sat between Jane and Brynne, and not beside Tito like usual.

Rosa watched him with the same sad expression she'd had the night before. "Why have you changed seats, Caden?"

"I'm not talking to Tito until Tuesday."

When Caden said nothing more, Rosa looked to Tito, but Tito stared at his eggs like he was under a hypno-turtle's thrall. With a slow exhale, Rosa looked back to Caden. "Will you tell me why?"

Not an order. "It depends."

Tito looked up. Brynne and Jane watched as well. Rosa kept her expression even. "On what, Caden?" Rosa said.

Suddenly, Caden wasn't hungry. He pushed away his whole-grain toast. He needed to stay with Rosa—if not for-ever, at least for two more days. What could he say? He took a deep breath. "It depends," he said, "on if you're sending me away like everyone else has. I trusted you."

He was trying for matter-of-fact, or maybe angry. Perhaps he'd not attained either, for Rosa looked as though she might cry, and he felt the same way. "Please keep me another two days. That's all I'm asking."

Jane and Brynne looked at each other, then at Rosa. They seemed to be waiting for Rosa to deny it. Rosa was quiet. Likely, she was shocked that Caden knew her plans, and more so that he'd confronted her.

After an awkward silence, Brynne started fidgeting. "Caden needs to stay with me," she said. "We're allies. We came here together."

"He's not really a bad influence," Tito said.

Caden wasn't talking to Tito currently, so he didn't acknowledge him. Tito was right, though. "I'm not a bad influence at all," he said. "I'm the opposite."

Rosa's expression went weary. "You overheard," she said.

"I did."

Jane set her fork down, though she looked at it thoughtfully before doing so, then frowned at Rosa. "Rosa," she said in the calm way of hers, "he's the one who saved me."

Rosa glanced at Jane, then back at Caden and held his gaze. Well, he deserved the brunt of her attention. He was the one she was giving away. He squared his shoulders.

"I want what's best for all of you," she said, and kept her gaze on Caden. "No one's being sent anywhere today."

"What about tomorrow?" he said.

"Monday you have school. And Tuesday afternoon we're talking to your social worker. That's all. It doesn't mean you're going anywhere. But you have to start behaving. Another incident, and I'll have to do what I think is best for you. Even if what I think is that you need more than I can give you."

Caden wanted to explain his quest again, but he had been ordered not to tell stories of his dragons, villains, or homeland. "I see."

With that, she started clearing the table. "I want what's best for you. Don't ever question that." An order. "Let's just enjoy Sunday together."

She didn't push the matter more and pardoned them

from their punishment chores for the day. Brynne, of course, took the pardon as an opportunity. "Can we get back our phones?"

Rosa must have felt particularly guilty because she returned them.

That afternoon, Rosa spent most of her time outside tinkering with her sculptures. The drizzle didn't seem to bother her. Tito fell asleep in the attic room while Caden was ignoring him. Caden went downstairs to visit the girls' room.

The sunny yellow walls looked dull against the gray light from the window. The billowy white curtains seemed to sag. Brynne was sitting cross-legged on the bottom bunk. Her hair hung long over her shoulders. Jane was at her desk.

As soon as he closed the door, Brynne ordered him not to be mad at Tito.

"It doesn't work that way," Caden told her. "That's why Tito shouldn't have ordered me not to talk about the Greater Realm. No curse can control how I feel. Just what I say and do."

"Too bad," Brynne said.

"No, it's not."

It seemed Jane had decided her breakfast fork unworthy of enchantment, for she had a large metal spoon—no, not a spoon, a soup ladle—on the desktop. She smiled. "Tito is trying to help," she said. She held up the ladle. "This one's new."

Outside, thunder cracked on the mountain. Caden crossed his arms. He pointed at Brynne, then the ladle. "You shouldn't encourage these enchantments."

"As long as Jane does small enchantments, she gains better control, and doesn't use so much life force. And she's part elf, so she has more life force to practice with. If the enchantments get small enough, the life force loss will be minimal," Brynne said. "It's a good plan."

"It is," Jane said. "The ladle is special, though. It deserves a lot of power."

Brynne creased her brow in worry. Caden shook his head. The ladle would be magic item number one hundred thirty-four, the Enchanted Ladle of Power.

Caden wanted to believe she and Brynne had a good plan, but if she hadn't held back on a ladle, would she really hold back on everything else? Wouldn't it be safer to concentrate on enchanting as few things as possible?

Caden couldn't hide his concern. "Don't enchant it, Jane."

Jane and Brynne exchanged a look. They were getting good at communicating like that. He considered them. "I see," he said, and sighed. "You've already enchanted it."

Jane didn't offer him the ladle as she had the paper clips that held things together, or the whisk that mixed things. He almost didn't ask. Still. "What does it do?"

He was expecting her to say "It ladles things," but she didn't. "It's complicated."

That made him more curious. "How so?"

Jane smiled, and it was a devious smile, indeed. "You'll see," she said. "And don't worry, Caden. It'll help us, and it's the last large enchantment I plan to do."

Caden opened his mouth to ask exactly how an enchanted ladle would help, but before he could, Brynne said, "Quiet, prince." She pointed at the floor and grinned. "Sit."

An order. He fidgeted. With a huff, he sat on the floor. Tito, at least, had the decency to feel guilty about the orders. Brynne looked amused. He crossed his arms and glowered up at her.

"Fine, you don't have to be quiet. But stop badgering Jane."

"He's not badgering me," Jane said.

Exactly. "I shouldn't have to sit, either," he said. Truth be told, he could get up now. She hadn't specified a time limit and Caden had satisfied her order already. The floor, however, was surprisingly comfortable.

"Don't worry about me," Jane said. "Worry about everything else." She moved away from the desk and sat on the floor beside him. "I've been thinking, There's no way to easily skip class. The teachers are getting wise to the bathroom excuse, and they'll be watching us after the vandalism incident. Lunch period is when we should snoop around the cafeteria. We're supposed to be there then."

"We've only got two days left," Caden said. Time was as much their enemy as the villains.

"That's why we have to be smart and get into the school kitchen," Jane said.

"I agree," he said, but he felt unnerved. Something was wrong, and he wasn't seeing it.

On Monday, the sky was a deep blue. Sunday's drizzle seemed to have washed and polished the city. The roads looked clean. The trees on the mountains were shades of green.

When they drove up to the school, there were no police or paramedics, no screeching alarm bells, but something wasn't right. The grass on the front lawn looked sickly. The blooms on the rhododendron had turned a slimy black. The trees looked burned. The just-planted roses that surrounded the building were brown and dry as if the weekend's rainstorm had never happened.

A few local students pointed at a tree, or mumbled sadly about the flowers. But none really seemed to understand what the dead plants meant. They were connected to plots against the school, Asheville, and the Greater Realm. And they were a bad omen.

Caden went to the side of the building, bent down, and picked a flower. It crumbled in his hand. The bloom reminded him of the dead rats in the science room, drained of life. He turned to Brynne.

"What do you think?"

Brynne crouched beside him, her brow creased, her

eyes narrowed. "Definitely ritual magic," she said. "Odd to sacrifice flowers and trees, though." She narrowed her eyes. "The Great Walking Oak is protector of the Springlands and spellcasters. To kill a tree is sacrilege."

Jane looked at the tree and clenched at something hidden in her coat. "This has to stop."

She'd never walked among the flower fields of the Springlands, nor climbed the great mountains of the Winterlands. Her skin had never felt the burning heat of the Summerlands deserts, nor seen the red, yellow, and orange fire forests of the Autumnlands. Yet Jane was half elf. Her mother was from the Springlands. The Walking Oak was as sacred to her as the Winterbird was to him.

"Then the three of us will stop it," Caden said.

Beside him, Tito sighed. "Are you really going to ignore me until Tuesday?"

Caden refused to look at him. "Why don't you order me to stop?"

"If I did, I don't think I'd ever hear the end of it."

Brynne stood up and took Caden's hand. "I will break the curse. Please believe me." She squeezed his hand. A passing group of girls pointed at their clasped hands and giggled. Brynne pulled away. "And I'm sorrier than even you know."

She sounded so sincere, so contrite, Caden believed her. "I know you will."

"Good," she said. Then her eyes glinted, and her brow

arched. "But for now, stop ignoring Tito."

"Fine," Caden said. "I'll ignore you instead."

"I'll order you not to." She brushed off her jeans. "I've no qualms about using any advantage at my disposal."

Tito nudged Caden's elbow and smiled. "And I'm the one you're mad at?"

Caden didn't smile back. "I expect better from you."

Once inside, the girls went to visit the bathroom. Tito leaned against locker twelve-three while Caden wiped down unlucky locker twelve-four. "Brynne and I will distract everyone at lunch," Tito said.

"How?" Caden grabbed his reading book. Another pink note fell out.

"Don't know yet. I'm thinking it'll involve magic." Tito bent down and picked up the note. "What's this, bro?"

Caden motioned to the neat stack of pink notes in his locker. "More trash. Someone keeps dirtying up my locker. I suspect it's Derek."

"Huh," Tito said, and held up the note. There was writing on the outside this time. "It's pink and it says 'PLEASE READ ME.' Sounds too polite for Derek."

The first bell, the warning bell, rang. If the note wasn't meant as an annoyance, Caden was curious. "What does it say?"

Tito unfolded it. "It's a heart with your name in the middle. Below it, it says 'Do you like me? Circle yes, no, or maybe.' Signed, Emma A."

Caden considered. "I don't know Emma A," he said. "Circle maybe."

Tito reached into his bag and pulled out his purple pen. "She's a sixth grader." He used the locker door as a desk. He circled the word with the *m* and *a*. Then Tito wrote something on the note.

"What did you write?"

"That you like someone else, but if you change your mind, you'll let her know." He handed it back to Caden.

"I don't like someone else."

"Get Tonya to give it to her," Tito said, ignoring him. "What is it with you and the sixth graders, anyway? They all seem to like you."

"My allies Ward and Tonya are in the sixth grade. They are an honorable group."

"Well, the seventh graders don't like you much at all. But we have to put up with you half of the day, so we know you better," Tito said.

"Nonsense," Caden said. "They like me. They just don't know it yet."

Derek walked up then. He stuck his hands in his pockets and fidgeted.

Tito glared at him. "What do you want?"

Derek leaned closer. "Mr. Rathis keeps calling my mom." He spoke near a whisper. "I thought he just wanted free legal advice, but Saturday he took her out to dinner. Do you think I should be worried about her?"

Indeed, Derek had once seen Rath Dunn threaten

Caden with his dagger. He knew Rath Dunn's true nature. He had reason to be afraid. "There is none more dangerous than Rath Dunn," Caden said. "You should be very worried. Be careful."

Derek looked pale. "My mom likes him."

Tito glanced at his cell. "We've got to get to class."

Caden peered at Derek. "We are trying to expose him." Then Caden thought of something else. "What type of advice did he want?"

Derek took his hands from his pockets. He crossed and uncrossed his arms. "He wanted my mom to look at his employment contract."

Caden turned to Tito. "Why would he have a lawyer look at that?"

Tito frowned. "To try to get around it?"

"Mom's great at finding loopholes in contracts."

"Try to keep her away from him," Caden said. "Do whatever you have to do."

"Yeah," Derek said, and squeezed his hand into a fist. "That's what I was afraid of."

After Derek left, Caden said, "His mother has been annoying Ms. Primrose again."

"Yeah," Tito said. "She wrote one of those letters, too."

"Rath Dunn is using her." As Caden turned for his class, he squared his shoulders and looked at Tito. Better to part ways with forgiveness. "Also, I've decided not to be mad at you."

"Great," Tito said.

"But only because I may die tomorrow."

Tito scrunched up his face. His expression became shrewd. "Bro, don't die tomorrow. For that matter, don't die today, either. That's an order."

BLOODRED NAILS

In Caden's morning literacy class, Mr. McDonald seemed to have taken Ms. Primrose's warning that they needed to learn something seriously. He tried to engage them, but no one was in a good mood. Ward scowled at Mr. McDonald. Tonya stared at her lap.

"You kids need to be good this week," Mr. McDonald said, but he'd abandoned them in the bee swarm. Such cowardice was hard to forgive.

Caden's computer flashed words, but he wasn't paying attention. His mind kept wandering. It was Monday. He'd but a day left to complete the quest. He was cursed. And one of his brothers was a traitor.

It was the last thought that he couldn't quite believe. He thought about the last time he'd seen Valon and Maden. It was the day before their father, King Axel, had sent Caden away in the middle of the night.

* * *

The snows had been heavier than usual, the temperature colder. The castle was draped in dark silks. It was six months since Chadwin's death. Since then, their father had been more distant than usual. He spent most of the days in the gardens staring at the frosted tulips and ice shrubs, or in his private room in the Western Tower.

First-born Valon and second-born Maden practiced indoors in the fifth training room. It was the largest of the ten training rooms, and the most ornate, with a vast domed ceiling and a floor tiled in marble. Three open balconies overlooked the practice area. Caden watched them from the second one.

Seventh-born Jasan stood to the side of the practice area, where the white marble switched to a dark stone border. His arms were crossed and his expression grim. In the center of the floor, first-born Valon and second-born Maden faced each other.

Valon was tall and lean. He held himself with the same gravity as their father. In one hand, he grasped a long sword. Its hilt was embedded with star sapphires and its blade looked sharp like a dragon's tooth. He clutched a ruby-encrusted dagger in the other. Gifted in leadership, he always moved with intent.

Three strides from him, Maden held a two-handed broadsword. It was massive and Caden doubted any of his other brothers could have lifted it. Maden swung it with ease.

Valon dodged, then countered. They broke apart and stared at each other.

"You should know your place," Valon said, and he smiled a king's smile.

Maden smiled back at him and charged. "You won't win this time."

Clang, clang, clang.

Jasan watched from the side. He seemed distraught.

Valon's and Maden's weapons clashed again. Had Caden not known better, he'd have thought it a real fight, not a practice. From across the balcony, Caden sensed movement. He saw their father peering down from the other side. He looked from Valon to Maden, then to Jasan.

Had the king known then that one of them had betrayed Chadwin? He'd sent Caden away that very night. Had it truly been to protect him? Maybe he'd just wanted Caden out of the way.

"Hey, pay attention," Mr. McDonald said. He reached over and tapped Caden's computer screen. "Stop daydreaming and read it, Caden."

Both orders. Caden paid attention. He looked at the computer. A brown mare was pictured above the words. The meaning took a moment to come. "The . . . horse . . ." Caden started. "Horse" was a word he liked. It made him think of Sir Horace. The computer voice was in a kindly mood today. "The horse runs."

He beamed and smiled at Tonya. "I read a sentence," he said.

She blushed behind her glasses. "G-good."

"I guess you are getting better," Mr. McDonald said. "Try the next one." Caden did as he was ordered for the rest of class.

At the changing bell, Mr. McDonald pointed Caden toward the front door. "Meet on the front lawn for your science class. Mrs. Belle is taking you on a nature hike."

It was shocking how much warmer it was outside. The air smelled of earth. Some of the students leaned against the small retaining wall. Derek caught Caden's gaze. He looked like he wanted to say something, but turned away when his friends walked up.

Mrs. Belle beckoned them with her bloodred fingernails. The one on the fourth finger was shorter than the rest. Perhaps a bit shinier, too. As if it had been filed and repainted. "This way, people," she said.

Caden had found a fingernail backstage. Mrs. Belle might be as guilty as Mr. Creedly, Ms. Jackson, and the others.

Brynne nudged Caden's shoulder. Her eyes were bright with mischief. She looked like she could hardly contain her excitement. "It's almost lunch," she whispered as Mrs. Belle took them around the building. "Tito and I will distract them."

"And Jane and I will seek evidence," Caden said.

"That's the plan," Tito said.

They walked past the auditorium. A small crack meandered up one wall. Caden touched it and it felt hot. Odd.

"Caden, come along," Mrs. Belle said. "There's nature to discover."

He did as told. The trees and grass on the slope were now black and rotted like the dead forest farther down. Jane stopped and stared at the trees. "Is this what Ms. Jackson did to my mother?"

How could Caden answer that? Jane's mother had fallen prey to the lunch witch. Burned-out husks and brittle bodies were all such dark magic left. Still, none of them had been there when Jane's mother had been taken. "I don't know," he said.

For the briefest moment, Jane seemed near tears.

Tito put his arm around her shoulder. "You were asleep when they took you, and you didn't feel anything." His words didn't really seem to make Jane feel better. "So, you know. No suffering, right?"

"She'll regret what she did to my mom," Jane said.

Mrs. Belle made them gather around a particularly rotten-looking oak trunk. It seemed to Caden the only nature they were discovering was grimy dead things.

Near the oak's roots, she dug into the ground with her red nails. On closer inspection, one of them had definitely been recently broken. Within moments, she unearthed beetles with shiny blue backs. "Even among rot, life finds a way. And it's important to understand the insect world. People often underestimate its value." She brushed dirt off her wrinkled skirt. "When we understand, " she said, "we can team up with it. Exploit it."

Was she thinking of Mr. Creedly when she said it? From what Caden had overheard in the blown-up science room, he suspected it was so. He caught his friends' gazes. If Mrs. Belle was allied with Mr. Creedly, did that mean she was against Rath Dunn, Mr. Bellows, and Ms. Jackson?

After the lesson, they trudged back toward the school and the cafeteria. Caden lingered near Mrs. Belle. He needed to know how she was involved. "Mr. Creedly caused the bee swarm," he said.

Mrs. Belle tripped on the grass. "What makes you say that, Caden? That was deemed an accident. It's springtime, you know. Nature and hormones are abuzz."

"I found your broken red fingernail backstage soon after."

The class walked up the hill, but she stopped and turned to face him. "Red is a very popular color. What makes you think it's mine?"

"I think you helped him," Caden said. "Why?"

She started walking fast up the hill. "I don't know what you could mean."

"Tonya was targeted. So was I."

She stopped and smiled sweetly. "You're both fine."

They'd survived due to luck and a magical whisk. It

wasn't that he expected Mrs. Belle to be on his side, but she'd been nice to him, then she'd helped a monster. Caden felt his blood boil. Betrayal. That's what he felt. His life seemed full of that right now.

Caden had to find out what she knew. He only had a day left. "You helped Mr. Creedly sabotage the spelling bee. Admit it."

"Caden . . ."

"Tell me why or I'll show Ms. Primrose the fingernail. She wants someone to eat. I bet I could convince her that you'd be a satisfying dinner. Are you feuding with Rath Dunn or Mr. Bellows? Did you endanger countless innocent people to make them look bad? Tell me or else."

The breeze blew down the hill. Mrs. Belle stared at him. "Calm down," she said.

It was an order, but no order could change his emotions. Still, he tried to quell his temper. "Just tell me why."

"Fine. But quiet." She laughed nervously and too loudly, then waved to the other students like nothing was amiss. "Look, I like it here. I like teaching. They destroyed my room and tried to blame me." The rest of the class was almost to the building. "So we ruined their little spelling bee. Like the gas accident, nothing can be proven."

"But why did they attack your room?"

"They know I'm loyal to Ms. Primrose. Only the foolish and brash wouldn't be."

"You're on opposite sides," Caden said.

"I'd rather serve Ms. Primrose than Rath Dunn or Ms. Jackson. That's all. Several of us feel that way. None more than Mr. Creedly." She glanced at Caden. "But as you've discovered, Mr. Creedly is jealous of you. So be careful."

So the teachers were split. There were those loyal to Ms. Primrose and those loyal to Rath Dunn, and it was those loyal to Rath Dunn who had caused the gas explosion. Those loyal to Ms. Primrose had caused the swarm in retaliation.

There was a mutiny brewing among the teachers. The villains were destroying the school. He just needed more proof. He needed evidence that damned Ms. Jackson and Rath Dunn.

Mrs. Belle touched one of her bloodred nails to his hand. "I'm sorry. I didn't want you or any of the students hurt in the swarm."

He held her gaze. "Yet you did nothing to help me."

She said nothing. There was nothing she could say. They walked up the hill in silence.

21

FLYING CORNISH HENS

The cafeteria smelled like baking breads and spring vegetables, and nothing of the mayhem Caden knew Brynne intended to bring. One wall of the cafeteria was carved from the mountain. It was granite, roughhewn, and speckled with flecks of gold-colored mica. Across from it, large windows overlooked the downslope of the hill. Last week, there had been oaks with new leaves and blooming cherry and dogwood trees.

Now, the trees were black, the grass sickly. Caden turned from the eerie sight and ran his hand over the wall made from the mountain. It felt cool and solid. Unlike the auditorium stones, which were oddly warm. Under the background noise, he heard something low and rumbling like thunder—or maybe like a dragon's growling stomach.

Ms. Jackson stood behind the serving line. Her skin

and hair glowed with health. Her dark eyes sparkled. She scooped locally grown collard greens. Truly, the lunch witch was evil. Rath Dunn stood beside her serving squash risotto and Cornish hens.

"Oh, the distraction I've got planned," Brynne said. She was happiest when she was about to cause trouble. "Are you ready?"

"Yep," Tito said.

Jane had returned to her stoic, confident self. If she didn't burn herself out enchanting kitchen utensils and office supplies, she had a good future as an Elite Paladin. "I am," she said.

No one had asked, but Caden was also ready. He and Jane waited by the side of the serving line, near the wide doorway that led into the kitchen proper. A partial wall hid most of the cooking area from the front.

Caden watched as Tito plopped down at their usual table. Brynne slid into the chair beside him. She slyly motioned to Mr. Bellows at the teachers' table. He'd been foolish to glue her hair to her chair. With a flick of her finger, his tray slammed into the ceiling. Risotto rained down. The small cooked bird splatted onto his head.

Almost every student and teacher in the cafeteria looked at Mr. Bellows. The table of sixth graders who always waved at Caden lost their trays next.

Rath Dunn walked out from the serving area. He dodged a flying cooked bird. "What is this?" Ms. Jackson stepped out as well. She didn't dodge the risotto pummeling her face.

Jane gave Caden a thumbs-up sign. Unlike in the Greater Realm, where it was an obscene gesture, in Asheville it meant "well done." Still, Caden didn't give Jane a thumbs-up back.

Instead, he whispered, "Let's go."

They darted past the serving counter and ducked behind the partial wall. The counters were metal, open, shining, and clean. The floors were without crumbs. In the science room, Brynne had found runes under the countertop. Caden leaned forward and looked at the underside of the counter. He tilted his head.

There was nothing.

Squeals and laughter came from the eating area.

Jane was crouched near the spoons and spatulas. Caden motioned to himself and to her, then pointed to the back area where there was a large refrigerator and pantry. Jane signaled for him to wait.

She reached in her shirt and pulled out her enchanted ladle. With an expression like wrath, she switched it with the one Ms. Jackson used for chicken soups, spaghettis, and other witchy brews.

Caden raised a brow.

Jane scooted over to him. "You'll see."

Whatever Rath Dunn and Ms. Jackson were up to, whatever they had plotted while leaving the city limits for their farm-fresh food, it appeared they wanted the school involved. They wanted it to happen here. There had to be evidence in the cafeteria. This kitchen was the witch's lair.

The plants had died recently. If she'd been casting spells, there should be evidence.

Caden peeked into the pantry. It was filled with breads, fruits, and vegetables. Evil or not, Caden had to appreciate Ms. Jackson's housekeeping and healthy foods.

Jane opened the refrigerator. Her face lit up. "Gross things," she said.

Caden looked inside, too. The shelves were filled with dead birds wrapped in plastic and rodents in ziplock bags. There were stacked tubs of grasshoppers, flies, and tofu. In the back, there were jars containing hearts and intestines.

"Spell ingredients?" he said. Maybe Brynne would know their purposes. However, according to Rosa, Ashevillians didn't eat dog, cat, or rodent; they didn't allow the gross things on these shelves in their restaurants. If that was true, he was certain they wouldn't be allowed in the school.

He considered the criteria of his quest. Ms. Primrose had said three things:

"Find the one responsible." Caden knew those responsible.

"Bring me Ashevillian evidence of their misdeeds." This was a misdeed and it was by one of those responsible for the science accident.

"Give me something I can act upon." Ms. Primrose could act on dead rodents in the school refrigerator. It might not have been her intent, she might not even care about the bugs and birds on the shelves, but it would satisfy the criteria she'd set. At least, Caden hoped it would.

He felt rising pride. This might work. Caden pulled out his phone. He took pictures of the gross things. When he opened the freezer, the light inside was off and the phone's camera flashed.

"Let's go," he said.

"Wait." Jane grabbed his wrist. "Do that again."

As it was an order, Caden waited and took another picture. Then he saw what Jane had seen. There was writing on the inside of the refrigerator. It was only visible under the white light of the flash. So there were runes here, hidden just like those in the science room.

The more evidence, the better. Caden turned, set the flash to on, and took pictures everywhere he could. The flash also illuminated runes on the shiny counters and floors that they hadn't seen before.

He froze. There, in the middle of the counter, he saw something that wasn't a rune. It was a word, written in Ashevillian letters. This could be Ashevillian proof. Carefully, he put the letters together in his head. He sounded out the word. And then his blood went cold.

It was a name.

Maden.

22

THE ORDERS OF ENEMIES

He reached out and traced the counter. Like the auditorium wall, there was a strange heat emanating from it. He felt frozen.

"Caden," Jane said. "We have to go."

He blinked at her. "Yes." They could decipher everything later.

"No more time," she said, and pulled him toward the doorway.

They collided with Ms. Jackson at the edge of the cafeteria proper. She had clumps of rice and squash in her hair. It seemed Brynne's distraction had worked. "What are you doing?" she said. "Get out of my kitchen."

An order. Caden stepped out.

Jane followed him. "Sorry, Ms. Jackson," she said, though she didn't sound it.

The cafeteria was not the orderly eating area he'd left. Half the tables were flipped over. Rice oozed down the rock wall. Mr. Bellows still had a bird on his head. Perhaps he was considering reanimating it. Mrs. Belle was a risotto-covered lump with bloodred fingernails. Derek had squash sticking out of his ear. For her part, Brynne was sitting in the middle of it all, spotless and smiling. She winked at Caden.

Rath Dunn was in the middle of the chaos like a red wolf in a field of cooked bird and white rice. His voice boomed through the cafeteria. "What is this school coming to these days?" There was a gleeful edge to his voice. "Students, get to your tables. Turn them upright. Sit. Now, people. I've had enough."

Both orders. Caden hurried to his usual table, sliding on squashed squash. Jane followed close behind.

Rath Dunn stalked over toward them. He leaned over Brynne. "This, young lady," he said as he waved over the destruction, "might help me. Throwing food is still against the rules, though. I'm going to have to give you detention. Good thing, too. I've been needing to see you alone."

Her smile faltered. "I was sitting here the whole time," Brynne squeaked out. "I threw no food."

"It was magic," Rath Dunn growled. "Mind magic, the magic of a sorceress. Don't play dumb with me," he said. "I'll teach you a lesson come this afternoon." Then a slow smile crept across his face. "Or we could see what

Ms. Primrose says. She might have tougher, toothier consequences in mind." He leaned down and spoke right in Brynne's ear. "First I need that hair, though. If you're good, I'll leave you your scalp."

Brynne turned the color of day-old snow. She smoothed her hair over her shoulder and clenched her fist around it. "Stay away from my hair," she said.

But she needn't be scared, Caden realized. He cleared his throat. "You're mistaken."

Slowly, Rath Dunn turned toward him. "You'll get your lesson soon enough, boy. And it will be painful."

No. It would be Rath Dunn who would learn a lesson. His ritual magic master would soon be on Ms. Primrose's dragon-sized plate. Also, the quest had taught Caden something. Ms. Primrose could only punish those who broke the school rules. He doubted there were school rules against telekinesis magic. Magic was myth to the locals.

"She's done nothing punishable," he said. "There are no rules against magic here. Magic is as unknown as ritual science sabotage. Ms. Primrose can't do anything if there is no Ashevillian evidence that Brynne's done something wrong."

Rath Dunn stroked his beard, then laughed as if it were the funniest thing he'd heard all day. Truly, he seemed in an alarmingly good mood. "I suppose I'll let it slide this time. I'll catch you four in class."

Jane made sure Rath Dunn was out of earshot before she spoke. "We found something."

Caden snuck his phone from his pocket and held it under the table between him and Brynne. He showed her the pictures of the refrigerator contents. Then the runes.

"What do you think?" he said.

"Ritual magic."

"I know."

"More than one spell."

"I know," Caden said. "I'll use the pictures to prove misdeeds."

Jane and Tito leaned forward. Brynne glanced around to make sure none of the teachers were looking, then took his phone and held it near her lap. She flipped through the pictures again, pausing on the one of refrigerator ingredients and again on the one with the name.

Caden's heart was in his throat. "What do you think it means?" he said.

Brynne frowned at the phone, then snuck it back to him. "There's a name," she said. She twisted her hands together under the table. "Maden."

Caden fidgeted. If his brother's name was part of a spell, that meant he was in danger. Maybe Maden was the next member of his family to be pulled from the Greater Realm to the happy Land of Shadow. Maybe they needed something from him for Rath Dunn's spell. Or maybe they'd curse or kill him. His name in the kitchen could mean many things. "Is my brother Maden being targeted?"

Jane and Tito exchanged a glance.

Brynne took a deep breath. "I don't know that much

about ritual magic. It's not my specialty, prince."

"You know enough," Caden said. "Tell me."

"On the counter, there are runes for 'roots.' Roots in the Greater Realm are thought to grow from one land to another. They are said to connect distant places. And it seems likely the dead plants were used to fuel the spell. Combined with the ingredients in the refrigerator, it could be a spell of complicity." She looked down. "We've suspected Rath Dunn was in contact with someone. This could be how. Dark magic for a dark goal."

Caden felt strangely numb. "You think he is communicating with someone about Maden?"

"No, prince. I think it is Maden he is communicating with."

Caden stared at her. "Maybe you're wrong," he said.

"Maybe," she said softly. "But it's a rare occurrence."

Caden wanted to argue. He stared at a cooked hen on the floor and resisted the urge to start cleaning.

Once, while teaching, Rath Dunn had spoken of Occam's razor. It wasn't an enchanted shaving device. It was the idea that the simple answer was often the best. Or worst, it seemed to Caden, in the case of his brother.

Maden was second born. Unlike eighth-born Caden, he was only one brother away from the throne. Maybe sixth-born Chadwin, agile of body and mind, had suspected Maden had ambitions and had gotten in the way of them? And if Maden was communicating with Rath Dunn, first-born Valon, all of Caden's brothers, and his father would be in great danger.

But why? Rath Dunn had tried to subjugate Razzon, subjugate the Greater Realm as a whole. His campaign left scars on the Springlands and Winterlands, his terror stretched as far as the turning deserts of the Summerlands. Maden had fought against Rath Dunn in that war. He'd fought with their brothers. Why would he now work with Rath Dunn? And how could he have blamed Jasan, who, while surly, had done nothing wrong?

Did they want to conquer the realm together, then try to kill each other for the throne? Was Maden capable of that? Maybe it was a mistake. Maybe the name and spell didn't mean what they suspected. Ritual magic, after all, wasn't Brynne's specialty.

Could Maden truly be the traitor?

Before long, the villainous teachers ordered everyone to clean up and prepare for their afternoon classes. Caden told his friends he'd meet them in math. He ducked between two rows of pale pink lockers. When he was certain no one was watching, he pulled his phone from his pocket, shielded it, and looked at the name on the counter once more.

Once, when Caden was very small, Maden had carried him on his shoulders. Neither Jasan nor Valon nor any of the others had done that. Not even Chadwin had done that. Even then, Caden could tell Maden was strong. Gifts were said to emphasize and reflect a person's natural predilections.

Caden reconsidered his family's gifts. His father was gifted in resolution. His will was iron; he was determined and steadfast. If Caden was honest, and he always was, his father was also unyielding when there was no reason for him to be so. He could be relentless. Not always in a good way.

First-born Valon, gifted with leadership, could be unbearably domineering.

Second-born Maden, gifted in strength, was strong of body, strong of will. He was ambitious. Had he also become power mad?

Perhaps the gifts reflected not only virtues but also vices.

Third-born Lucian was stealthy but also sneaky, fourth-born Martin had accuracy but was a terrible perfectionist, fifth-born Landon was gifted with fortitude yet was stubborn. Sixth-born Chadwin had been agile in mind and body. He'd also been indecisive. And Jasan was quick in all things, including his temper.

Caden, eighth born, was gifted in speech. As far as he knew, it had no dark side.

He put the phone in his pocket and pushed away thoughts of Maden and the Greater Realm. If he gave Ms. Primrose the evidence, it would surely put his brother Maden in danger. It would implicate him in Rath Dunn's evil plans.

But a prince must always complete his quest.

Before the math bell rang, he needed to see Ms. Primrose. She'd not been in the halls lately, but the school had been colder than usual. Students kept hearing rumbling like thunder, but they'd heard it when there were no storm clouds. He feared she would eat someone, anyone, soon. He hurried down the long hall.

Despite his despair, he also felt a glimmer of pride. Not only was he going to complete the quest, he was going to do it a day early. At the end of the hall, Mr. Creedly sat behind his mahogany desk. When he saw Caden, he stretched up and sneered.

"You are foolish, young one, to venture near me," he said.

Caden stayed beyond his reach. He stayed beyond the reach of the shadows on the walls behind him also. Mr. Creedly and his swarm wouldn't attack during school hours. At least, Caden didn't think he would. The oak door to Ms. Primrose's office was closed. "I must speak to her," Caden said. "She's waiting for me."

"She isn't."

"She is. Let me in."

Mr. Creedly cocked his head. "She's not here today," he hissed. "She's talking to parents. Away. Downtown." He took a step closer to Caden. "You can't see her."

Perhaps it was time for Caden to smartly run away. He moved back. "When will she return?"

Mr. Creedly slunk closer. The shadows behind him

lengthened. He paused to check the planner on his desk. "Tomorrow," he said, and stretched ever closer.

With a nod, Caden turned and sprinted back down the long hall.

He made it safely to unlucky locker twelve-four. As he reached for his math book, the blood-dagger wound on his arm started to throb. A moment later, Rath Dunn grabbed his arm and pushed him back against his locker. It made a noticeable bang.

Two girls from Caden's science class stood nearby. One, Victoria, with blond hair and tanned skin, gasped. The second, Tamera, with chin-length dark hair and medium brown skin, reached into her pocket as if to pull out a cell phone.

Rath Dunn peered at them. "Nothing to see here, ladies," he said in a low growl. "And if that's a cell phone, Tamera, it'll mean detention."

Caden smiled at them. "I'm okay," he said.

They inched away and whispered to themselves.

"For now," Rath Dunn said. He spoke harshly in his ear. "I need to speak with you alone. You see, boy, I've decided to make you one more offer. Well," he said, and sighed dramatically. "Your brother insisted. He wants me to woo you to our side. Thinks you're malleable."

"I belong to the side of the righteous."

"Yes, you're hopeless. That's been established." He raised his other arm and put it over his heart. "But a deal is a deal. And I agreed to try. You should be happy. He only wants you dead if necessary." He leaned closer. "Now, listen, son of Axel."

It was an order. Caden had no choice but to listen, his heart pounding.

"Here's the deal." He knew Caden would not agree to any deal. "I still need that sorceress's hair. She trusts you. Tell no one." An order. "Bring me the sorceress's braid. Cut it near her neck."

A weird tingling shot through Caden's arms and fingers. Oh, no. Those were orders, too.

"That is, unless you want me to do it. I can't promise not to take her scalp with her hair, however. Or even the head with the scalp." Rath Dunn raised his brows. "You look terrified," he said. "Finally. As you should." He released Caden and stepped away. "But do that, and I'll consider you useful. Maybe I'll even spare you some pain, once I'm in power." He leaned closer. "If not, well, you can't say I didn't offer, can you?" he said, and laughed as he let Caden go and walked away.

Caden stood stunned. Rath Dunn knew not what he'd just done. Truly, Caden was cursed. Three orders:

Tell no one.

Cut her hair near her neck.

Bring it to Rath Dunn.

If Rath Dunn didn't kill him, Brynne certainly would.

But even as he panicked, he knew he would obey.

23

WHAT CAN'T BE UNDONE

Caden tried to force himself to cut Brynne's hair in the middle of class and, later, at the kitchen table—both at times he expected someone would stop him. But he couldn't do it. It was as if doing so with assured failure was the same as disobeying. He tried to tell them, but found that the orders prevented him from doing that, too.

Rosa had made him his favorite Ashevillian meal: trout tacos. It had the uncomfortable feel of a last meal.

"You're not eating," she said.

"I'm not hungry."

Likely, Rosa thought his lack of appetite was because of his impending visit to the caseworker the next day. It was true that he was nervous about that. Now, however, he was more worried about what he might do to Brynne—and what Brynne would do to him if he succeeded and cut her hair. He looked across the table at her. He needed to warn her somehow.

Her hair hung loose around her shoulders. Here with Rosa and her friends, Brynne seemed to feel safe. But she wasn't, not tonight. When Caden kept staring, she arched her brows.

"Is my beauty blinding you?"

"Take care of your hair," he said.

Rosa's frown deepened. Likely, he was doing nothing to persuade her that he was sane. But the curse gave him no choice.

Caden leaned forward. "You must be careful, Brynne."

Tito was on taco number five. He leaned over and whispered, "Stop saying weird stuff."

"As you wish," Caden said.

"Caden," Rosa said gently, "is something wrong? You can tell me. I do want to help."

But he couldn't tell her. He couldn't tell any of them. "A kind offer. But I can't say what's wrong." His friends didn't even seem suspicious. They probably thought he couldn't speak because of Tito's order. He turned to his taco. A future Elite Paladin needed to keep a healthy diet, and he hadn't eaten much this week. Rosa wouldn't believe him anyway.

After dinner, while Rosa tinkered with her art, they sat on the porch. The air was cool, and there was an earthy smell in the evening mist. The half-moon hung low in the sky. Caden scowled at it.

He had to make the others understand. He tried mimicking something like hair cutting, but it seemed the closest he could do was sword form number three.

"It's too late to practice," Tito said.

It was never too late to practice, but that wasn't Caden's aim. "No," Caden said. He pointed to Brynne, then spelled out "C-A-R-E-F-U-L" on his phone. He showed the others.

Jane looked at it and smiled. "You spelled a word," she said.

He sat a little straighter. Perhaps spelling contests had some value after all. "Careful," he said.

Brynne seemed less impressed. "Careful? You're making even less sense than usual."

Caden couldn't say "I'm going to cut off your hair tonight and take it to Rath Dunn" although he felt most certainly that he was going to do so. "Rath Dunn still wants your hair. It's an ingredient in his spell."

"We already know that," Brynne said.

"You're in danger."

"I know. But you know who will be in real danger. The person who tries to cut my hair." She patted him on the shoulder. "Don't worry. Anyone trying will regret it."

Caden already regretted it. He got a paper and pen, but all he could write was "be vigilant" in the common tongue. It seemed writing and speaking both counted as telling.

Tito leaned forward. "Okay, weirdo, I order you to tell me what's wrong."

An order. But Rath Dunn had given him the order first, and as he had learned, the order given to him first was the one he must obey. The clearest Caden could communicate was "I'm worried for tomorrow."

"You have your proof," Brynne said. "It will be enough. All you have to do is get it to Ms. Primrose tomorrow." She smiled. "Then you and Prince Jasan will be saved."

"What you need to be worrying about now is the meeting with the caseworker," Tito said.

"There are more pressing matters."

"If you're hauled away, the other matters won't get solved, bro. Not by you, anyway."

Brynne stretched and looked at the sky. "I'm going to bed." She pointed to Caden. "You go to bed, too. You need to rest. Admit it, I'm right."

That was an order. It didn't seem Brynne, Tito, or Jane realized it. Caden got up to head to his bed. "You're right," he mumbled.

In one last-ditch effort before bed, he asked Sir Tito to tie his hands with the laces of his shoes. "Bro, no," Tito said. "Go to sleep already."

Caden went to sleep. He awoke in the middle of the night. Tito was sprawled across his bed, his eyes were shut, his face slack and peaceful. His purple quilt was in a wad at the corner of his bed.

Caden felt his rebellious legs swing out of the covers. He gripped the sheets until his fingers were numb. He had to stay in bed. He didn't. He got up.

As he passed Tito, he tried to knock the bed, hit the wall, slam the bathroom door. Do something to wake him. But his body wouldn't do as he wanted.

In the bathroom, he grabbed the sharp scissors he used to trim his hair every two weeks. Then he sneaked down the stairs. The creaky step didn't even creak.

The door to Rosa's room was open, and he heard her snoring. If he could just wake her somehow, she'd know something wasn't right. With all his willpower he tried to turn into her room. As soon as she awoke and saw the scissors, she'd stop him.

He didn't walk into her room. His feet turned. His hands quietly opened the door to the girls' room. It was dimly lit from a nightlight in the corner and the moon out the window. Brynne slept in the bottom bunk curled up like a wind cat. Jane was in the top, a small lump under the pink-and-white quilt. He tried to scream. To bang into the nightstand. He tried to stomp on the floor but ended up simply doing a light-footed dance. He'd trained with third-born Lucian in stealth. No matter how hard he tried, he made no sound.

The girls didn't wake.

Like usual, Brynne had braided her hair to sleep. It hung across her face. He crouched and willed her to awaken. She didn't. With three swift cuts, her braid was in his hand and he was creeping back upstairs.

He felt the deep heat of shame on his cheeks. Maybe

Brynne was right to like Jasan so much more than him. Jasan had saved Brynne's hair. Caden had cut it.

He tucked the hair in the pocket of his coat and climbed into bed. Tomorrow, he'd give Rath Dunn the hair. He looked at the half-moon shining from the window. Caden would help his enemy and his enemy would wonder why. If Rath Dunn figured his curse out, the next order might be to hurt Brynne or Jane or Tito. Or maybe he'd order Caden to collect Jasan's blood, and Jasan would be betrayed by yet another brother.

Caden awoke to screaming. He hadn't realized he'd fallen asleep. The hair. He jumped from bed and ran down the steps. He heard Tito run behind him. Rosa was out of her room, baseball bat in hand, nightgown crooked. She stood at the door to the girls' room.

"Brynne, calm down." That was Jane. "It . . . it doesn't look that bad." She did not sound convincing.

Caden stopped in the hall. Tito ran past him until he was standing beside Rosa. He looked into the room, then out at Caden, then back into the room. Tito creased his brow.

Brynne burst from the doorway. "My hair!" She was crying. Her hair frizzed in short strands. It was uneven and longer on the left than the right. "My hair . . ." She turned and saw Caden standing at the end of the hall. She knew at once. "You did this."

Everyone stared at him. Rosa's mouth was agape. Caden felt a flush fill his cheeks. It was his fault, but if Brynne hadn't cursed him, this never would have happened. He hadn't wanted to cut her hair. He would never hurt her. "I tried to warn you." Suddenly, he felt angry, too. "It's because you cursed me."

Brynne looked ready to tackle him.

Rosa grabbed Brynne by the shoulder to stop her, then made her take several deep breaths. With great care, she released her. "You're just as lovely with short hair," Rosa said. "You girls get dressed and wait for me downstairs. You too, Tito."

"I didn't have a choice," Caden said again. What use was it? Rosa wouldn't believe him.

Brynne hadn't moved. Rosa gently pushed her toward her room. "Get dressed," she said. She gave Jane and Tito pointed looks, and they ambled toward their respective rooms and day clothes. "You three have school." She hadn't included Caden in that.

Soon, Caden and Rosa were alone in the hall. "Did you cut Brynne's hair last night?"

"Tell no one." Caden frowned. "I can't say."

"What does that mean?"

"Nothing good."

Brynne opened her bedroom door and said, "I can't go to school like this."

"Brynne, you can't miss school. The awards ceremony

is today. We'll fix it." She motioned her back inside. "I need to talk to Caden."

She was going to take him to the nuthouse. He'd lose his friends and his horse. And if he didn't go to school today to give Ms. Primrose the evidence and complete his quest, he'd lose his life.

He felt his heart plummet.

Brynne took a shaky breath. Through gritted teeth, she said, "It's not his fault, not really. Please don't send him away." Brynne sometimes withheld information. She teased him and tormented him. But she would never truly let harm come to him. They were allies. They were friends. "It's . . . I cursed him. Someone must have ordered him. Rath Dunn, no doubt. Or Mr. Bellows." Her tone became scathing again. "He already tried to get my hair once. He'll regret that."

Rosa looked even more concerned.

While Caden appreciated Brynne finally admitting he was telling the truth, this wasn't the best time to do it. "You're doing nothing to convince her I'm a good influence," he said.

Brynne put her hands on her hips. "I'm trying to help you, prince."

Rosa looked at Caden. "Go get dressed, too, while I figure out what to do with you."

An order. "As you wish."

Tito was dressed and pacing the attic room. "What the

crap, Caden?" he said. "Rosa will send you away for sure now. How did this happen?"

"I can't say."

Rosa called for Tito. She probably didn't want him alone with Caden, lest Tito start talking about tyrants and witches, too. Tito turned toward the steps. "Be there in a minute."

Caden sat on the bed. The hair was tucked in his coat pocket. "Bring it to me." The order was like a physical pull. He couldn't let anyone keep him from the school today.

From under the bed, he saw the edge of the escape rope. The pull of compliance was strong. He had to get to the school before he was carted away to the Ashevillian nuthouse.

He chose the blue T-shirt with pictures of snowflakes. It reminded him of home. In the mountains of the Winterlands, there was always snow. Asheville was turning warm. There hadn't been snow in weeks. Perhaps the flakes on his shirt would give him luck. He pulled on his coat, his cell phone and magic paper clips in one pocket, his compass and Brynne's hair in the other. Hot or not, he would wear it.

Tito watched him. "What's going on?"

"I told you, I can't say."

Tito frowned. "Don't do it."

Like before, Tito's order seemed to have no precedence over the earlier one. "I'm going to do what I'm going to do."

Of that, Caden was certain.

"Okay. I order you not to do it."

"It doesn't work that way." How Caden wished it did. "You know whatever order I get first, I have to follow. Especially if it's from someone of higher rank."

Tito walked back and forth across the room. He seemed to be thinking hard. "Yeah, okay," he said. He was sharp. Surely, he'd guessed what was happening with Brynne's magical locks, whose order Caden was following.

"And you know what I'm about to do," Caden said.

"Based on Brynne's new hairdo, I can guess." Tito looked worried. "I could try to stop you," he said.

Caden wasn't sure if that would work. "I feel like I'd fight you on that." As good as Tito was with training, as much natural talent as he possessed, Caden still had years of experience on him. Years where he'd trained with brothers gifted in leadership, strength, stealth, accuracy, fortitude, agility, and speed. "I feel like I'd win."

Despite Tito's worry, he snorted at that. "Yeah, you just keep telling yourself that, Your Smugness."

"I feel like I'd win," Caden said again. He grabbed the escape rope. "I feel like I'd win." With exasperation, he turned to Tito and gave him a look. "I feel like I'd win."

"You can stop now."

Caden stopped. He placed his hand on Tito's shoulder. After stealing Brynne's braid, Caden had spent the night in fitful dreams. But he'd also come up with a plan, one that might help them on this dark day. He might have no choice but to give Rath Dunn the hair, but maybe he could use it to his advantage.

"I've an idea," Caden said, and he sounded more confident than he felt. "It should work."

Rosa called for Tito once more. She seemed impatient.

"I'll be right there!" Tito yelled down. He turned back to Caden and peered at the escape rope near Caden's boot. "You're going to bolt."

"Bolt" was Ashevillian slang for "run." And, yes, that was the exact thing Caden was going to do. "I'm going to the school. Look for me there."

Tito shook his head. "Nah," he said. "I'll come with you."

"That's a bad idea."

"You sure about that?"

Caden was sure. "Rosa will be beyond worried if you run away with me," he said as he lowered the rope out the window.

"Bro, she's beyond worried already."

"Then help me by distracting her."

Tito grabbed his phone. He texted someone—Jane, it seemed. "I told her to stall Rosa, but that won't last long." He frowned his lopsided frown. "Are you sure I shouldn't come with you?"

"For now," Caden said, "it would raise suspicions. Trust me."

As soon as he said it, Caden realized how much he wanted someone to actually trust him, for someone to believe he could handle himself. To believe in him.

Tito hesitated. "Okay."

"Okay?"

"Yeah, weirdo, okay. I trust you." Tito took a deep breath. "Look, meet me right after you get done doing this thing you can't tell me about. We'll come up with a plan. Rosa will be looking for you, and trust me, she won't let you out of her sight again."

"Where?"

Tito took a breath. "Outside, behind the auditorium. I'll get there as soon as I can. And don't talk to anyone until you get there. Go immediately after you do the thing. Those are orders."

And they were good ones. Truly, Tito would make a formidable Elite Paladin. Caden would have to leave as soon as he gave Rath Dunn the hair. He would be able to escape the tyrant's power.

"Then I'll go with you to talk to Ms. Primrose, bro."

"There's a chance my evidence won't satisfy her." Caden held Tito's gaze. "It will be dangerous."

"Bro," Tito said, "as future Elite Paladins, isn't danger our middle name?"

"My middle name is Axelochson. It means eighth son of Axel." He made sure his compass, enchanted paper clips, and cell phone were secure. "But we do face danger with courage." There was, however, one thing Tito did fear more than all others. "What about Rosa?"

Tito stared down at his sneakers. "Maybe she'll understand one day?"

That was a big maybe. But there were terrible things afoot. Stopping them was more important than having a warm bed and loving mother. "You are a true friend, Sir Tito."

"You've got that right," Tito said.

Three minutes later, Caden scaled down the side of the house. It was early. The sun wasn't even over the mountains yet. As such, he used his compass to navigate through the woods to Sir Horace's horse prison. He crouched at the edge of the trees and whistled. Within moments, Sir Horace was leaping the fence, a magnificent gray-and-white athlete.

Caden reached the school before most other students. The blackened roses looked particularly ominous in the deserted early morning. This day, the school looked like a tomb. Sir Horace bucked as they approached, spooked by the dark magic and dead trees.

"It is important that you wait here for me," Caden said. "If I don't return, take care of Brynne and the others. Continue to fight."

Sir Horace nudged his cheek.

Soon after, Caden pushed the double doors at the entrance.

As expected, Rath Dunn was in the math room. He

had his back to Caden. In red marker, he'd written problem after problem on the whiteboard until it looked as if it was dripping blood. Obviously, he was preparing to torture his first-period class.

Caden aligned his posture. He focused on the back of Rath Dunn's head.

"And what might you want?" Rath Dunn said without turning.

Caden had to bring Rath Dunn the hair. The pull of compulsion was like an energy moving his body. He had to obey, and he had to do it this morning to satisfy the curse. No one would be able to stop him and save him now. He was here. He was going to give him the hair. But with the objective certain, Caden could speak before he handed Rath Dunn the hair. Rath Dunn hadn't said, "Bring me the hair immediately." The other students wouldn't enter until the warning bell rang. Until then, until others found Caden, he could keep the hair.

Rath Dunn called the order a deal. Hair in exchange for his good favor. In exchange for not killing him.

The thing about Rath Dunn was he liked making deals. He liked talking and deceiving. He foolishly believed he couldn't be outwitted. That was his mistake. No one should be underestimated. Especially Caden.

"I've come for the deal," Caden said, although he doubted Rath Dunn understood that he had actually completed his end of it.

Rath Dunn turned and looked suitably suspicious. The scar across his face pulled at his mouth as he peered at Caden. "This is unexpected. You want to join me?"

"I'd never join you." Caden let some of his anger show. "But I don't want you hurting Brynne for her braid." That was absolutely true. "And I need to know something." Also true. "Tell me, and I'll give you the hair."

Caden could feel the curse pressing down on him. The old clock on the wall was three ticks from the warning bell. When it reached it, when students entered, Caden knew he'd be compelled to hand over the hair.

Rath Dunn was unhurried. "You'll cut your little sorceress's hair in exchange for information? Really, boy?"

"It's only hair."

Rath Dunn peered at him. Then he grinned like a wolf. When he spoke next, he sounded amused. Well, Rath Dunn did enjoy games. "What is it you want to know?"

A minute had passed. Two ticks left.

Caden reached into his coat. He didn't grab the hair—he could resist a bit longer—but squeezed his phone instead. He started the record app. "You and my second-born brother, Maden, are communicating. Why?"

Rath Dunn wore the slightly impressed look he had when Tito or Brynne or Derek answered a particularly difficult problem in class. But there was nothing in his reaction to Maden's name to suggest Caden was wrong.

So that was it. Maden was the traitor.

Caden's breath caught. Despite the evidence, he'd still expected to find out he was wrong, that it wasn't one of his brothers who had turned traitor. Rath Dunn's casual acceptance seemed to make it real.

"I tell you, and you cut her hair?" Rath Dunn said. He was definitely amused now.

Caden knew exactly what to say to that. "I cut her hair." Matter of point, he had, and it was in his pocket.

Rath Dunn's eyes took on a greedy glint. His smile could have frightened a fear wraith. "Why not?" he said. "After all, it's too late to stop me, son of Axel."

Rath Dunn leaned back against a front-row desk. Jane's desk. "I am communicating with Maden," he said, "to shatter the boundary between worlds. Perhaps you'll get to see your homeland again before I burn it to ashes."

Was this the purpose of the spell ingredients? Ritual magic required sacrifice. What type of destruction would a spell like that wreak? It would kill more than plants. That Caden didn't doubt. And maybe more. Caden didn't want to get home like that. "With ritual magic?"

"Well, I do have a ritual magic master in my sway, and a city of unwitting sacrifices for such a spell," Rath Dunn said. "And Maden has an equivalent across the realm."

He intended to destroy the city, to kill its inhabitants— to sacrifice Asheville—to get home. And Maden planned the same on the other side. Caden stood speechless.

"There are many who would follow Maden."

Caden's fingers were beginning to tingle. The curse would demand he hand over the braid soon. "It is first-born Valon who is gifted in leadership."

"Some follow charisma, others follow strength." He gave Caden an appraising look. "Some will even follow charm."

A second minute had passed. There was but a minute left. "But why destroy the science room? What does that have to do with spells and kings and realms?"

"Is that part of our deal?"

"You want the hair," Caden said. "Tell me."

Rath Dunn leaned into Caden's space. Caden leaned back. He felt his coat smear the red numbers and letters and grimaced at the thought of his coat's embroidered Winterbird pushed against the mess. "This city needs to see this school's poorly run."

"Ms. Primrose won't like that."

"Then she should control her school. Or be replaced with someone who can."

Rath Dunn wanted Ms. Primrose replaced? If he caused it without breaking her rules, would she not be able to stop him or punish him?

Rath Dunn had collected complaints. He'd encouraged the feud between the teachers. He'd set up evidence that there was negligence. And he'd had Derek's lawyer mother look over his employee contract. These were the things that Caden knew about. No telling what else Rath Dunn had done.

Students were waiting outside the door now. Hapless souls who didn't know their instructor intended to torture them with math and, later, sacrifice them for dark magic. Caden had mere seconds left and still had no confession of guilt. He held Rath Dunn's gaze.

"That's why you conspired with the others to sabotage the science room? Just to make her look bad?"

For a second, Rath Dunn didn't speak. Then he grinned. "That's right. Someone needs to bring her house down." He seemed particularly amused with that. "She won't be a villain keeper for long. Now, go get me the hair."

With a shaky hand, Caden took Brynne's braid from his pocket and handed it to him.

"Already?" Rath Dunn said, and thoughtfully turned the hair over in his hand.

Caden didn't answer. He turned and dashed from the room. Several people said hello to him in the halls, but he was a flash of speed on the dirty tiles. Rude though it was, he acknowledged no one. In his pocket, he clutched his phone. "That's right," Rath Dunn had said. Certainly that would count as a confession. He had the evidence he needed.

24

CRACKS IN THE WALL

aden only stopped running when he was safe and hidden behind the auditorium. There was a crack meandering up and around the stacked stones. Lately, there seemed to be cracks in everything. Despite Ms. Primrose's care, the school seemed to be falling apart. Maybe her hunger distracted her from its upkeep. Maybe some of the complaints had merit.

Downslope, Sir Horace peeked out from behind a dead tree. Sir Horace sniffed at the ground as if uneasy. Caden motioned for him to stay hidden. If Ms. Primrose didn't accept Caden's evidence, he and Jasan might need to try to outrun her. Likely, it would be a futile attempt, but neither Caden nor Jasan would simply stand and be devoured. Better they die while running and fighting.

In his pocket, Caden felt his phone buzz. It was tangled

in the enchanted chain of paper clips again. Five missed calls: all from Rosa. He also had five new messages. She didn't deserve the worry he was causing her. She'd treated him well. Then again, if she'd believed him, he wouldn't have had to sneak away.

If Caden survived this day, he would have to one day repay Rosa's kindness. First, though, he had to find Ms. Primrose. He had to play her the recording and show her the pictures of the cafeteria to save Jasan, to save himself. Today was a day of unknown fate. Caden hoped to live to see tomorrow.

He took a deep breath. The air smelled of ash and rotted grass. He prepared the photos and files on his phone the way Tito had taught him. Caden paced back and forth. The class-changing bell rang. He was getting impatient, but Tito had ordered him to wait. Wait he did. Finally, Tito ran around the corner with a blue bathroom pass in his hand. "Hey," he said, and breathed in and out, in and out.

"Time is running out," Caden said.

"Mrs. Belle wouldn't give me a pass until the class was seated for the ceremony. Hurry up. I'd like to be back in time for the awards. Let's go find your Elderdragon before it starts."

"She's not my Elderdragon," Caden said.

From within the auditorium, he heard music start to play. It was muffled but loud. With each beat, the stacked stone walls vibrated. Fine dust of plaster puffed from the cracks. The sun's rays illuminated it and made it look like smoke from a summer chimney.

Tito flapped his hands to disperse it.

Caden reached out and touched the wall. It was damp from the humidity. The stones were warm but not from the spring sun. It was a strange warmth. It was like the warmth of the counters in the cafeteria kitchen.

"Bro," Tito said, and grabbed Caden's sleeve to pull him along. "If you want to talk to Ms. Primrose, we've got to go find her now."

Caden looked at the walls for a moment longer. "Something's wrong here."

"Well, yeah," Tito said. "The math teacher wants to kill you, and the vice principal wants to eat you."

"More than that." Caden traced his hand along the crack. "Rath Dunn said he'd bring down Ms. Primrose's house. And he's already been involved in one not-accident."

Tito looked at the crack and frowned. "Yeah? What are you thinking?"

"Maybe he's going to cause another." Caden took out his phone and shone the flash against the stone wall. Behind him, Tito gasped.

"Whoa."

Caden clicked the flash again. Runes were scribbled across the stones. The wall looked like a filled scroll. As soon as the bright light went out, they weren't visible. A ritual spell had been cast. With the next beat of music, a piece of stone tumbled from the wall. Then another.

From the sound of the music and noise within, the auditorium was full. Likely, Tonya and Ward were in there. As were Jane and Jasan. And Brynne. Caden felt a cold chill and he knew. He just knew.

"He's going to collapse the building."

Then he reconsidered. Rath Dunn wouldn't dirty his hands; he wouldn't risk blame if his plotting failed. "I take that back," Caden said. "He's going to get Ms. Jackson to make it collapse."

"Now? He's in there."

Quickly, Caden took pictures of the stone walls. "Where was he seated?"

"Left front?"

Caden looked over the pictures he'd snapped on his phone. "Near the exit? He could easily escape if the walls were to collapse."

"But why would he want to destroy the building?" Tito said. "For his spell? I didn't think he had everything. I mean he doesn't have your brother's blood or Ms. Primrose's perfume."

"I don't believe so," Caden said. "This is a different spell. He needs to do this one in order to begin the next one."

Caden pounded and yanked on the door nearest them. It didn't budge. The exits only had to be open to those on the inside. He yelled for someone from inside to open it, but the music seemed to drown out his warnings.

Another stone tumbled from the top of the wall. "Crap," Tito said. "I think you're right. Warn the girls."

Caden called Brynne. She didn't answer. Tito texted Jane. She didn't reply either. If the teachers were watching, they wouldn't answer their phones. "Try Ward and Tonya," Caden said as they hurried to the main building and the hall's side entrance.

No one was in the corridor or the classrooms. It seemed all were at the awards ceremony. Before Caden found the Elderdragon, he and Tito had to warn those inside. The fire alarm was on the wall near the English room. Caden lifted the cover and pulled the lever. He braced for screeching bells and bright flashing lights. Nothing happened.

Tito frowned. "You did it wrong," he said.

"I did not."

Tito tried pushing and pulling the lever. "It's not working."

Caden understood how to flip the alarm. "My point exactly." He pulled out his phone again. This time he called Officer Levine. He answered immediately.

"Caden." Truly, he sounded worried. "Where are you, son? Rosa is worried sick."

"The auditorium is going to collapse. Get help."

"Are you at school?"

He hung up and turned to Tito. "Call Rosa, too. She'll be more likely to believe you." Maybe they'd believe them, maybe not. Tito called Rosa. "She's at the horse rescue look-ing for you."

"Did she believe you?"

"Don't know," Tito said. Then he dialed nine-one-one on his cell phone.

Caden doubted anyone would get to them in time. He and Tito ran into the auditorium from the back hall entrance. They needed to evacuate it.

Almost every seat in the auditorium was filled. Parents occupied the back rows. Students sat in front with their morning classes. Two empty rows separated them. The potential victims were many.

"Evacuate. Now!" Caden yelled from the doorway. "The building is going to fall!"

No one heard him over the music.

Tito nudged him and pointed to the stage. There were three chairs set up. One was occupied by an overly tanned man in a wrinkled shirt, another by an older woman with medium brown skin and a green pants suit. Mr. Creedly stood center stage, setting up the microphone.

If he or Tito could get to the stage, they could warn everyone. Caden looked at Tito. He was thinking the same thing.

"Go!" Caden said. "I'll warn our friends."

Tito darted toward the stage. Mr. Bellows tried to grab him from a front aisle seat, but Tito dodged and climbed up to the stage. The man in the wrinkled shirt stood up and tried to block him, but Tito was too quick.

Brynne and Jane were seated in the middle with Mrs. Belle. Already, Brynne seemed to sense something. Her short dark hair hung loose to her neck and tickled the top of her purple high-collared shirt. She was looking up at the ceiling. Tonya and Ward sat on the other side, but Mr. McDonald wasn't there. Ward's father was, however. He, too, looked at the ceiling. Those from the Greater Realm knew how to spot magic and danger.

Near the front middle, Caden saw Jasan. He was flanked by villainous teachers: Mr. Bellows and Rath Dunn on one side, and the sixth- and eighth-grade math teachers—solemn-faced Mr. Faunt and stocky Ms. Grady—on the other. For a split second, Caden didn't know whether to warn Brynne and Jane, Tonya and Ward, or Jasan first.

He ran to Brynne and Jane. They were the closest. When he got to their row, he reached across Mrs. Belle. "Brynne! Jane!"

The loud music came to an abrupt stop. The room went silent. On stage, Tito held the cords to the speakers. Everyone looked toward him.

Ms. Primrose appeared at the curtain's edge. Her dress was the color of thick ice. Even from afar, her skin seemed to shimmer with blue scales. She and Tito stared at each other. When she licked her lips, her teeth gleamed. Tito, however, was brave.

And, apparently, a bit of a liar, for he said, "There's a

bomb threat! Everyone out!"

In the fleeting quiet that followed, the ceiling groaned. The middle rafter dropped several feet and debris showered down from it. That convinced everyone to get out.

Students scrambled for the exits. Parents scrambled for their kids. Manglor pulled Ward and Tonya from their seats. The two well-dressed people on the stage hurried to the door. From somewhere outside and farther away, sirens wailed.

Ms. Primrose looked mortified. She eyed Tito for one long, horrible moment, then scanned the crowd, her icy gaze looking from one of her villains to the next. Then the ground shook. In a flash of blue, Ms. Primrose disappeared.

Mrs. Belle directed her class toward the back exit. Before they could all get free from the middle section, the drooping rafter crashed down. Twenty would be crushed, a quarter of the seventh grade. Caden braced himself. Brynne reached up. The beam stopped a thumb's length from her hand and even closer to their classmate Olivia's head.

Telekinesis magic.

Derek pulled Olivia out from under the beam. It hovered eerily in the air. Brynne was strong, but she couldn't hold it there for much longer. The class surged from the row. Caden fought against the flow of people.

Soon, only Brynne and Jane remained. "Brynne! Jane!" Caden said. "Get out from under it!"

Jane tried to pull Brynne away, but Brynne didn't move.

Instead, she flicked her wrist. The rafter flew straight up, burst through the ceiling, and tumbled out of sight. It left a large hole. The sun shone in and onto the dirty seats, the aisle, and the screaming students running out the exits.

Caden heard someone calling him. "Caden!" It was Tito. He ran across the stage. "Look!" Frantically, he motioned toward the front, toward Jasan. "Your brother!"

Jasan, of course, hadn't run away. He was a trained Elite Paladin. He would help others first. But he wasn't the only teacher who remained. Those around him did as well.

With the auditorium almost empty and Ms. Primrose gone, they blocked him from all sides. Rath Dunn had his blood dagger drawn. Mr. Bellows had his arm outstretched. The black aura of necromancy emanated from his fingers, and a large bag sat by his feet. Ms. Grady had a spiked bone club. The solemn-faced Mr. Faunt raised his hands and flexed his fingers. His fingernails looked like long, sharp knives.

Toward the back, a rear beam started to fall. Brynne's eyes turned so silver they glowed. She reached up. Power emanated from her. The rafter flew up, twirling madly like the blade of a helicopter, and disappeared into the sky. She wobbled from the effort.

Jane held her up. "We've got this," Jane said. The walls all around them crumbled. "I'll get Brynne out. Hurry, help your brother."

Dainty termites fluttered past them in the dust. What

was going on? Caden was certain attacking Jasan with daggers, nails, and clubs was against even Ashevillian rules. Where was Ms. Primrose? Caden dashed to the front.

Jasan grabbed Mr. Faunt by the wrist and flung him to the stage. The top of the stage, it seemed, had fallen in when the second rafter fell. Mr. Faunt crashed amid the splinters and termites.

The other three villains pounced on Jasan. Ms. Grady swung the club. It cut through the air with force. Rath Dunn slashed with the dagger. Mr. Bellows waved his hand. Something dead rose up from his bag. Bone by bone, it clicked together. Patchy muscle and flesh knitted together. Within a second, a corpse-like Ashevillian bear roared beside him.

THAT WHICH BINDS

$\mathfrak{I}$t didn't matter if Caden saved Jasan from Ms. Primrose if Jasan died here by Rath Dunn's hand, Mr. Bellows's bear, Ms. Grady's club, or Mr. Faunt's knife-like nails.

Ms. Grady rammed the club at Jasan's middle. Rath Dunn attacked from the other side. Mr. Bellows raised his arm to command the bear to rush Jasan. Just as he did, Caden lunged and grabbed his elbow. Instead of Jasan, Mr. Bellows now pointed at Ms. Grady and the corpse-bear charged. Better that she fight the bear.

"You!" Mr. Bellows sneered. So close, he smelled like death. He flung Caden off him. Caden skidded to a stop a few feet away.

Ms. Grady turned her club on the charging reanimated bear. Rath Dunn and Jasan fought. Above them, the front rafters groaned. Mr. Bellows glanced up.

He stepped back, then ran for the exit. Without its master, the corpse-bear fell into a puddle of bones and sinew. Ms. Grady looked at Jasan and Rath Dunn's battle, then looked at the groaning ceiling. It seemed she was done with both, for she, too, ran out a front exit.

Right above Jasan, a piece of heavy plaster fell. Caden was forced to jump back. Jasan was trapped between it and Rath Dunn. He dodged both but was knocked off-balance, and Rath Dunn charged him. They fell backward to the floor.

"No!" Caden yelled.

Rath Dunn brought the dagger down to Jasan's chest. Just as he did so, though, Jasan blocked with his right hand and punched Rath Dunn in the jaw with the left.

Rath Dunn stumbled back.

For a moment, the fight stopped. Then Jasan was screaming and grabbing for his right wrist. As he'd blocked the killing blow, the dagger—sharp, magical, and powerful—had severed his hand. Blood pooled on the floor, stark red against the grayish-white tiles. Caden rushed to his brother's side. The walls around them creaked. Sunlight shone in from above.

The slash in Caden's arm was also bleeding. Air seeped in through the rip in the coat, the rip that had been made only months earlier by the same blood dagger that had severed Jasan's hand. It was the only imperfection on his enchanted coat—one enchanted item countering the effects of another.

Slowly, Rath Dunn stood. He backed toward the exit and wrapped his dagger in a handkerchief from his pocket, sealing in the blood, and hiding the dagger.

"Not my initial intention, but I'm content to let you bleed out, Prince Jasan."

Caden glowered at him. "This is against Ms. Primrose's rules."

"Such teacher-to-teacher conflict must be arbitrated by the principal." He raised his arm as if taking an oath. "I'll get my day in court, you understand. He'll be dead then."

With sudden sickening clarity, Caden understood. Jasan's right hand had been severed by Rath Dunn's blood dagger. A wound made with it would never fully heal. It would reopen in its presence. No Ashevillian medicine could keep Jasan from bleeding to death. Rath Dunn finally had Jasan's blood—the blood of the seventh son.

"She'll still eat you," Caden said. "You broke the rules."

"We shall see, shan't we?"

Without the support of the beams, the right wall of the building tilted inward. Jasan stifled his screams with a grimace. There was a red pool under his right arm. He held his right wrist with his left hand. His right hand was on the floor.

Caden tried to help his brother up. Something in Caden's pocket tingled. He reached in and his hand touched his magical chain of paper clips. They felt warm and hummed against his fingers. Jane said they held things together. A simple enchantment with a simple purpose.

Before Jasan could bleed out, Caden reached down and grabbed the severed hand. It was a strange and icky sensation to hold someone's hand when it wasn't attached. Jasan's golden eyes flashed. He didn't move. He looked ready to pass out dead.

Quickly, Caden used the chain to join Jasan's right wrist to his right hand. He wrapped the paper clips around and around again, until the chain was tight against his skin.

Jasan's golden eyes looked dim, his matching hair matted and sweaty. He was covered in blood. He stared at his right hand. With the strangest of expressions, he wiggled his fingers.

His expression wasn't one of gratitude nor of relief. It was shock. He looked at the chain of paper clips at his wrist. Caden knew what his brother was thinking: Where did you get these things?

Enchantment was magic made stronger by giving. Jane had given the enchanted paper clips to Caden, and Caden had given them to Jasan. Surely, that would make the magic more powerful.

A firefighter, a woman, ran in the exit. "Hurry out, now! The building is falling." She scanned the space looking for others.

"Don't remove those," Caden said as he and Jasan

stepped onto the lawn. "Don't let the Ashevillian medics remove them either. They won't understand."

Dust-covered people ambled around on the lawn like the lost souls of the Sorrow Planes. A paramedic reached for Jasan, but he jumped away. Jasan didn't easily trust. Even so badly injured, he was fast.

"If you can ride," Caden called out, "Sir Horace waits at the woods' edge."

Jasan was out of sight a moment later. The poor paramedic seemed perplexed. There were others to help, though, and the paramedic moved on to them.

Caden looked for his friends. They were hard to find when everyone was covered in crumbled plaster. Soon, though, he found the girls. Brynne sat on the grass, her hands in her lap. They were trembling. Sometimes when Brynne overdid it, she'd shake or pass out afterward. She seemed close to that now.

Jane was on her knees beside her, rubbing her back. "She had a fit," she said.

"Only a small one," Brynne said.

Caden crouched down. "You've used too much magic," he said.

"Perhaps, prince," she said.

"Are you okay?"

"I have Ashevillian medicine that helps with them," she said. Her face brightened. "So I can do more and recover quicker than before."

"I don't think that's the purpose of the local medicine."

"And did you see?" She beamed. "Nothing exploded. I controlled it."

"You saved the seventh grade," Jane said, and smiled.

Caden sat beside the girls. He saw Derek and Olivia by a rotted tree. Tyrone stood near them looking stunned. Victoria and Tamera hugged each other by the dead rhododendron bush. He saw the villainous and terrible teachers who had tried to kill Jasan moments earlier. Mrs. Belle wandered by, several of her fingernails looking chipped. Tonya and Ward sat together on the grass.

In the crowd, a figure in a purple T-shirt and orange pants darted from one dust-covered person to another. Rosa. She went from student to student, face tight and tense, and called Caden and his friends' names. Her hair was tied back but frizzy from the heat. Officer Levine chased after her, trying to calm her down. "My children were in there," she said with a voice like rusted iron. "Move out of my way."

When she spotted Caden, she hurried over and grabbed his shoulders as if ready to pull him into an embrace. Her gaze slid down to Brynne. Rosa reached down and brushed dust from her short dark hair. The tightness in Rosa's jaw seemed to loosen, her breathing seemed to slow some. Caden followed her gaze to Jane.

Rosa's brow creased. She looked at the three of them once more, alarm returning to her face. "Where's Tito?"

Jane stared at the building as if in shock. Then she looked up at Caden, clearly distressed. Caden felt his heart begin to race. Tito had run onstage to warn everyone. And the stage had collapsed. And he wasn't on the lawn.

Rosa looked around again. "Where is Tito?"

Caden would go back inside. He'd dig Tito out. "I'll find him."

The right wall was tilting farther, about to fall. Plaster and stones tumbled down. Caden sprinted back toward the building. He heard Rosa and Jane running behind him.

Out of the corner of his eye, he saw Ms. Primrose. She was standing on the side of the lawn. Her special guests were nearby and covered in dust. They were yelling at her. She looked at him and licked her lips.

Well, she and her quest could wait until Tito was safe and free from the building. She'd said he had until today. Today was not over yet.

Firefighters blocked the way. "Get back, get back!" one yelled.

Those were orders. Caden fought against the pull of the curse. His feet stopped. He stepped back. Rosa zoomed past him. A firefighter grabbed her by the waist.

Officer Levine caught up to Caden's side. Jane was beside him. They watched in horror as the building collapsed inward. A wave of dust rolled across the lawn. Only the back wall, which connected to the hall, remained.

From the dust, and backlit by sun, a large figure emerged. It was hard to make out anything but a bulky silhouette. The man carried a boy under one arm. With the other, he pushed away a heavy chunk of rubble like it was gnomish feather stone. For a brief moment, Caden thought it was second-born Maden, gifted in strength, come to find him, or tempt him, or kill him.

But of course, it wasn't Maden. He was in Razzon, plotting against family and the Greater Realm. As the dust settled, Caden could see that it was Ward's father walking toward them. Caden watched how easily Manglor pushed another stone from his way.

Gifted with strength, Caden thought. Like only royals were. And like Maden. Like Maden, who had killed Chadwin and sent Jasan here to bleed.

Ward's father shifted the boy he carried until he was cradled against his chest. His hair was covered in dust and splinters of wood, but Caden could see that it was black and in a ponytail. His clothes were also dust covered, but that didn't hide that they were shades of gray and boring. Tito.

Rosa and Officer Levine were running to him. So were the paramedics.

Caden felt light-headed, like everything around him was fading, like he'd felt when he'd found Chadwin lying unmoving but still warm on the Winter Castle's tower path. Like he'd lost yet another brother. Then he fell to his knees.

26
THE DRAGON IN THE ROAD

The paramedics loaded Tito into an ambulance. Rosa climbed in, too. Caden's gut was in knots. This was his fault. Sir Tito had been helping him. And Tito hadn't even gotten his grade award.

As the ambulance pulled away, Caden looked around for Jasan but didn't see him. How much blood had Jasan lost? Was Jasan all right? Had he found Sir Horace?

Caden was being pulled in too many directions. He took a deep breath. Tito was being helped. So Caden needed to find Ms. Primrose. He'd yet to give her the evidence. He'd ignored her, no less. He looked over the dust-, rock-, and plaster-covered lawn. She wasn't there.

He'd have to search. Before he could, Officer Levine reached out and stopped him. He squeezed Caden's shoulder. "Come on, son," he said. Then he motioned to Jane and Brynne. "Get in my car. Let me drive you all to the hospital."

All orders. "I need to talk to Ms. Primrose," Caden said, but his traitorous feet were already following Officer Levine.

"Do that later. We'll meet Rosa and Tito at the hospital."

Beside him, Brynne was still dazed. Jane looked scared. Truth be told, Caden was a bit stunned, too. Officer Levine had them in his patrol car—Brynne in the front, Caden and Jane in the back—before Caden had time to process everything. Jane grabbed his hand and squeezed.

Officer Levine drove down the small side roads. "It'll be quicker."

These streets were small and quiet. They lacked the yellow-and-white lines painted on more prominent Ashevillian roads, and there was room for only one-way traffic. Along their edges sat small houses with overgrown grass, green trees, and flowering bushes. Officer Levine turned, and the car bumped onto a gravel road.

Caden closed his eyes and leaned against the upholstery. He had evidence that would work. It fit the criteria given. And he had evidence Rath Dunn was involved. Tito would be okay. He had to be. With fortune's favor, they all would.

He sensed the sun shining through the backseat window and filtered by overhanging branches. He felt its warmth. His whole body felt weary.

Then it was like a great shadow had swooped in and covered all. The car became cold. He snapped open his eyes. A stern figure stood in the middle of the road. Brynne gasped. Jane braced herself.

Officer Levine swerved his patrol car into a ditch by the shoulder. "What the . . ." He seemingly took a deep breath. The car was slanted to the left. He tried to pull back onto the road, but they were stuck in the mud. After a moment, Officer Levine got out. He helped Brynne slide over and hop out the driver's side. Then he opened the back door and let Caden and Jane out.

The air smelled of roses. Ms. Primrose stood three strides in front of them. The heels of her old-lady shoes were stuck in the gravel. Her gray hair was pulled taut. Her skirt was deep blue. Her blouse was the same shade. Her skin looked reptilian, and the whole road had buckled as if a great beast had landed on it.

Caden clutched his phone as he stepped from the car. It seemed his fate, and the fate of his seventh-born brother Jasan, would be decided on a small gravel road beside an overgrown lawn and a beautiful pink rhododendron bush.

Officer Levine stared at her. "Are you okay?" he said. "You're in the middle of the street. Ms. Primrose, do you know where you are? Did you get hurt in the collapse?"

Caden was certain she knew exactly where she was. "This doesn't concern you," Ms. Primrose said to Officer Levine. "This isn't about you."

Jane stood to Caden's left. She looked calmer than she had in the car. She still held his hand. Brynne stood to his right. She had dropped into a fighting stance. Despite appearances, Brynne was always ready to fight. At times, Caden thought she even liked it.

In the soft blue sky, there had been a shadow. Then she'd stood before them. "Did you fly here?" Caden said.

"Don't ask inane questions, dear," Ms. Primrose said, and straightened her blouse. "Yes, of course I flew here." She flicked her hand down at the rocks. "It's too bumpy to walk in these shoes."

So she had wings. Caden hadn't realized that. Normal, non-Elderdragon dragons didn't fly. Of course, they didn't talk, collect villains, or run middle schools either. "I see."

She arched a brow. "Do you, dear?" she said. The ground seemed to rumble. "Well, maybe you do get a glimpse, now and then. But why weren't you in my office first thing this morning?" She pointed a gnarled finger at him. "I am far too hungry to be amused by any of this."

"Now, Ms. Primrose," Officer Levine started. He held up his right hand as if it might appease the hungry dragon.

She was having none of it. "Quiet," she said. It got colder.

"Caden has your proof," Brynne said. "He does."

She turned her icy stare to Brynne, and Brynne shrank back.

"I do," Caden said.

Her anger seemed intense. The ground shook. Her voice came out inhuman. "It's too late. I'll eat you. And sour Jasan, too. No one outruns me."

As Brynne inched back, she locked her elbow with his. "She eats you, she eats me, prince."

Jane was wide-eyed. This was the first time she'd seen Ms. Primrose act like an Elderdragon. Jane stepped toward him and Brynne. "She'll have to eat all three of us."

Ms. Primrose stared at them like a predator stalking prey, then licked her lips.

"Perhaps you two should reconsider that," Caden whispered.

"Trust me, prince," Brynne said, "we are," but she didn't move away and neither did Jane.

Behind Ms. Primrose there was a massive blue shadow. It stretched to the sky itself. "My ceremony was ruined. My school is in shambles. The school board put me on leave." She pointed at Caden. "You were supposed to stop this from happening. But you failed."

"Technically," Caden said, because his survival, Jasan's survival, and possibly Jane's and Brynne's, depended on technicalities now, "I was tasked with finding the saboteur responsible for the gas explosion, not stopping an auditorium collapse."

But Ms. Primrose had disappeared.

Caden felt a freezing breath behind him. He had the impression of something sharp near his neck. A dark blue shadow fell across him and stretched beyond the gravel road. He turned back. Ms. Primrose had appeared behind him.

Caden stood in the jaws of the Elderdragon. He couldn't see them, but he could sense them. And she would swallow him whole.

Yet she didn't gobble him up, and he didn't die.

Caden sensed a second power around them—one that wasn't hers.

"Oh, drat," Ms. Primrose said.

The air grew heavy like it had when he'd agreed to the quest. That's right. It was the forgotten language that decided whether Caden had failed or completed his quest, not Ms. Primrose. She'd said so herself.

Officer Levine covered his ears and sank to his knees. Jane and Brynne did the same. Caden felt as if the sky were low and crushing him down. He tasted blood. It was the power of the forgotten tongue. This was the quest's formal conclusion.

Ms. Primrose switched to a language of power—the guttural one in which they'd made the agreement.

"Have you completed my quest?"

The words hurt. Jane was screaming. Caden took off his coat and threw it over Jane's head to cover her ears. Perhaps if she didn't hear it, it wouldn't hurt her. Officer Levine crawled toward his car and reached for something within it. Brynne had her arms wrapped around her head.

A trickle of blood came from her nose.

"Find the one responsible." Caden knew Ms. Jackson and Mr. Bellows had caused the gas accident, that she was the one responsible, and that Rath Dunn was their accomplice.

"Bring me Ashevillian evidence of their misdeeds." He had pictures of Ms. Jackson's refrigerator. He had proof she'd conducted misdeeds. And, more important, he had Rath Dunn's voice on tape admitting their guilt.

"Give me something I can act upon." Ms. Primrose could terminate Ms. Jackson for unsanitary practices. Hopefully, terminate them all for conspiracy.

Would the forgotten tongue deem it enough?

"Answer me."

The words beautiful and terrible, and phrased as an order. He held out his phone. One word was forced from his lips. It felt like a spear to the temple.

"Yes."

The moment his phone was in her hands, the air crackled. Caden felt spit dribble down the side of his mouth. Brynne slumped against him. All returned to normal. A small yellow car turned down the street, pulled slowly around them, and puttered away. The spring breeze blew through the long grass.

Ms. Primrose switched back to English. "What am I supposed to do with this?"

Caden stumbled forward. He showed her the pictures.

"These things aren't allowed in the cafeteria." He played her the recordings. "They conspire against you. He admits it." He gulped. "There are many for you to eat."

Caden shouldn't encourage her to eat anyone. Sometimes, at night, he felt conflicted and strange that she'd eaten the other lunch witches after he'd proven them rule breakers. Now he'd given her the needed information to eat their sister. Still, better Ms. Jackson and Rath Dunn and Mr. Bellows than he and Jasan.

"I guess I can't eat you then." Ms. Primrose seemed annoyed. "Pish," she said. "I didn't want to eat you anyway. Not enough meat."

Caden was relieved, but also a bit insulted. He was plenty meaty, and everyone knew royal meat was the tastiest. He was also hurt. She acted like she'd wanted him to fail.

"Don't misunderstand, dear," she said. "Maybe I can't eat you or your brother now, but if he doesn't do his job, I'll turn him into a rabbit and give him to the science students."

Caden wiped his mouth with his sleeve. She'd threatened that once before. "You can do that? Really?"

"I can turn myself human. You don't think I can turn humans into pets? Besides, it wouldn't harm him, and he'd still be able to serve the school." She looked Caden up and down. "You might make a nice hamster."

Caden highly doubted that, but now wasn't the time to

argue. "I understand," he said, and he did. Ms. Primrose remained angry. And hungry. Best he be respectful and try to quell both.

"You can eat Ms. Jackson and Rath Dunn," he said. "Not to mention Mr. Bellows."

"Rath Dunn caused no accidents."

Caden blinked at her. "You heard the file. He's orchestrated them."

She pulled her sunken heel from the gravel and shook the rocks away. "I can act on proof of who has caused the accidents, not on who has encouraged them. We all make our own choices. Those causing the accidents made theirs."

While cursed, Caden's own choices were severely limited. "Not always," he said.

Rath Dunn was planning to destroy the barrier between worlds, and he planned to sacrifice Asheville and its people to do it. Ms. Primrose needed to know his evil intentions. Caden told her.

Brynne was climbing to her feet. "The letters," she mumbled.

Caden took his phone and loaded a picture of a complaint. "Not to mention, Mr. Bellows, Rath Dunn, and others attacked Jasan today. That, too, is against the rules. They've broken many."

She seemed surprised and angry. "Perhaps you're right, dear. Maybe he would make a good meal." Her silver phone rang.

"Likely more complaints," Caden said.

With a step forward, she reached out and put her finger under his chin. Her skin felt smooth, cold, and tough. She looked into his eyes. "I'm hungry and I'm tired. Don't anger me."

A moment later, there was a flash of blue, the sun disappeared behind shadow, and she was gone. Jane tossed Caden's coat off her head, though she remained on her knees. Farther away, Officer Levine stared at the spot where Ms. Primrose had been standing.

"You've completed the quest." Brynne offered a tired smile. "You've saved yourself and your brother from an Elderdragon."

Brynne was right. Caden had completed an Elderdragon's quest. Jasan was now safe from Ms. Primrose, safe even though he was quick-tempered and surly. And surely Caden could argue against turning him into a school rabbit.

"Even if she doesn't eat Rath Dunn," Brynne said, "he'll soon lose his ritual magic master. That will make the spell a lot harder to cast."

A spell like the one he was planning would take months even after the ingredients were collected. And he didn't have Ms. Primrose's perfume. Without Ms. Jackson, even if he could get the ingredients and figure out how to do it himself, it would take much longer. These were victories. Weren't they?

"Good," Jane said. "My mom's gone because of her.

And now Tito's hurt."

At the mention of Tito, Caden felt his smile fall. His friend and foster brother was injured. They needed to get to the hospital to see him.

Officer Levine used the car to pull himself to his feet. He looked from Caden to the sky and shook his head. "Well," he said. "That was interesting."

"No," Caden said. "That was an Elderdragon."

27

A SURPRISE VISITOR

They spent the afternoon at the hospital. That night, Rosa stayed there with Tito while Officer Levine stayed with Jane, Brynne, and Caden at the house. They sat around the kitchen table and ate French fries. Officer Levine listened somewhat less skeptically to Caden's tales from the Greater Realm.

"You can tell Rosa I'm telling the truth," Caden said.

"I could," Officer Levine said.

"You've now seen an Elderdragon."

The policeman was being difficult.

"She'll believe you," Jane said.

Brynne swiped three of Caden's fries.

Officer Levine leaned back in his chair. "Maybe," he said. "But there are some things you have to see to believe. We may need to ease her into it." He chuckled. "I may need to ease myself into it."

Caden sighed. The kitchen and house seemed strange without Rosa and Tito. "Then she'll still think I'm crazy. She'll try to send me away. Who knows what Ms. Primrose will do to me then?"

"That," Officer Levine said, and picked up a fry, "I can talk to Rosa about. Son, she's not going to send you away. Not with all this going on. And you were right about the building falling."

Wednesday afternoon Tito was released from the hospital, and he and Rosa came home. Officer Levine still didn't leave. Well, he left to work, but found reasons to stop by and see them. So far he'd brought them doughnuts for breakfast. Then more doughnuts and pigs in blankets for lunch. While the pigs in blankets weren't woolly like Caden expected, he still refused to eat them.

Officer Levine also brought Tito a framed grade award. "When I went by the school, I picked this up for you," he said before he and Rosa went out to the porch to talk in private.

Tito was thrilled. He sprawled on the living room's green couch with his twisted leg elevated, a doughnut in his hand, and his grade award leaning against his side. Sugary crumbs looked like sand on his black T-shirt. "The doc said that two of my injuries would've been fatal if shifted a centimeter either way." He seemed proud of this troubling information, and he'd been in a good mood since seeing the framed award. "The doc wasn't sure why the knock to the head didn't damage my brain. But, hey, it didn't."

"Better you not be injured at all," Caden said.

Caden sat on the floor, which he didn't like, and beside Brynne, which was not bad. Officer Levine walked past the front window. Caden couldn't hear what he or Rosa was saying, but they were speaking in low, serious tones. No doubt discussing Tito's injuries or reconsidering Caden's imminent—and eminent—nuthouse trip.

Jane sat on the coffee table. She smiled at Tito. "I'm just glad you're all right."

"Of course he's all right," Brynne said. She reached up and pulled Tito's necklace out from his shirt. "He wears the enchanted necklace . . . oh."

Caden leaned over to look. The usually shimmering necklace was dull against Brynne's fingers. The black stone was cracked. The interwoven wires had no luster. The doughnut looked more magical.

"I thought enchantments were forever," Caden said.

Jane, too, looked confused. "My enchantment is gone?"

Brynne creased her brow and pushed her short hair behind her ear. She'd magicked herself so the new length looked planned and stylish. "Perhaps the only way to break an enchanted item is to drop a building on it?"

Jane reached for the necklace. "I didn't think it would wear out. I wonder why?"

Brynne bit her lip. "There have never been many enchanters. Not all of their enchantments worked the same way. Some could only enchant fabric. Some only metals, like you. And we've been experimenting with controlling it. Maybe these things have affected the enchantments?" She shrugged. "We'll have to experiment more."

Jane nodded. "And we'll experiment with mixing our magic."

Brynne's face lit up. "We will, indeed."

Soon Caden would probably have a cursed Enchanted Fork of Eating. He turned to Jane. "What matters is the necklace you made likely saved Tito's life." He looked up at Tito. "But it's useless now." To make sure Tito understood, he added, "Don't rely on it for protection."

"I don't wear it because it's enchanted," Tito said. "I wear it because Jane gave it to me."

Jane smiled. "But I gave it to you to protect you."

After that, they seemed content to smile and stare at each other across the gap from coffee table to couch. Brynne made a disgusted face.

The school was closed Wednesday. Caden's curse faded along with the moon. His will became his own again. Thursday it was announced the building would open again on Friday. The seriousness of the collapse seemed to diminish from people's minds with an almost magical speed.

Tito spent Thursday sleeping. As did Brynne. She remained weakened from all her magical moving of large rafters. Caden practiced fighting styles three, four, and six with Jane. He grew more restless with each strike. Where was Jasan? Officer Levine had promised he'd check on him, but he'd yet to do so. Ward had texted that he'd seen lights in the yellow town house, but not his brother. Sir Horace hadn't visited.

After dinner a large Suburban pulled into the driveway. The windows were tinted, the paint the color of desert sand. Officer Levine and Rosa went to greet the driver while Caden and Jane watched from the window. Tito dozed on the couch. Brynne had fallen asleep in the chair.

Jane pointed outside. "Perhaps they've come for you," she said.

Caden felt his cheeks pale.

"It was a joke, Caden," she said. "They're not going to take you away now."

Outside, the driver's door opened. Manglor, Ward's father, stepped out. He towered over Officer Levine and Rosa. Officer Levine reached out to shake his hand. Ward's mother, Desirae, got out of the passenger's side, holding a casserole dish. She greeted Rosa warmly. The rear door opened. Caden expected to see Ward hop out.

But it wasn't Ward who stepped out. It was Jasan. He was wearing a slate-blue T-shirt and dark jeans. He squinted up at the house with a look of disdain. His right hand was bandaged and wrapped to his chest. He nodded at Rosa and Officer Levine.

Caden ran out, leaving Jane at the window, then ran down the porch steps to his brother. They stared at each other. Jasan tensed, but reluctantly patted Caden's back with his left hand. Caden peered into the Suburban. It was big, but not big enough to carry Sir Horace.

Caden spoke in Royal Razzon. "Where's Sir Horace?"

Rosa reached out to pull Caden to her. "Caden," she said gently.

Jasan seemed perfectly content to have him pulled away.

"Caden," Rosa said. "He isn't your brother."

"He is," Caden said.

Jasan's expression brightened like he recognized the word. He motioned from himself to Caden. In a thick accent, he said, "Brothers," in English so Rosa could understand.

Rosa looked skeptical.

Manglor cleared his throat. His deep voice sounded like velvet. He pointed to Jasan. "His English is limited, but he and I share another language." He pointed to Caden. "He says that one is his little brother."

"What language is that?" she said.

Manglor didn't answer. Likely, he'd also translated wrong. "Little" wasn't the word Jasan would use. "You mean half brother," Caden corrected.

The janitor peered down at Caden. "That one"—he pointed again at Jasan—"said little."

Desirae looked between them. "There is a resemblance."

Officer Levine turned to Rosa. "We can do a DNA

test," he said. "Find out what's what."

Rosa shot them glares and looped a protective arm around Caden's shoulder. "Maybe. Assuming it's a match, I'd like to know where his family has been for the last few months."

"They've been looking for him," Desirae said.

"Then why didn't he come directly to me?"

Jasan seemed to be losing patience. Of the seven Elite Paladin virtues, it was his weakest. This he and Caden shared. Jasan glowered at Manglor, stomped his foot, and pointed from Rosa to Caden. Manglor didn't seem inclined to do or say whatever it was Jasan wanted.

Not that Caden was surprised. In his experience, stomping at people rarely made them inclined to do anything. Well, Manglor did look as if he might want to squash Jasan. Jasan, however, was likely too quick to be squashed. Who had won when Jasan and Maden practiced? To Caden's memory, Jasan's speed and Maden's strength had been evenly matched.

Desirae spoke gently. "Would it be possible for Caden and his brother to speak in private, just for a moment?"

Caden untangled from Rosa and smiled at her. He wanted to speak to Jasan alone, away from the prying eyes and ears of the others. "Just give us a moment," he said in English. "Please."

Rosa hesitated. "You can talk on the porch," she said. "But I'll be watching the entire time. You signal if you need anything."

Once on the porch, Jasan spoke in Royal Razzon. "Did you make a deal with that Elderdragon? This is what she told me. Right before she told me she sadly couldn't eat me despite my delicious temperament."

Caden answered in the same tongue. "Only to protect you and the school."

"You don't make deals with beings like that, Caden. They are dangerous."

"If I had refused," Caden said, "she would've eaten us both immediately." He paused. "There's something I've found out." He told Jasan of Rath Dunn's plan to destroy the barrier between worlds, of his communication with Maden. As Caden spoke, Jasan's expression grew stonier and stonier. His body tensed. For a long moment after Caden finished, Jasan was quiet.

From the drive, Rosa watched them with obvious concern.

When Jasan spoke, his words were low and harsh. "Why should I care?"

"Our family is in danger."

"Our family betrayed me."

"Because they were tricked."

"Because they believe me capable of killing my brother."

Jasan frowned at the mountains, likely thinking they were too small and too warm when compared to their homeland. Caden motioned to them. "The spell would also destroy this land. These people are innocent. Just consider it. Please."

Jasan inhaled deeply. His nostrils flared. "Fine. But I don't want you making any more deals with dragons."

Desirae was hugging Rosa. "I've worked with children." She gestured at Caden. "And I've counseled people in his position before."

Rosa glanced at Officer Levine. "It's your choice," Officer Levine said.

"I'll think about it." Rosa said.

"Please do." Desirae smiled. "Ward doesn't have many friends. And I like Caden. I'd be happy to help."

Manglor snorted. It seemed he didn't share her affection, but he was warming to Caden. Most people did. Jasan had. Eventually, Manglor would as well.

28

ALLIANCES

The school reopened Friday, as promised. As Caden ate a breakfast of milk and grains, he mentioned the oddity to Brynne, Tito, and Jane.

"Maybe there's some of your world's freaky magic in the forms," Tito said. "You know that Rosa had to sign something when she enrolled each of us. All the parents did."

Caden suspected that as well.

"I was sent back after the lunch people kidnapped me," Jane said. "No one said anything. No one even seemed that bothered by it. Not even Rosa."

"I gotta say," Tito said, "I thought that was strange, especially for Rosa. She sent us back after all the accidents, too. And I don't think a single student has ever moved away." He grabbed his crutches from where they leaned against the wall. "Graduation. That's the only way out."

At the school, the auditorium was cordoned off behind bright orange netting and barrels. There were men and women in hard hats removing debris and working. On the lawn, there were more people—they wore matching green T-shirts. They were replacing the sickly looking grass with new bright green grass squares. Many of the black-barked burned trees had been removed. Other green shirts were planting new trees. Crimson-colored roses were planted where the dead yellow ones had been.

In Caden's first class, Mr. McDonald kept hidden behind a thick book. His brow was sweaty despite the chill from the air conditioner, and his fingers shook when he turned a page. Tonya and Ward were seated at their computers. Ward leaned over. "Pa had a talk with Mr. McDonald."

"I'm surprised Mr. McDonald is still alive, then," Caden said.

"We are, t-too," Tonya said.

"Pa has sworn off killing people," Ward said. "He says he doesn't do that anymore."

Like Mr. McDonald, Mrs. Belle was jittery in science class. She showed the class a video on the secret life of bugs. Caden sat at the front of the class with Tito and Jane. Brynne's desk was in the back.

"Perhaps this will give us insight into Mr. Creedly," Caden said.

Tito looked skeptical. Jane shrugged.

Caden was about to say more when the speaker system interrupted. Mr. Creedly's raspy voice filled the room. "Send Caden to the principal's office." Like Mr. McDonald and Mrs. Belle, his mood sounded worse than usual.

Mrs. Belle tapped her bloodred nails on the white board. She looked from the wall speaker to Caden like she was going to argue with Mr. Creedly over the intercom, or insist he not go. It was a fleeting thing, though. After a moment, she raised her chin like she was defending herself, tapped his shoulder, and walked him to the door.

As they passed the back row of desks, Brynne leaned over. Her silvery eyes glinted. Her short dark hair framed her pretty face. "Be brave, dragon charmer," she said, and grinned.

Caden smiled back, but Mrs. Belle pulled him away. At the door, she stopped. She looked conflicted about sending him down the hall. "Be careful, Caden," she said. Then a strange expression crossed her face like there was something devious under her makeup and gentle words. "And tell your brother you've been summoned."

That sounded like a warning. "Why?" he said.

She pursed her lips. "The enemy of my enemy is my friend. Trust me."

A moment later, she went back into her classroom and closed the door. He was alone in the hall. Trust her? He wasn't too sure about that. She conspired with Mr. Creedly, an inhuman and cruel creature. Whatever she was worried about, she hadn't spoken up for him, or asked any questions. She'd still told him to go.

Jasan had given Caden his phone number the previous day. Before Caden turned down the long hall, he snuck his cell phone from his back pocket and called Jasan. He didn't answer, so Caden left him a voice message.

At the end of the hall, Mr. Creedly had his too-long arms folded over his chest. His hair was slicked back. He looked like a spider huddled in a corner. A sad spider. Caden wasn't sure how to feel about that.

"What's wrong with you?" Caden said.

Mr. Creedly untangled his long limbs and stood. Behind him, his shadow reached across the wall. "The pest control comes today," he said, and his voice sounded as if it ached. "They come to kill my kind." Then the shadow behind him seemed to stretch, to grow darker. "One day, you will be engulfed by us."

Not a pleasant notion. Caden stepped around him and toward the office. He squared his shoulders. "Not today, though."

"Not today." Mr. Creedly sank down into his chair. The long shadows drew back toward him. He pointed a too-long finger at the office. "Today, they wait for you."

They. They waited for him. And this time, neither of them was Jasan.

The office smelled faintly of roses and heavily of paint. The walls were red. The bowls of beads, buttons, and cheap plastic things on the shelves were gone, and replaced with books—many with pictures of food on the covers. There was a stack of boxes in the one corner like someone was moving in or moving out.

It wasn't Ms. Primrose who sat behind the carved desk. It was Rath Dunn. Ms. Jackson stood beside the tyrant. She held Jane's ladle. Caden stood stunned. She should have been eaten. She should no longer be a threat.

His stomach twisted, and he looked at her. "I thought you'd been devoured."

She leaned forward. He saw gray bands in her hair, wrinkles on her forehead. "You'd have liked that, wouldn't you?"

"I wouldn't have not liked it." The book-filled shelves worried Caden. "Where is Ms. Primrose?"

Rath Dunn's eyes brightened. "During the auditorium incident, she was removed as principal," he said, and grinned. "Don't worry. The locals have full faith I'll be able to perform exemplarily in her place. And she still has all her other jobs: vice principal, placement counselor." He flapped his hand. "Whatever else." He stood and put his hands on the desk. "I have plenty of work for her."

Ms. Jackson cackled.

Caden studied Ms. Jackson's face and motioned to the ladle. "Why are you holding that?"

Her face scrunched in fury. The wrinkles seemed to make her once-glowing skin look saggy and dull. "I can't let it go," she said.

So this was Jane's plot. A ladle enchanted with age. A dark enchantment.

There were few enchantments known to cause harm. After all, enchantment was a magic of giving, of sacrifice. It wasn't selfish and evil like ritual magic. Nor was it neutral like Brynne's mind magic.

But there were some such dark items. Rath Dunn's blood dagger was an example of one. Caden peered at the ladle. Was it draining her of her stolen youth? Perhaps it wasn't evil, then, but fair. Enchanted item number one hundred thirty-four, renamed the Aging Ladle of Justice.

He gave Ms. Jackson his most charming of smiles. "You're looking old, Ms. Jackson."

She raised the ladle as if she was going to strike him. Rath Dunn, however, caught her arm. "Now, now. It seems that little enchantress is more devious than we thought."

Ms. Jackson then looked ready to strike Rath Dunn. He released her arm.

"Don't be upset; as acting principal, I've pardoned all teachers and staff from the events of the last week," Rath Dunn said. "Don't make me reconsider."

Ms. Jackson looked at him coldly.

"And you can have her soon enough. The others, too. As many children as you need."

That seemed to appease her somewhat. Not Caden, however. He straightened his posture. "No," he said. "You can't have Jane. You can't have any of them."

"Of course we can. You'll help us," Rath Dunn said.

Caden felt cornered, but he had to stay brave. "I'll stop you."

Rath Dunn walked around the desk. "You will do as I tell you."

An order. But the moon was days past half-full. "I must decline," Caden said. Suddenly, he felt vulnerable in the office. He stood in front of the desk, trapped between the heavy door, an enraged lunch witch, and the gleeful math tyrant. "I should return to class."

"I'm not done with you yet," Rath Dunn said, his voice a wolf's growl. He looked Caden up and down, then turned to Ms. Jackson. "What do you think?"

She sniffed Caden's hair. "There's definitely some magic attached to him. It's faint, at the moment."

From outside, there was a loud thud and a screech. The door swung open a moment later. Jasan stood there. He was dressed in black slacks and a long-sleeved blue shirt, the cuff pulled over his magically attached hand.

"What's going on here?" he said in the common tongue.

Rath Dunn motioned to Jasan's hand. He, too, spoke the common tongue. "Nice trick. You'll have to show me how you did that one day. Not that it will matter in the end. Now, get out. You've got a class to prepare." He smiled. "And I've a student to discipline. I can't let this school's reputation fall into even deeper disrepair, can I?"

Blood trickled around Jasan's sleeve. It wasn't like his hand was severed, however. It was more like a modest cut—the enchanted paper clip chain countered the blood dagger, but not completely. Jasan took a step forward. "I'm taking my brother. Best you let him go."

"Don't try it, boy," Rath Dunn said. "I'm head of this school. Show some respect, or you'll be terminated. Ms. Primrose remains part of that committee."

"Before she lost this position," Caden said, "Ms. Primrose gave Jasan special accommodations."

"Excuse me?" Rath Dunn said.

"He has permission to be difficult as long as he teaches his class."

Rath Dunn looked curious. "Is that so?"

"Like you," Caden said, "I don't lie."

"That won't keep you from being punished."

Caden knew what to say to that. He raised a brow. "Disciplining students is the vice principal's job. Not yours." He moved back to Jasan. When he was out of reach, Caden said, "She'll eat you one day. You understand."

Rath Dunn laughed. "I've broken no rules."

"You cut off Jasan's hand!"

"One, it looks like it's still attached. Two, I've pardoned everyone for those events. It's my discretion as acting principal. With everything that happened, many people were confused. I won't hold their behavior against them. And, three, let's be honest," he said, and motioned to the place where Caden had been cut by the blood dagger months earlier, "a little blood's never bothered her." He walked back to the desk and made a show of stretching in the chair. "If you want, I'll put an incident report in both our employee files." He opened the desk drawer and pulled out two purple forms. Then he looked in the drawer again.

"Now, what's this?" He reached back into the drawer and pulled out a bottle of perfume. He sniffed it, then tossed it to Caden. "Take that to our dear vice principal. I've taken what I need from it."

Caden looked at the bottle in his hand. It was medium sized and of beveled crystal. The liquid inside had a pinkish tint, and smelled strongly of roses.

"Let's go," Jasan said.

Before they closed the door, Rath Dunn yelled out, "You two aren't nearly as much fun as your brother Maden," and broke into booming laughter.

Jasan froze for a moment, then slammed the door shut behind them. They walked back down the long hall. Once they were alone, Caden turned to him. "I'm surprised you didn't lose your temper and attack him."

"Desirae is counseling me on anger management. Besides, I'm uncertain how stable my right hand is. With his current position, your Elderdragon might be obliged to guard him." He turned. "Still, she's angry at him."

The halls were so cold, Caden's skin pimpled, his breath fogged. "I can tell."

"The minute he makes a mistake, she'll act on it."

"He makes few mistakes, Jasan."

"Don't overestimate him," Jasan said. "He's already made mistakes. He failed to kill me. That's a mistake. He's trying to control the Elderdragon. That's like leashing a blizzard. It won't last. He's foolish."

Jasan was sounding less like his banished surly self, and more like his normal surly self. Was his brother ready to fight? The obstacles were many. "As foolish as he is," Caden said, "Ms. Primrose is still under Rath Dunn's control."

"Only as much as he was under hers. No one can truly control an Elderdragon. We should talk to her. She might not be able to remove Rath Dunn, not yet, but she could give us information on magic, on the realms, on how to contact home. If Rath Dunn can do it with dark magic, it can be done, and maybe in less-wicked ways."

"He has allies here."

"So do we." Jasan rubbed his wrist, thoughtfully. "We've got an enchantress and a powerful spellcaster. We've the allegiance of the Conqueror and Ninth King of the Seven Deserts." At Caden's confused expression, he added, "Manglor. Ward's father."

"And we have Sir Tito," Caden said. "Don't forget him."

Jasan ran his hand through his hair. "But we must stop Rath Dunn here, and Maden there. Too many perished in the last war. And this city and these people would be the first casualties in another."

Caden looked at him. "Does this mean you'll forgive Father and the others?"

Jasan's eyes flashed. His cheeks turned red. "I'll never forgive them." He clenched his fist and glared at a locker like he was about to hit it. He breathed in and out for a moment. Counting, Caden thought, like Rosa did when she was angry. After a moment, he spoke again. "But I don't want the city destroyed or Razzon conquered." He let out a breath. "I don't want our father and brothers dead."

Perhaps there was hope for Jasan and the others to reconcile.

Jasan clenched his jaw. "I want them to beg me for forgiveness," he said, his voice a pitted blade, "and I want to refuse them."

Perhaps not. Caden looked up at his brother and raised his brow.

"They need to be alive for that," Jasan said.

At least Jasan would fight, would protect those he loved even if he couldn't forgive them. In this dark time, with Rath Dunn close to his goal, they must unite. They must stop the villains to save both Asheville and the Greater Realm.

With Brynne, Tito, and Jane, they would be formidable. Maybe Ms. Primrose would help them. If Caden said the right thing, offered the right words, she might. If Caden couldn't prove his honor by slaying a dragon, perhaps he could by charming one.

ACKNOWLEDGMENTS

My sincerest thanks to my awesome agent, David Dunton, and to my excellent editor, Jocelyn Davies. Thanks to everyone at HarperCollins who helped me make this book happen and to the wonderful cover artist, Eric Deschamps.

I'd like to tell my family—my mom, Pat; my brother, Orren; my sister and also critique partner, Sarah; my brother-in-law, Stephen; and my nephew, Edward, and niece, Marie—how much I appreciate all they do for me.

Also, I appreciate the support from all the Balls, from Quin and Tamera, and from my good friends Janie, Adrienne, and Amy, who are always great company for a Friday dinner; from my writing buddy Kat and fellow writer Dawn Reno Langley; and from my friends

Lorrie, Krista, Laura, and Sam.

I'd especially like to thank my good friend Christine for being the type of friend I can see every day or every decade yet who I always feel like I just spoke to yesterday.

Nothing was more important than slaying a dragon...until now.

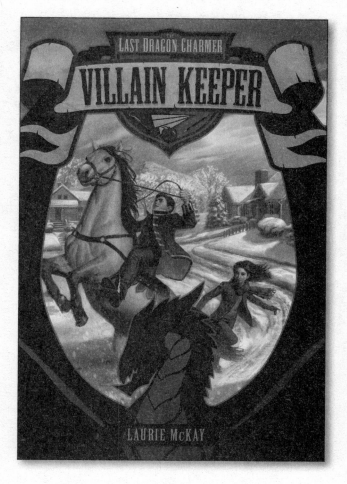

Don't miss the first book in
The Last Dragon Charmer series!